A Mother Goose Chocolate Kissed Christmas

A Mother Goose Chocolate Kissed Christmas

MARTA L. MAXWELL

Published by Peace River
A division of Lamb of God Creations
peaceriver777@outlook.com

Printed in the United States of America

All Bible scripture taken from the
 Self-Pronouncing edition The Holy Bible
Containing the Old and New Testaments
Translated out of The Original Tongues and with The Former
Translations Diligently Compared and Revised
Authorized King James Version
The World Publishing Company
Cleveland and New York

Library of Congress Control Number: 2014953930
First Edition

Cover Design by Kevin Carden

ISBN 978-0-9909218-0-6 (Paperback)
ISBN 978-0-9909218-1-3 (Hardcover)
ISBN 978-0-9909218-2-0 (Ebook)

A Mother Goose Chocolate Kissed Christmas

This book is dedicated to my mom, {Mettie Louise Maxwell} whom I never got a chance to say goodbye to. She, was a kind sensitive woman, whom I miss, and love very much. I was blessed to have her as mother. She also was an artist and a writer. Here is one of the poems she wrote long ago, that I would like to share with you.

> Come loose your desperate hold
> Upon the golden, gossamer thread of life;—
> Your frantic grasp but strains
> The fragile wisp the more.
> The cord is yours,
> Held fast to your allotted time;
> And when the strand must break,—
> Soft, - as thistledown on the air,—
> Will steal away
> To its eternal fate.

Where ever you are mom, I pray that I will see you again someday and that all will be forgiven.

Acknowledgements

First off I would like to thank Lisa B. for reading the entire second draft of my manuscript and for leaving me an encouraging message on my answering machine. I referred back to the message often. Her, words {your words Lisa} spurred me on to completion. Thank You!

Thank you, also Melody for all of the time you put into editing

My dear friend Kris, I can't thank enough for her listening ear and for having faith in me and my, ability to write this book. Thank you, my friend.

And to my cover designer, Kevin Carden. I sincerely thank him for taking the time to design the cover exactly to my specifications. I have the utmost appreciation for his digital artwork. To see more of his awe inspiring digital photography go to https://www.google.com/?gws_rd=ssl#q=kevin+carden+photography or just google Kevin Carden 500px

For putting this whole manuscript into the correct form for printing and publication, I thank Darlene Swanson for her expertise and for going the extra mile to correct, some poo-paas. You can contact her at http://www.van-garde.com or just google Darlene Swanson van-garde

Above all I Thank God, Lord Jesus Christ and his Holy Spirit for giving me the words to put on paper and for guiding me through this entire process. With all my heart in Jesus name, Thank You God.

Chapter One

Softly, the Holy Spirit whispered, "Have a Christmas party."

After Mother Goose read from her book of daily meditations, she reminisced about years gone by as she drank her morning cup of strong brew.

She thought of the children who had once been in her care and her other friends who all used to get together over the holidays. She kept in touch with those who still lived in and around the community but it had been years since she had seen the kings and queens over in England along with her dear friend, Humpty Dumpty; to whom she wrote often and prayed for a miracle. Many of her friends had moved on with their lives and now lived far away.

"Have a Christmas party," whispered the Holy Spirit again.

Mother Goose got up from her grey, speckled, Formica-topped kitchen table to pour herself, another cup of dark French roast when the idea occurred to her.

"What a great idea," she said aloud. "This year I will throw the biggest, grandest Christmas party ever!" The question was… where to have it?

She sat back down; compelled she gazed out her kitchen window to the forested hills north of town. She listened now, more intently to the Lord's guidance and tried to shut out her own rambling thoughts.

The answer to her question was right before her eyes. The Christmas party would be held out where the forest mingled with the foothills, just north of town. Out there was a large clearing and, right in the middle, stood the most majestic old fir tree you have ever seen. It seemed to be preternatural, as if to hold all the wisdom of the universe within its being. The mystical clearing was embraced by a melodic little creek which sang its song merrily around as if to entertain the wise old tree and rejoice in its solitude before retreating into the woods to share its joy.

Mother Goose knew of this mystical place only because her best friend, the Old Woman Who Lived under a Hill, whom she affectionately called the Old Woman, had showed it to her after they became close friends. The moment Mother Goose saw the clearing, she fell in love. It had a cathartic effect one's soul.

This clearing is where the Old Woman went to pray and meditate. She was a very spiritual woman. Some people said that she was theocentric, which wasn't totally off base, because God was her main focus in life. Some said she was superstitious while others believed that she was just outright crazy. Often, Mother Goose went with her to the clearing to pray and meditate also.

One time, when they were together in the mystical clearing, they built a labyrinth using rocks, which they had gathered from the creek. From then on, whenever Mother Goose went to visit, they liked to walk through it together and count their blessings. For the Old Woman, this became an important ritual.

Every evening, just before dusk, the Old Woman also ran a mile or more up the creek and then came back to bathe in this running vein of God's out-reached hand to humanity. She said this kept her blood flowing and it washed away any negative energy that had invaded her being. Besides, she just loved the warm chill of her muscles being rejuvenated in the cleansing water.

Since the two of them were the only ones who knew of this mystical place, Mother Goose thought, "What a wonderful gift it would be to share the mystical clearing with all of our, friends."

With Christmas only two weeks away, she needed to contact everyone immediately. Although she had most of her friend's phone numbers and addresses, she did not have them all. Even if she did, it would take too long to write out invitations and get a response in time. Taking her last drink of coffee, she anxiously pondered what to do until, once again, she was able to calm her own thoughts.

"Ask Little Bo Peep to look your friends up online for you, then send everyone an email," said the still small voice. Mother Goose smiled, in awe of her personal relationship with the almighty God, Jesus.

After Little Bo Peep and Little Boy Blue got married they became very responsible shepherds. They then opened their own wool clothing and yarn business and purchased a computer, which allowed them to reach clientele they never would have known about. Although Mother Goose despised computers herself, she was not beyond asking for Bo Peep's help.

Chapter Two

Mother Goose was so excited about her encounter with the Holy Spirit that morning, she felt the need to walk off some of her excess energy. Instead of giving Little Bo Peep a call or flying out to see her, as she normally would, she decided to walk out to the Blues' farm instead and talk to Little Bo Peep in person. On the way, she would stop in and talk to The Butcher, The Baker, and The Candlestick Maker.

These fine men each had profitable little businesses in old town, which ran along the river on the south side of town. Each of the storefronts along the river had its own unique, colorful, awning drawing customers in. Sapphires, rubies, emeralds, gold, dark and light shades of amethysts and white diamonds lined the sidewalk like a kaleidoscope. The sight was enough to brighten any winter day.

Each shop also had its own little seating area out front with its own unique wooden furniture, much of which was made of bent willow, hand carved oak or knotted myrtle wood. With this invitation to sit down available, the shop owners had multiplied their clientele.

Rub a-dub-dub
Three men in a tub.
And who do you think they be?
The Butcher, The Baker, The Candlestick Maker,
Turn 'em out, knaves all three.

Mother Goose's first stop was the Butcher's market. As she approached, she saw the Five Little Piggy's in front hanging jerky out to dry under the bright orange and purple awning. They were all fat and very happy now since they had come to live with the Butcher, who sold only kosher meats. He had rescued them from a slaughterhouse and then put them all to work. When the Five Little Piggy's saw Mother Goose, they all squealed with delight. She had this effect on animals, as well as on humans. Even her daffodils and tulips seemed to rise early just to be with her a little while longer.

When the Butcher came outside to see what all the hoopla was about, his weathered features stretched out into a big smile. His Jewish nose seemed to reach out to greet her as he took her hand, in his right, and then covered it with the warm touch of his other hand.

"Well, good morning Mother Goose," he said. "What brings you out and about so early this fine winter's day?"

Mother Goose did a little jiggedy-jig with the sheer abandon of a child. Her tap dancing abilities were right up there with the likes of Gregory Hines.

"I am so excited," she said.

"I see that," said the Butcher. His resin-colored eyes gleefully watched her.

"Lately, I have been thinking about all of our old friends and the children I used to take care of and this morning the thought occurred to me to throw a Christmas party. Remember how we all used to have get-togethers not only at Christmas, but anytime, just for the fun of it?"

"Yes, I do," said the Butcher his expression reflecting his memories.

"Well, this morning I decided I wasn't going to let another year pass by. I am going to throw the biggest, grandest Christmas party ever. After the idea hit me, the Holy Spirit whispered in my ear and said, "Good choice my child, I promise that you will not be disappointed. Now get a move on!"

Mother Goose wiggled around again, doing a little tap shuffle with her feet, itching to spread the word. The Butcher and the Five Little Piggy's tried to mimic her fancy feet but they couldn't quite pull it off.

> *This little pig went to market.*
> *This little pig stayed home.*
> *This little pig had roast beef.*
> *This little pig had none.*
> *This little pig cried, "Wee, wee, wee,"*
> *All the way home.*

"Well, now," said the Butcher rubbing his hands together, "if the Holy Spirit's involved in this, I definitely want to be involved too."

"Please let me contribute to your party, or should I say, yours and the Holy Spirit's party. I will bring the best Butterball turkeys you have ever eaten plus some top-notch prime rib, a mouth- watering leg of lamb and some blazing hot buffalo wings."

"Oh, I can't let you do all that," said Mother Goose.

Before she could say anything more, the Butcher replied, "I insist! You just concentrate on the other details and I will supply the main dish."

Mother Goose hadn't expected such generosity. In fact, she hadn't expected anything at all except enthusiasm. "Thank you! Thank you so much," she said beaming from ear to ear. "Please be sure to let your wife and son know about the party also. I will let you know later in the week what time the party will start and where to meet."

The Butcher gave Mother Goose a big hug and said, "Merry Christmas, dear." Then he went back inside to make a list of what he needed to order. Feeling high on the Butcher's generosity, Mother Goose did a little twirl and then with a hop, shuffle and a carryover she tapped on down the sidewalk.

Her next stop was The Baker's shop. She could smell the sweet aromas drifting down the sidewalk. For the last several years, it had become a habit for Mother Goose to drop in just about every weekend in order to satisfy her sweet tooth. Although she did do some baking of her own, it was in no way comparable to The Baker's irresistible temptations.

His shop had the most enticing window display you have ever seen. His scrumptious creations were artfully lined up: mango-kiwi-pineapple-sliced upside down cake. Sidecar, Penthouse, Margarita, or Piña Colada virgin mousse. Blueberry-frosted cream cheese angel food cake. Truffles and tarts and pies of every kind. And that wasn't not all.

The Baker also made the most wonderful bread you have ever

chanced to eat. There were round, oblong, twisted and braided loaves. Some were stuffed with olives and cheese, others with artichoke hearts, pine nuts and peas, dried tomatoes, herbs and spices. Some had cherries and honey too; cinnamon-dipped and buttered blue!

Before Mother Goose ever entered The Bakers shop, she would first stand outside to look over his seductive selections while, at the same time, reciting to herself a bit of wisdom written by Lao Tzu:

The snow goose need not bathe to make itself white. Neither need you do anything but be yourself.

She did this in order to gather her emotions that often seemed to go haywire with lust in the presence of The Baker's stature. She wanted so much to impress him.

Could it be his suave demeanor that enamored her so or was it the dulcet tone of his voice? No, it was much, much more.

Unexpectedly, Mother Goose was greeted at the door with a Big Chocolate Kiss on the cheek from The Baker, himself. Satisfied, he backed off and looked at her appraisingly. In the filtered light of the sun, with her wool coat slung over her arm and her cheeks pinched by winter, she looked so fresh and innocent. Her mid-length peasant dress and tight leggings revealed her strong, youthful legs. Her harness Fry boots, which she almost always wore, added to her natural charm.

The Kiss was a first and it nearly dropped her to her knees.

She blushed, and with her heart all aflutter, she started to tell him about the Christmas get-together.

The Baker looked into her eyes with a knowing smile, and gently interrupted her. "Doll, I already know all about it. The Butcher gave me ring and told me you would be passing by shortly. I wouldn't miss your party for the world. I'd love to stand around and chat with you now, but I have a lot of baking to do since I will be providing all of the desserts. If there's anything else I can do to help, you just let me know."

"I'll see you on Christmas, love!" He called as he headed back to his pantry.

Mother Goose was elated. She tapped down the sidewalk to the Candlestick Maker's shop singing to herself, "Pat-a-cake, pat-a-cake, Baker's man, bake me a cake as fast as you can."

The soles of her boots accompanied her like a snare drum in rhythm with her heart. Giggling, she then walked into the light.

> *A swarm of bees in May*
> *Is worth a load of hay;*
> *A swarm of bees in June*
> *Is worth a silver spoon;*
> *A swarm of bees in July*
> *Is not worth a fly.*

Chapter Three

MOTHER GOOSE LOVED GOING into the Candlestick Maker's shop. It was like being descended upon by the Holy Spirit. The illuminating, warm light along with the soft, melodic hum of the busy bees making wax and honey reminded her of angel wings in motion.

The Candlestick Maker sold honey and flowers along with his beeswax candles. A few years back, he enlarged his business when he caught a Swarm of Bees and set up hives in his shop for them to live. With all the light and warmth from the candles, along with the fertile flowers, his bees produced year round now and he no longer had any need to order his wax from outside the country.

He bought his flowers from Mary Quite Contrary, who now lived out on the Coast. She had enlarged her selection of flowers to include roses and posies, blue lavender and green, along with her prized silver bells and cockleshells. Besides her arrangement with the Candlestick Maker, on weekends she also sold her array of beautiful flowers at the local Saturday market

Now, just like the Butcher had called The Baker, The Baker in turn called the Candlestick Maker. Bless his big sweet heart! So, unbeknownst to Mother Goose, as she basked in the glow of his beautiful shop, the Candlestick Maker was already busy bundling up little candlesticks to light the tree.

Showing them to her he said, "Now, a Christmas tree wouldn't be a Christmas tree without lights, would it?"

"Absolutely not," she said her eyes twinkling with joy.

"Thank you so very much. You three rascals are more generous than a free tub of buttered popcorn at the matinee."

"Well, with you and the Holy Spirit starring in the show, a person would be foolish not to be." The Candlestick Maker picked a posy and put it in her hair while smiling at her whimsical sense of humor; which, meshed well with her humble intelligence and common beauty.

"I'll have Jack Be Nimble deliver the candles in time to decorate the tree. I will also see you at the Christmas party, my dear."

As soon as Mother Goose was out of sight, the Candlestick Maker made a beeline to The Baker's shop to chide him about the Big Chocolate Kiss!

> *Jack be nimble, Jack be quick,*
> *Jack jump over the candlestick.*

Jack Be Nimble loved working for the Candlestick Maker and the Candlestick Maker loved having Jack around. He fully trusted Jack. Not once had he ever knocked over a candle; not even when he was a little tyke and began coming to the shop to visit.

When Jack wasn't pouring wax into molds, scraping the hives for honey or watering the flowers, he ran errands for the Candlestick Maker. Included in his errands were trips to the Coast to pick up flowers from Mary Quite Contrary. Mary didn't know it yet, but Jack planned to marry her as soon as he had his little house paid for.

He was also building a solar greenhouse for her in his backyard, complete with hydroponics. She would then be able to extend her selection of exotic flora which, had always been a dream of hers.

As you can see, Jack was a man with a plan and was really counting on Mary's acceptance of his proposal.

> *How many miles is it to Babylon?*
> *Three score miles and ten.*
> *Can I get there by candlelight?*
> *Yes, and back again!*
> *If your heels are nimble and light.*
> *You may get there by candlelight.*

When Jack got off of work in the evening, he went straight home to eat supper and then went back out at night to lead guided tours through Babylon. That's what people called the poor part of town where there were many little shanties and rundown apartment dwellings. There were also beggars who lived under the bridge, including both men and woman. He conducted these tours in hopes of gaining donations to fund a housing project for the needy. He came up with the idea all by himself.

He envisioned a place that was clean, safe and warm for these less fortunate people to live. A lot of people took his tour; not just people from out of town, but also residents of this seemingly well-off community.

Some of the town's people took the tour more than once out

of sheer curiosity. For many others, it was to get in touch with reality. And for some, they were hoping to gain some humble gratitude for what they already had. It was a real eye-opener to see how these people lived and even more mind blowing, to hear what they had to say.

One time, one of the homeless men who lived under the bridge said to a woman on Jack's tour, "Lady, please don't look so distraught, I may be homeless but I am not hopeless." The lady burst into tears.

Jack always ended his tour with the same quote, one of many that Mother Goose had recited to him over the years.

This one was written by the Reverend Martin Luther King Jr. and was very appropriate to Jack's mission.

> *"True compassion is more than flinging a coin to a beggar…
> it understands that an edifice which produces beggars needs
> to be restructured."*

Chapter Four

MOTHER GOOSE CONTINUED DOWN the sidewalk, along the river heading south out of town, tapping all the way. No wonder her legs looked so fine. She could clearly see the blue-grey marbled river just a few feet below the sidewalk. Most of the year, the view was obscured by the overgrowth of native plants and trees with their foliage out in full force. She stopped for a moment when she spotted a great blue heron on the west bank, right across the river from where she stood. He was preening his wings to take flight. She scanned the river and saw an osprey in full flight headed her way.

At the same time, both large birds swooped down to the river to pluck a shimmery winter steelhead from its journey north. The osprey won the contest and flew off triumphantly while the blue heron retreated to a nearly submerged rock to contemplate its loss.

Approaching a little park, Mother Goose saw a few children playing around the Mulberry Bush, while a few others played on the playground equipment. Naturally, she went over to say, "Hello."

Here we go round the mulberry bush,
The mulberry bush, the mulberry bush.
Here we go round the mulberry bush,
All on a frosty morning.

While listening to the children enthusiastically tell her about their latest knowledge of life, she heard the courthouse clock strike one and saw a mouse run down from the old courthouse roof, right over the face of the clock. Amused, she said, "Goodbye," to all of the children giving them each a little tickle that left them smiling for the rest of the day.

With joy, she continued on her way to the Blues Farm. She wanted to be home by dark so she would have time to eat her dinner and feed her pets before she went out in her backyard to relax on her worn, wooden porch swing and watch the Cow Jump Over the Moon.

Moving right along she made up a new rhyme as she often did.

Hickory, dickery, dock;
The mouse ran up the clock.
The clock struck one,
The mouse ran down,
Hickory, dickery, dock.

As Mother Goose rounded the last curve in the river going out of town, she could see Little Boy Blue and Bo Peep's farm. It was only about an acre and a half big, but it was just the right size for them and their small flock of sheep.

It was nestled against a thicket of red alder trees that grew along the river providing shelter for their sheep during the hot summer months and an escape in the winter from the rain and snowfall. Their home was a grand old farmhouse painted blue with white trim. Like a lot of old farmhouses, theirs also had a big screened-in porch that ran all the way around it.

> *Mary had a little lamb*
> *Its fleece was white as snow.*
> *And every where that Mary went*
> *The lamb was sure to go.*

Out back was a darling little cottage also painted blue, and white. This is where Mary and her Little Lamb lived. They came to live with the Blues after Mary had gone through a long string of bad relationships. First, she had hooked up with a musician, then a biker, then a potter. Then, to her surprise, she hooked a doctor, but he was almost always gone so she moved on to another man. This time she thought her mild mannered mechanic might be the one.... only to find out that he was gay.

Out of concern at this time, Mary's mother, who had divorced her father when Mary was only five years old, claimed that Mary was either bipolar or she had an attachment disorder. She told Mary that she thought she should seek professional help. Mary got a real rise out of her mother's last diagnosis; like her mother was one to talk! She couldn't stay attached to any one man any more than a child could stay attached to its umbilical cord.

Mary went to Mother Goose, after this confrontation with tears blurring her view and asked her what she thought.

Mother Goose wrapped her in her arms, just like she did when Mary was a child and asked, "What do you think sweetheart?"

"I think I just haven't found the right guy yet." Said Mary.

"Well that's for sure. I don't think I would say you have some sort of mental illness either. Your behavior at times does seem to mimic bipolar disorder, but there again, a lot of people behave erratically due to stress or trauma. I think this may be a good time for you to stop searching for a man and just spend some time alone with your Little Lamb and pursue your own interests. Let God calm your emotions and be your guide and counselor. I believe He will bring the right man to you when you're ready."

"But then, I'll be all alone, Mother Goose. I don't have any friends any more since I have spent all this time looking for Mr. Right"

"Mary," said Mother Goose, "you will never be alone with that Little Lamb of yours-and Jesus is always with you, too. I know for sure, also, that you still have a very good friend in Little Bo Peep. She misses you. In fact, she and Boy Blue are looking for help; why don't you run on out to their farm and see them?"

"Thank you, Mother Goose, I knew I could count on you to tell me the truth and to give me some good advice. I'm going to head over there right now."

Mary hugged Mother Goose and as she headed out the front door, Mother Goose added a few words of wisdom from our admirable late president, Thomas Jefferson.

> *"Neither believe nor reject anything because another person or description of persons have rejected or believed it. Your own reason is the only oracle given you by heaven."*

Mary had known both Bo Peep and Little Boy Blue ever since they were little. They had all grown up together and at one time she and Bo peep had been close friends, until she started searching for a husband of her own. When they offered her a job, plus a place to live rent free, she couldn't have been happier.

Little Bo-Peep, she lost her sheep,
And didn't know where to find them;
Let them alone, and they'll come home,
And bring their tails behind them.

Mother Goose broke into a run when she saw Little Bo Peep and Little Boy Blue out in the pasture shepherding their sheep. She ran toward the wooden fencing surrounding the pasture, waving her arms frantically. When the Blues saw her, they threw down their staffs and ran out to meet her by the roadside. At first, they thought something was wrong. Until they noticed that she was glowing and she had a posy in her hair. Her smile went from ear to ear with a Big Chocolate Kiss stretched out on her cheek.

After Mother Goose caught her breath, she told them about the Christmas party in the forest and how she had already spoken to the Butcher, The Baker, and the Candlestick Maker. With excitement in her eyes and voice, she told them about all of their generous contributions and enthusiasm also.

She then said to Bo Peep while tap dancing around, "Honey would you do me a favor and email my friends whom I don't have numbers for? I have a list of names right here." Mother Goose handed Bo Peep a crumpled piece of paper.

Bo Peep looked at Mother Goose's list and shrieked, "Yeah, sure! I'll email them!"

She said this with her eyes wide open, like an owl as she looked at the Queen of Hearts name and the other kings and queens over in England along with Humpty Dumpty and Brian O'Lin, who lived in Ireland. Bo Peep had never emailed anyone overseas before, let alone royalty.

"I do have The Queen of Hearts' phone number," Mother Goose said, "but I thought it would be more fun for you to send her an email especially since she knows how much I dislike computers; this will really send her for a loop!"

Bo Peep was more than happy to be of assistance. Besides loving her husband, Little Boy Blue and their sheep, she loved that keyboard and mouse!

> *Little Boy Blue, come blow your horn,*
> *The sheep's in the meadow, the cows in the corn.*
> *Where's the little boy who looks after the sheep?*
> *He's under a haystack, fast asleep.*

Little Boy Blue patiently listened to the conversation while contemplating the Big Chocolate Kiss on Mother Goose's cheek.

When he got a turn to talk he said, "Hey Mother Goose, if you'd like, I could bring my horn to throw in some music."

He had become quite an accomplished musician. While Bo Peep was busy with her hobbies, he played music out in their little red barn with a few of his friends. He also played around town at the local nightclubs. Jazz and blues had become his favorite musical forms and enabled him to blow a pretty mean horn!

After thinking about his offer a little more, he asked Mother Goose, "Would it be alright for Bo to ask Old King Cole to bring his fiddlers three and the rest of his band with him when she sends out the email?"

"This will be one merry ole jam session," he thought to himself.

"Oh Boy, that's a great idea! I can't wait to hear you play," said Mother Goose. "I am sure that Old King Cole would love to bring them along. This is going to be such a wonderful party. The Holy Spirit has already provided everything we need for a glorious event."

> *Ride a cock horse*
> *To Banbury Cross*
> *To see a fair lady upon a white horse;*
> *With bells on her fingers,*
> *And bells on her toes,*
> *She shall have music wherever she goes.*

They were still standing out by the pasture talking when the Fine Lady from Banbury Cross and Yankee Doodle rode up on their horses. The Fine Lady looked as pretty as ever with all the rings on her fingers and bells on her toes. She was also wearing a beautiful new wedding ring. Yankee Doodle also had on a shiny gold wedding band. He looked very dapper sitting up on his horse next to his Fine Lady with his peacock feather swaying in his cap.

The Doodles were just out for a ride when they happened to see Mother Goose at the Blues' farm so they stopped to say "Hello". It wasn't often that they went into town; you know how newlyweds can be.

> *Yankee Doodle went to town*
> *Upon a little pony;*
> *He stuck a feather in his cap,*
> *And called it macaroni*

Yankee Doodle tipped his cap in greeting with a garish flair. "Good morning, Mother Goose, what a pleasant surprise. My Fine Lady and I have been meaning to come visit you but, well, you know how it is."

"Well I haven't ever been married myself," said Mother Goose, "but I can imagine. How is every thing going for you two? You sure look happy; just like a bowl of macaroni and cheese."

Yankee Doodle, Boy Blue and Bo Peep all laughed. Leave it to Mother Goose to compare their marriage to a bowl of drenched noodles. The Fine Lady from Banbury Cross smiled shyly and positioned her hand on her horse's neck so that they could all see her wedding ring. Mother Goose immediately picked up on the gesture.

"Oh darling, your rings are so beautiful; your wedding band is exquisite. My goodness, Yankee, you must have spent a fortune on it!"

Boy Blue put his arm around Bo Peep and gave her a little squeeze. Both Yankee and his Fine Lady sparkled with pride. Their marriage over in Europe hadn't been voted the most likely to succeed, seeing as the two of them came from such different walks of life.

After they all chatted for a while, Mother Goose invited the Doodles also, to the Christmas party. They said they would be there after she told them that she was expecting the queens and kings from overseas to attend. Yankee could hardly wait to show them all how well off and happy he and his Fine Lady were now.

The Doodles bid farewell to Mother Goose and the Blues, then cantered off up the country road to their home. Their farm was quite a bit larger than the Blues; large enough to accommodate Yankee's team of high breed horses, along with his beloved pony and all of their other pets.

They raised peacocks on their farm because of the unique feathers which Yankee favored for his caps. He came to find out that their molted feathers also made great cat toys when he waved one in front of one of their many kittens. In this way, the peacock feathers became the main source of income for the Doodles when they began selling them to pet stores. They even had to buy more peacocks to keep up with the supply and demand.

Three little kittens
They lost their mittens
And they began to cry,
Oh, mother dear, we sadly fear
Our mittens we have lost
What! Lost your mittens
You naughty little kittens!
Than you shall have no pie.
Mee-ow, mee-ow, mee-ow

The Doodles also had a lot of grown cats on their farm. It started out with the Three Little Kittens who lost their mittens and then, they all had kittens of their own.

The north wind doth blow,
And we shall have snow,
And what will poor Robin do then?
He'll sit in the barn
To keep himself warm,
And hide his head under his wing,
Poor thing!

Poor Little Robin also came to live with the Doodle's when, he found his way to their farm one winter when the north wind did blow.

Lady Bird found her way there as well after her house caught on fire and the authorities took Little Anne away. Although Lady Bird still thought of Little Anne often and missed her, she felt in her heart that God was with Little Anne and that she would see her again some, day.

Before Mother Goose went on her merry way, she hoped to talk to Mary and her Little Lamb but the Blues told her that she wasn't out back in her little cottage. She had gone into town to pick up some spun wool from My Maid Mary and Cross Patch. With this information, Mother Goose decided she would go on over to their home and at the same time, tell all the gals about the Christmas party.

After saying, good bye to Bo Peep and Little Boy Blue, Mother Goose hustled back across the road to head back into town.

Bo called out to her, "I'll call you, Mother Goose, as soon as I get your return emails. I love you!" Mother Goose turned around and blew her a kiss.

Chapter Five

BOTH MY MAID MARY and Cross Patch also worked for the Blues. After Mary and her Little Lamb dyed the wool, they spun it into yarn for the Blues. Neither, My Maid Mary or Cross Patch had ever married. Their love in life was spinning wool and eventually, they came to love each other.

> *My maid Mary, she minds the dairy,*
> *While I go a –hoeing and mowing each morn;*
> *Gaily run the reel and the little spinning wheel,*
> *While I am singing and mowing my corn.*

My Maid Mary never did like living on a farm, especially a dairy farm. Once while in town, running some errands for her boss, she stopped in to talk with Mother Goose about her situation and, like always, Mother Goose listened thoughtfully.

"You know, Mother Goose, I hate living on that dairy farm. It stinks and I am so far from town. And besides that, I really am not one to truckle, especially to a man."

Mother Goose looked at her with raised eyebrows and said,

"Honey, this weekend there's going to be a celebration in town just for women. I heard there will be different speakers and art displays and even live music. Melissa Etheridge is supposed to be highlighting the event.

"Oh, my God, are you kidding me? Melissa Etheridge is my favorite, I'd love to see her."

"Well, sweetheart, why don't you come into town on Saturday and we will go together. You can even spend the night, if you'd like, so we can talk some more."

"I'll be there, Mother Goose. Thank you for inviting me. I can't wait to get away from that ole cow poker."

That weekend, at the celebration, Mother Goose introduced My Maid Mary to Sukey and Polly and to My Pretty Maid and Bonny Lass, and also Cross Patch.

Cross Patch and My Maid Mary instantly hit it off. Needless to say, she didn't spend the rest of the weekend with Mother Goose but, instead, with her new love and new girlfriends. They all got along so well they decided to all pitch in and buy a big Old Historical Gingerbread House in town.

Thanks to Mother Goose's intuition, My Maid Mary now had a partner and other gals she could relate too.

Cross Patch
Draw the latch,
Sit by the fire and spin;
Take a cup and drink it up,
And call your neighbors in.

Cross Patch was also happy now to be living in town with My Maid Mary and the other gals. She, like her friends, had also been a farm girl and longed to be closer to town.

My Maid Mary and her, would sit by the fire together for hours spinning wool and drinking tea. They did well for themselves working for their good friends, the Blues. It was as good, or maybe even better, than being self-employed. The Blues also provided them with health insurance, separate from their earned incomes, which they greatly appreciated.

The big Old Historical Gingerbread House sat just a block over from the old town shops that ran along the river. This was a very convenient location, not only because of the shops and restruants close by on the river front, but also because the library and a favorite clothing shop and a Safeway store, were within walking distance. Everyone in town called their house the Women's Retreat because there was a constant flow of woman coming and going from the home who liked to just hang out at the charming old structure visiting with whoever was around. The gals always had a ready ear to listen and something interesting to say.

Straight women seemed to especially appreciate their time spent there. The gals were all very self-confident in their womanhood. They didn't get hung up on trivial matters and they did not cater to gossip. If you were feeling doubts about your own womanhood, you were sure to feel empowered when you left. Now, I'm not saying all lesbians are like this; these gals were just exceptional human beings.

Polly put the kettle on, Polly put the kettle on,
Polly put the kettle on, we'll all have tea.
Sukey take it off again, Sukey take it off again,
Sukey take it off again, they've all gone away.

Polly and Sukey especially loved it when people stopped by. The two of them made their livelihood hosting tea parties at the country club, and also catered private bridal showers and baby showers. They loved to experiment with different recipes by adding their own special touches. Sometimes, when they had company, they would try out their new creations on their visitors before incorporating them into their menu.

"Where are you, going my pretty maid?"
"I'm going a milking, sir she said."
"May I go with you, my pretty maid?"
"Yes, if you please, kind sir," she said.
"What is your father, my pretty maid?"
"My fathers a farmer, sir," she said.
"What is your fortune, my pretty maid?"
"My face is my fortune sir," she said.
"Then I can't marry you, my pretty maid."
"Nobody asked you, sir!" she said.

My Pretty Maid, like the other woman, preferred living downtown also. Farm life was definitely not her style. She did not want to hear one more proposal for marriage from some man hoping to get a big inheritance if he married her. This happened a lot while she was still living on the family farm. Her dad owned the largest wheat field and apple orchard in the county. Fortunately, when she moved in with her sisters (that's what she called the other gals at the house), her problems with men seemed to disappear. What these men didn't realize was that she was all woman, even when it came to her sexual preference.

Her thing was, and still remained, all about beauty. Although her mannerisms were quite ladida, her beauty was real. Bonny Lass and the other gals loved her in spite of her pretentiousness. She really was a kick to be around. To watch her was like watching Lucille Ball on the Lucy show trying to be sophisticated and glamorous.

Selling Mary Kay products, she made it to the top of the company. She even drove her own pink company Cadillac that she received as a gift after her outstanding sales one year.

> *Bonny Lass, pretty lass, wilt thou be mine?*
> *Thou shalt not wash dishes nor feed the swine;*
> *Thou shalt sit on a cushion and sew a fine seam,*
> *And thou shalt eat strawberries, sugar and cream!*

Now, Bonny Lass, like the other gals, grew up in the country. She had decided a long time ago that she didn't want to be married either and had turned down a few proposals of her own; including a proposal from Bryan O'Lin. He had promised her a life of luxury sitting around all day eating bon bon's and chocolate-covered cherries, but she treasured her freedom and independence. Even more, she enjoyed the company of other strong women.

Like them, she was quite capable of providing for herself. She was a fine seamstress and had her own in-home tailoring business.

She also designed some of her own fashions. Her dream was, to someday move to Hollywood with My Pretty Maid. There, she would design clothes for the rich and famous and My Pretty Maid would be a cosmetologist to the stars.

Chapter Six

MOTHER GOOSE STROLLED BACK into town, along the river, with an occasional tap-tap-brush-slide while humming the melody of *Amazing Grace.* She passed back by the park where children were still outside playing, untouched by the chill of winter. She could see them jumping rope and hear them singing. Being unable to resist, and like a child herself, she skipped over to them swinging her arms and jumped right in.

"One, two, buckle my shoe; three, four, shut the door," she sang. The children's joyful giggles spurred Mother Goose's childish antics along. She held up her dress and hopped over the rope like a grasshopper on steroids fleeing from a predator. Surprisingly, she made a graceful exit, and continued on her way thanking the Holy Spirit for not letting her fall flat on her face.

Next to the area where they were skipping rope was a water fountain with varying heights of water geysers. In the summer, this was a favorite place for the children and their parents to have some good clean fun and to cool off.

Mother Goose thought about little Johnny as she passed by

the geysers. There was a time when he was little that he wouldn't go out to play with the other children if it was wet outside.

> *Rain, rain, go away,*
> *Come again another day;*
> *Little Johnny wants to play.*

Now married to Jill and having three children of his own, Johnny enjoyed taking walks in the rain and playing in the fountain with his family. Jack, Jill's brother, also lived with them. After his fall, he never was quite right mentally and was confined to a wheel chair. When Jill and Little Johnny got married, Johnny had no objections to Jack living with them so Jill could care for him. After all, he was family.

After a long search Jack was able to get a part-time job working at Goodwill, which was very helpful in keeping his spirits up.

> *Jack and Jill went up the hill,*
> *To fetch a pail of water;*
> *Jack fell down and broke his crown,*
> *And Jill came tumbling after.*

Jill, like her brother Jack, also had a little problem of her own. After years of carrying all those pails of water she developed chronic tennis elbow which at times was very painful. Johnny now did all the fetching and heavy lifting. He was such a wonderful husband.

Mother Goose saw a couple sitting on a bench down by the river's edge, just past the playground, water geysers, and skate park. She recognized the crooked cane leaning up against the bench and headed towards it.

As she passed by the skateboard ramp, she saw a couple of young men down in the basin calculating their next moves.

"Hey, guys!" she hollered."

"Hey Mother Goose," they yelled back. It was Tom Tom the Piper's Son and Willy Boy. They were both skaters now and were practicing for the state skating championship. She adored them both. They were the youngest, and the last, of the children who had been in her care before she retired.

> *Willy boy, Willy boy,*
> *Where are you going?*
> *I will go with you, if I may.*
> *I am going to the meadows,*
> *To see them a–mowing,*
> *I am going to see them make the hay.*

Willy Boy, when not skateboarding, took online classes in agriculture and worked part-time for a farmer mowing his fields of hay. He dreamed of one day having his own grass seed farm.

Tom Tom, on the other hand, wasn't quite as ambitious. He would get a job and hold it for a while and then he either got fired or quit in order to run off and find something new and more exciting. Some might say he had ADD, but Mother Goose said he was just adding spice to his life.

> *Tom, Tom, the piper's son,*
> *Stole a pig and away did run;*
> *The pig was eat, and Tom was beat,*
> *And Tom went roaring down the street.*

Mother Goose watched as Willy Boy and Tom Tom showed her a few of their stunts as they roared up and down the basin ramps. Tom Tom did a flip in the air coming off the top of the ramp and landed safely on his skateboard. They both could jump over the cement obstacles with ease and slide along the steel poles as if they were surfing. Mother Goose oohed and aahed while she clapped for them.

After showing her their amazing feats, she invited them and their families to the Christmas party. At first the guys didn't seem too enthusiastic, but they got really excited when Mother Goose told them that she expected all of their old friends to be there.

Saying goodbye to the young men, Mother Goose yelled down to them, "Keep on rolling dudes!" The guys laughed and bowed. They really got a kick out of it when Mother Goose tried to sound hip.

As Mother Goose approached the river's edge, just as she thought, on the bench sat the Crooked Little Man and the Old Woman Who Lived in a Shoe. She had a cigarette hanging out of her mouth, as usual. The Crooked Little Man hooked up with the Old Woman some time ago after her husband ran off and left her all alone to raise their children.

Who comes here?
"A grenadier."
What do you want?
"A pot of beer."
Where is your money?
"I've forgot."
Get you gone,
*You can't have a drop.****

For years, her husband was nowhere to be found, but later it was learned that he had moved to Britain and became a grenadier in part of the regiment of British Guards. That was short-lived, though, for his alcoholism soon reduced him to a vagrant living on the streets. The Old Woman Who Lived in a Shoe prayed and prayed but she could never get him to stop drinking all that beer.

One day, shortly before the Old Woman Who Lived in a Shoe's husband disappeared, the Old Woman was over at Mother Goose's house visiting and said to her.

"He's incorrigible, Mother Goose. You wouldn't believe what he did at church last Sunday. When the communion tray got to us, he took one of the little plastic thimbles filled with the blood of Jesus and, in his obnoxious voice so everyone could hear, said, "This is the smallest **#@+: *---**&^% shot glass I have ever seen.""

"Then he waved the little wafer around in the air and tried to dip it in the little plastic cup and it crumbled too pieces and he got grape juice on his good white slacks. I have never been so humiliated and embarrassed in my life!"

> *There was an old woman who lived in a shoe*
> *She had so many children she didn't know what to do.*
> *She gave them some broth without any bread;*
> *She whipped them all soundly and put them to bed.*

The Old Woman was now very content with her lover and companion, the Crooked Little Man. He had always been very thoughtful to her and her children and he never drank a drop. They never did get married because she didn't want to lose her welfare check and he didn't want to have his disability check cut.

Often, though, she snuck out at night and went over to spend the night with him. She just made sure that she was home before her children woke up.

Most of her children were grown and out of the shoe but she still had several children at home: a sixteen, fifteen, fourteen, eleven and nine year old. She didn't want them to think she was sleeping around. God knows, she would marry the Crooked Little Man if she could and he would walk much further than a crooked mile to be with her.

There was a crooked man, and he went a crooked mile,
He found a crooked sixpence against a crooked tile,
He bought a crooked cat, which caught a crooked mouse,
And they all lived together in a crooked little house.

As Mother Goose approached the charming little couple she had to laugh remembering a conversation she and her best friend, the Old Woman Who Lived under a Hill, once had with the Crooked Little Man.

"I really would like to get out more, Mother Goose. You know, I'm sweet on the Old Woman Who Lived in a Shoe but with this ankylotic arthritis and my IBS, I can hardly do anything. Either I'm in pain or I'm sitting on the pot or both! I've been prayin' but I just don't get any relief and the pills I take just seem to make me worse off."

Listening carefully, the Old Woman Who Lived Under a Hill said to him, "God has a way of presenting what we need when we are ready to receive it. Mother Goose and I have some natural remedies we know could help you if you would just trust us."

The Crooked Little Man, in all his pain and orneriness replied, "I'm not about to try any of you two's voodoo potions!"

Mother Goose and her best friend looked at one another then, with a sudden wave of her hand, as if to clear the air, Mother Goose said, "Listen here you stodgy old man. You need to do something different now! You're bound up tighter then the devil being cast into hell!"

With that, the Crooked Little Man grimaced and with a slight smile said, "Well, what do you two old biddies suggest?"

The Old Woman Who Lived Under a Hill said "I will pick up some glucosamine tablets for your arthritis and also some psyllium husk powder, for your bowels, at the Co-op."

Mother Goose told him that she would bring over some of her homemade apple cider vinegar and also some homemade yogurt, both of which would also help his arthritis and his colon problems. Grudgingly, he agreed to try their remedies, but secretly, he was grateful for their interference.

Within six months after quitting the pills his doctor had prescribed, he felt much better and continued to exercise more and follow Mother Goose and her best friend's antidotes.

While Mother Goose talked with the Crooked Little Man, each taking turns sharing their encounters that day, the Old Woman Who Lived in a Shoe hacked and coughed while chain smoking throughout their whole conversation and thought about how Mother Goose had been such a great friend over the years.

Mother Goose knew that she wasn't really paying attention to her and her companion's conversation, but that was normal. Her mind was always going a mile a minute. Having so many children, distraction had become a habit.

Before Mother Goose continued on her way, she said to her friends, "You know, those who govern really make no sense at all.

It's a game of Russian roulette. They preach to us about the rising health costs, the dangers of smoking, the increasing number of people with diabetes, the many types of cancer contracted through the chemicals in our household products and the additives in the food we buy, but they do nothing to shut down the companies who supply these smoking guns and bloody bullets."

She then folded her hands together and said directly to the Old Woman Who Lived in a Shoe, "Honey, I know you're smarter than to continue playing their game. I would really, really miss you if you died from those white devils between your fingers. Is there anything I can do to help you quit?" The Old Woman smiled at her as she stubbed out her last cigarette and said, "No, I'm done." "That's all I needed to hear."

The Crooked Little Man gave his companion, the Old Woman Who Lived in a Shoe, a hug and said, "I'd miss you too, sweetheart." She snuggled in under his crooked arm and he winked at her turning his attention back to Mother Goose. They both were now focused on the Big Chocolate Kiss on Mother Goose's right cheek. Neither of them said a word. Instead, they just smiled and grinned.

Mother Goose hugged them both goodbye and then headed on over to the Women's Retreat. Intentionally, she walked back along the sidewalk by the river in old town. She would not admit it, but she was hoping to catch a glimpse of The Baker if he just happened to be outside… and he was! She blushed with goose bumps springing up all over her body. Quickly, she crossed the street over to the next block. Just little further north on the west side of the street, sat the Women's Retreat.

Chapter Seven

WHEN MOTHER GOOSE ARRIVED, she stood out front for a few moments gazing up at the big Old Historical Gingerbread House. It was absolutely awesome! The gals had painted the body of the house emerald green and, with sapphire and amethyst they colored the gingerbread trim. All the way around the house wrapped a big southern style porch with plenty of seating for themselves and anyone else who came to visit. In addition to the steps leading up to the porch, they installed a wheelchair ramp for their friend Jack and for anyone else who was wheelchair bound. They also installed a new front door large enough to accommodate any size scooter or chair. It was gorgeous, made of solid oak. They stained it a reddish-orange. English Chestnut it was called. Right in the middle, just above the center, was a bright yellow stained glass window in the shape of a heart.

Mother Goose stepped on up to the porch and rang the doorbell. My Pretty Maid opened the door and threw her arms around her.

"Come in, come in," she said and then hollered to the other gals, "Guess who's here? It's Mother Goose!"

They all loved it when she came to visit. She was the most spiritual, down-to-earth person they had ever met besides her best friend, the Old Woman Who Lived Under a Hill. Unfortunately, they rarely saw the Old Woman except when she came along with Mother Goose for a visit. She was pretty much an, eremite and preferred communing with God and nature out in the forest.

Polly and Sukey were in the kitchen when they heard My Pretty Maid's announcement. Polly immediately put on the kettle for tea while Sukey gathered cups and saucers. Bonny Lass was in her sewing room mending a pair of trousers for one of her clients and My Maid Mary, Cross Patch, Mary and her Little Lamb were all in the living room rolling up balls of yarn. Everyone stopped what they were doing to come out and greet Mother Goose. One thing was for sure, when you visited with Mother Goose, you were guaranteed to never be bored. She had a full reservoir of experience to draw from, not excluding what went on in her everyday life. Her knowledge came not only from reading but also from her extensive travels. After she retired, she and her best friend had traveled all over the world together.

Having done quite well on her own running the nursery in her home and writing children's books, Mother Goose was able to splurge on these adventures.

She and her best friend now made extra money selling medicinal herb potions which they concocted themselves.

The Old Woman Who Lived Under a Hill was especially knowledgeable of the healing potential of herbs and taught Mother Goose all about them. Together, they tended to their herb garden at Mother Goose's house like two Japanese women tending to their bonsai trees. Mother Goose's specialty was making aromatherapy bath crystals using Dead Sea Salts which she imported from Bethlehem. She also enjoyed making her own all-natural soaps. Plainly speaking, she was just very interesting and a joy to be around.

They had all just sat down on the gal's inviting sectional couch in front of the glowing fireplace to enjoy their tea and visit when, Mother Goose's ears perked up at the crooning voice of Mahalia Jackson. She was just about to launch into one of Mother Goose's favorite old time gospel songs, *Walk Across Heaven*. Quickly, Mother Goose jumped up and went over to the stereo and turned up the music.

"*Balmba-Balmba, Balmba-Balmba, Balmba-Balmba, Balmba-Balmba,*" Mother Goose tapped her booted foot and snapped her fingers to the beat. Then, with the swaying of her hips and the rocking of her shoulders and arms, she began to move across the room with a jazzy gait singing,

> *"I got shoes, — you got shoes, all of God's chil-dren got — shoes, my Lord."*
> *"When we get to heav-en goin' to put on our shoes, — we goin' to walk — we goin' to talk All — oo--ver heav'n oooohhh oooohhh! HEAVEN!"*

Mother Goose continued to sing one more round.

> *"All of Gods chil-dren got a robe my Lord."*

Along with Mother Goose's singing, her gestures made Mahalia Jackson's old spiritual come alive. Let me tell you, Mother Goose's voice was as smooth and soulful as a gator moving through the bayou, unexpectedly at times, raising its ancestral head to grab its prey.

While tapping their feet, the gals all watched Mother Goose perform with an ecstatic awe and profound reverence as if they were watching the Queen of Soul herself, Ms. Aretha Franklin.

Mother Goose flung herself back down on the couch with her legs wide open and her arms cast over her head and said, "Whoo, Whee! That Mahalia, she sure can get my motor running."

Sukey shook her head while looking at Mother Goose and said, "Unbelievable! A little ole white woman like you with a voice like that; it's amazing!"

Cross Patch then piped up and said, "Tell us again how you learned to sing and dance like that."

Mother Goose got serious, but with a twinkle in her eyes, said, "Well, there's really not much to tell. Like I told you all before, I was born in London but grew up in Louisiana where jazz and Cajun music and dancing is a way of life. When I was little I couldn't sing or dance worth beans, so my mother, who loved music, took me to a witch doctor and he laid a Mo-Jo on me. He bugged out, his already buggy, praying mantis eyes at me. And then, with one hand full of rooster tail feathers, he tickled me, while in his other hand, he wildly shook a rattlesnake's rattle. He then threw down his rooster feathers and jumped around me like a wild man yelling what sounded like garbled obscenities. Then…." Mother Goose bugged out her own eyes and looked at each of the gals menacingly. "Then, he hit me upside the head with a bullfrog!"

All of the young women doubled over in laughter. Cross Patch fell on the floor in stiches with her arms wrapped over her stomach and tears trickling down her cheeks. After everyone regained their composure, the gals told Mother Goose what had been going on in their lives.

Mother Goose always enjoyed visiting them and listening to what they had to say. Each of them had such a distinct personality. They were nothing like the women you would meet at some social club who all dress alike, talk the same pseudo-intellectual talk and try desperately to be politically correct. Although, in their minds there was much static.

After learning something new from each of the gals, Mother Goose filled them in on her day and the upcoming Christmas event. Naturally, they also wanted to contribute to the party and told her that they would bring their favorite salads.

"Oh, that would be wonderful," said Mother Goose. "Could one of you make my favorite, you know, the one you make with spinach, asiago cheese and croutons?"

"Sure, I'll make that one," said My Maid Mary.

Polly said that she and Sukey would make their favorite feta, pear and watercress salad. Also, Bonny Lass offered to make her delightful, tangy, marinated coleslaw and grapefruit salad with champagne dressing. Just thinking about these yummy salads made Mother Goose's mouth water.

Before she left for home, the Holy Spirit urged her to buy some of Pretty Maid's Mary Kay products seeing as she only had dried up mascara and a few other ancient cosmetics in her vanity drawer at home. She picked out a soft, black mascara to enhance her long lashes and a little compact of light brown eye shadow to set off her deep-set hazel eyes flecked with gold. She also indulged in a misty pink lipstick for her little rosebud lips and a compact of glitter dust to brush over her already rosy cheeks and glowing complexion.

After her purchase, she offered to pay Bonny Lass to make her a new dress. All she had at home were some very outdated party dresses that she just hadn't been able to let go of even though they were faded and some even had little moth holes in them.

"No, No!" Bonny Lass said refusing to take her money. "I would be honored to design something special, just for you."

They went back to her sewing room where Bonny Lass took her measurements several times. Bonny Lass wanted the dress to fit perfectly, and besides, she was a perfectionist. Earlier that day, she had purchased some beautiful new fabrics. She didn't know why, exactly, she bought them but that little voice inside her head said, "Buy them, buy them." And so she did.

She had learned to listen to her inner voice. Mother Goose told her that this was the Holy Spirit whispering to her and that she, herself, referred to his guidance often.

Bonny Lass had seen the results of this union between Mother Goose and the Holy Spirit and she wanted the same for herself. So far, listening to this still, quiet voice had been working quite well for her.

"I have the perfect material for your dress," Bonny Lass said to Mother Goose swooping up the luxurious fabric. "Just look at this. Isn't it just heavenly?"

Mother Goose looked at the fabric in awe. "These are exactly the colors and types of fabrics I had envisioned!" she trilled. Bonny Lass beamed and, placing her hand over her heart, silently thanked the Holy Spirit.

"I'll have your dress done by Christmas I promise you. I can hardly wait to get started on it! I guarantee that you will be the sexiest, most ravishing woman at the party."

Mother Goose wasn't sure what to make of this but she didn't want to interfere with Bonny Lass's creativity, so she let it be.

All of the gals walked Mother Goose out to the porch where they hugged her goodbye. Together, they watched her stroll on down the sidewalk until she disappeared from sight, then quickly went back inside where it was warm. The winter sky had turned a silver grey and threatened to snow at any time.

Like everyone else that Mother Goose had seen that day, the gals at the big Old Historical Gingerbread House did not remark on her sweetened cheek. They did not want to make any assumptions or pry into her personal affairs.

Chapter Eight

Goosey, goosey, gander, whither dost thou wander?
Upstairs and down stairs and in my lady's chamber.
There I met an old man, who would not say his Prayers;
I took him by the left leg and threw him down the stairs.

WHEN MOTHER GOOSE GOT home, she was still flowing with adrenalin and yet exhausted at the same time. She fed her Fine Gander, who was honking his little head off, and then fed his mate, Madame Goose. She fed Goosey Goosey Gander, her Fine Ganders childhood friend next.

He and her Fine Gander had become good friends when they were young while, Mother Goose visited her friends, the kings and queens over in Europe.

On one occasion, Mother Goose had bailed Goosey Goosey out of jail for throwing some man down the stairs in the lady's chamber because he didn't say his prayers. She had taught both the ganders, when they were little, to say their prayers but Goosey Goosey took it too far.

"You can't force people to say their prayers," Mother Goose told him after he was released from jail. Unfortunately, he was kicked out of his home after his run-in with the law and it also prevented him from finding a mate of his own. No eligible goose in her right mind would want a jailbird. Mother Goose knew that Goosey Goosey, in his heart, had good intentions so she invited him to come and live with her and her other pets.

She fed her Fiddling Cat last who was waiting patiently by his bowl. He, like her geese, was having a meal of commercially bought pet food that night. She was just too tired, to prepare them all something special as she often did.

For herself, she made a chef salad smothered with her favorite blue cheese dressing and then threw on some of her homemade garlic and herb croutons. She also took out of the refrigerator a stuffed Portobello mushroom filled with wild rice, chopped onions and wild asparagus given to her by the Old Woman Who Lived Under a Hill. She warmed it up a little and then topped it off with a dab of sour cream and tomato pesto. She also warmed up a small cup of shitake miso soup, made by her best friend. As you can see, she was very hungry.

The Old Woman Who Lived Under a Hill believed that everyone should have at the least one serving of mushrooms a day. In an earlier conversation with Mother Goose, she relayed her extensive knowledge of wild fungi and their health benefits.

"All mushrooms contain polysaccharide and beta glucan. These are anticancer agents that carry the will for our white blood cells to grow and survive any attack. They also have health promoting qualities that improve the immune system. Which over-all improves wellness and vitality. Reishi mushrooms, in particular, carry the highest anti-cancer and anti-inflammatory properties, but mainly due to their triterpene fraction. Triterpene is a natural steroid." She found it fascinating that in China, Reishi mushrooms were known as Ling Zhi, the mushroom of mortality. And in Japan, they were sometimes referred to as the herb of spiritual potency.

When the Old Woman Who Lived Under a Hill mentioned spiritual potency, Mother Goose thought of her visionary abilities. When they first met, she thought that maybe her new friend was eating peyote or the little psychedelic liberty cap mushrooms so common in the area but she soon found out that her best friend's days of experimentation with drugs were long gone and that she truly was a gifted seer.

"I mainly make tea using the Reishi mushrooms," the Old Woman had said, "because they're too tough and bitter to cook with. I just add some fruit juice and a little bit of honey and then they're tolerable. I drink at least two cups a day. The benefits far outweigh the bitter taste. I'll be happy to make a jug for you. You'll see within a few weeks, or it may take a couple of months for you, but you'll soon notice that if you drink it regularly, you will have more vitality. Oh, and that hint of arthritis you have been feeling, will go away too. I've also heard that these mushrooms have a healing effect on the lungs. Maybe we can get the Old Woman Who Lived in a Shoe to try some also. You know, she smokes like a chimney."

The Old Woman Who Lived Under a Hill also shared, in- depth, with Mother Goose her knowledge of maitake, shitake and porto-bello mushrooms and even told her some of her secret recipes.

"One of my favorite concoctions is one that my Old Man used to make using my bread and butter mushrooms. The big portobellos. First, you grill the mushrooms on both sides then you stuff them with turkey sausage flavored with oregano and thyme, salt and pepper and gorgonzola cheese. They are to die for!" she gushed.

"Oh my goodness. Those sound delicious," said Mother Goose. The Old Woman Who Lived Under a Hill chortled. She was delighted that her new friend, Mother Goose, not only shared many of her other interests and spiritual beliefs but that she also was brave enough to try out her bitter reishi tea along with other fungi. The two of them were truly kindred spirits.

Whenever they got together, they had the most enthralling conversations. Anyone would be blessed to be able to sit in on one. Their close relationship also enabled them to sit together for hours in complete silence without feeling the need to say a word.

As Mother Goose fondly thought of her friend, she sat down at her beautiful mahogany dining table she had purchased on one of her trips to the Virgin Islands. She enjoyed her supper while she wrote out a list of things she still needed to do before the party. She used her favorite quill pen that Madame Goose had given her.

After her meal, she washed and put away her dishes and then went into her bathroom to take a nice, hot soak in her claw foot bathtub which she filled to the brim and enhanced with some of her lavender mineral salts.

When she looked in the mirror as she pinned her hair up, before climbing into the tub, she was flabbergasted! There on her right cheek, was a Big Chocolate Kiss!

"Oh that Baker!" she said out loud. "I could just kill him! I can't believe that not one of my friends, not even one of the kids, said a word about it. No wonder they all seemed to have a mischievous look in their eyes". She flushed and got goose bumps all over again.

She soaked for almost an hour just relaxing and praising God for all his goodness. When she got out, she gathered up her clothes and put them in the hamper beside her pedestal sink. She then went into her bedroom and put on her favorite flannel nightgown and blue velvet bathrobe while, at the same time, she slipped into her fleece-lined slippers. She then headed for the back porch swing.

It was completely dark outside now with the moon in full view resting over the big old maple tree in her back yard before it completed its journey around the earth once again.

> *Heigh, diddle. Diddle,*
> *The cat and the fiddle,*
> *The cow jumped over the moon;*
> *The little dog laughed to see such sport,*
> *And the dish ran away with the spoon.*

She sat down on the old, wood slat swing and rocked back and forth while her cat played his fiddle and she watched the Cow Jump Over the Moon. She was so tired and relaxed from her soak in the tub that she fell asleep right there in the swing. Her Fine Gander woke her up and guided her to her bedroom where she climbed into her white, rod iron canopy bed and nestled under her goose down comforter. She said her prayers and then drifted off to a goodnight's sleep filled with sweet, sweet dreams.

Chapter Nine

W HEN M OTHER G OOSE GOT up the next morning, she went into
the bathroom like most of us do when we first arise. When she
looked in the mirror, there it was again, that Big Chocolate Kiss!
She had forgotten to wash it off before she got out of the tub the
night before.

"Oh for heaven's sakes!" she said to herself and grabbed a
washcloth. But first, she touched the Big Chocolate Kiss with her
finger and licked it! She then, scrubbed it off her face.

Hurrying, she went back into her room and got dressed for the
day. Her Baby Ben clock on the nightstand said it was already five
a.m. She wanted to call Bo Peep before she and Boy Blue went out
to tend to their sheep or before Bo Peep sent out any of the emails.
She had forgotten to tell Bo Peep what time the Christmas party
would be and where everyone would meet.

Since she and the Old Woman Who Lived Under a Hill were
the only ones who knew of this mystical place in the forest, she
decided to have everyone meet at the little abandoned chapel that
still stood on the left side of the forest's edge. Everyone knew of

this special landmark. From there, she would have Jack Be Nimble lead her guests through the forest to the clearing without disclosing where her best friend lived.

Fortunately, she caught Bo Peep just in time, she had already been out to tend to the sheep and was just getting ready to send out the emails.

"Good morning, sweetheart. I hope I'm not too late. I just called to tell you what time the party will start and where to have everyone meet. I completely forgot those little details yesterday when we talked."

"Oh geeze, I was so excited about the party and emailing everyone, that I forgot to ask," Bo Peep said.

"You haven't sent them out already have you?" Mother Goose asked.

"No. Boy and I went out last night to Tommy's Bar and Grill. They were having an open mike night so Boy and his friends got to show off their stuff. We got home pretty late and I was tired so I just went to bed. No need to worry, Mother Goose. Even if I had sent them out, I could just email them all again with the details in time. Computers are great! They're faster than the speed of light."

"Yeah, yeah, yeah," said Mother Goose. "What do you have-a gazillion biggy-giggy bites or something like that?"

Bo Peep cracked up. "Hey, sweetheart, I hate to cut this conversation short but I need to run. Someone's at my door. I'll talk to you again soon. Love you. And thanks again for doing this for me," said Mother Goose.

"No problem. I love you too, Mother Goose. Talk, atcha later."

Whenever Mother Goose's doorbell rang, it sounded just like

church bells chiming because it actually was church bells. After the little chapel had been abandoned, someone had taken the bells down out of the steeple. Nobody seemed to know who did it. Years later, Mother Goose found them discarded in some tall grass surrounding the desolate old structure. She took them home, polished them up, and then hooked them up to her doorbell. The sound reminded her of when she was a little girl and her family attended chapel services at a small church in Louisiana. The bells from their church chimed every day, and not just on Sundays, to remind people of the Lord's presence. Mother Goose loved the sound of them chiming in the presence of the Lord.

When she opened the door, there stood Little Miss Muffet pink-cheeked and panting. She was out for her morning jog and decided to run by and see Mother Goose. Little Miss Muffet knew that she would already be up since she continued to be an early riser even after she closed down her nursery.

> *Little Miss Muffet set on a tuffet,*
> *Eating some curds and whey;*
> *Along came a spider and sat down beside her,*
> *And frightened Miss Muffet away.*

"Well, good morning little lady," Mother Goose said to Miss Muffet, giving her a big hug. "Come on in. Do you have time to stay for breakfast? I have some curds and whey simmering on the stove."

"I'll make time," said Little Miss Muffet. "You know how I love curds and whey,especially when you make them."

Mother Goose poured them each a cup of freshly brewed French roast and they sat down at her old grey speckled kitchen table to eat.

Miss Muffet told her about how she had gone out the night before with her close friends, Polly and Sukey. They had gone to a poetry reading at the Whiteside Theater. Everyone knew that there was going to be a surprise guest speaker, but no one could have imagined that it would be the famous Maya Angelou.

"Dr. Maya Angelou? *The* Maya Angelou?" asked Mother Goose.

"Yes! Maya Angelou; the writer. I had heard of her before but had never read any of her poetry," said Miss Muffet.

"Oh, my gosh, Mother Goose, I wish you could have seen her! She is so poised and elegant and her voice is so soothing and yet so strong."

"Shame on those people at the Whiteside," said Mother Goose. "Keeping a visit from someone as esteemed as Maya Angelou a secret is just not ethical. In fact, it's downright criminal."

"I would have told you, Mother Goose, if I had known she was going to be there," Miss Muffet said.

"I know that, sweetheart. I have loved Maya's Angelou's writing ever since I was a young woman. My mother gave me my first book written by her, *I know Why the Caged Bird Sings*. It's an astounding autobiography. After I read it, I saved my money up and bought every book I could find of hers. Her poetry reaches deep within your soul and pulls out the dry and withered fruit, which once was fresh and alive. She has such a command of words, such harmony with life. Like you mentioned, her voice is incredible. I imagine that if mountains could speak, they would sound like her and if she were a tree rooted by a roaring river with rings of ageless elegance and divine wisdom encircling her soul, her words would flow over the jagged edges of one's being soothing and smoothing."

"That's beautiful, Mother Goose," said Miss Muffet. "I can tell that you really respect and adore her. I sure wish you had of been there."

Mother Goose was very disappointed that she missed the event since Dr. Maya Angelou had been an inspiration to her all of her life, but she was very happy, that the three gals got to have the experience of a lifetime listening to her wisdom. Pure poetic justice.

"Polly and Sukey told me about the Christmas party last night and said that they would be bringing salads. Can I bring something too?"

"It really isn't necessary, sweetheart, because there is already going to be way more than enough food."

Mother Goose could tell that after saying this, Miss Muffet felt left out. She didn't mean to make her feel that way so she thought a minute.

"I know," she said with a bright smile, "how about you bring some of your unique little tuffets for the children to sit on? I'm sure we will be in need of extra seating. Miss Muffet lit up and straightened her posture. She would be proud to bring her little handmade tuffets.

Before Miss Muffet went on her way, she asked to use Mother Goose's bathroom. She walked down the narrow hall stopping to look at the markings of the children's heights that were still on the walls. She found hers and, although she was still quite petite, she couldn't believe how small she was back then, at least five inches smaller than all of the other children.

After using the restroom, she came back down the hall and noticed on the wall in front of her a gilded framed quote by Rumi.

It read:

> "Be certain that in the religion of Love
> There are no believers and unbelievers.
> Love embraces all."

"Wow, that's heavy," Miss Muffet said to herself.

In the living room she also stopped to admire Mother Goose's eclectic collection of art. Her furniture was a collection of mixed mediums. She had a big, velvet, overstuffed burgundy couch with an old captain's trunk, posing as a coffee table, in front of it. Diagonally, to one side of the couch, two velvet floral and tapestry wing back chairs strut their stuff. Across from them, a gold and green satin love seat, with little round marble-topped tables on either side, waved hello to the two textured chairs across the way. There was also an old, rustic Adirondack rocking chair in one corner of the room by her old crank style stereo that still worked.

In the living room, dining room and kitchen you could find a piece artwork that had been made by each of the children while in her care.

Some of the children's drawings and paintings she had specially matted and framed. They hung on the walls marking space with colorful memories. Little clay sculptures and paper mache animals also sat around the living room and dining area on their own individual pedestals. She found these unique pillars of stone while visiting ancient ruins around the world.

> *Bye, baby, bunting,*
> *Daddy's gone a hunting,*
> *Gone to fetch a rabbit skin*
> *To wrap his baby bunting in.*

Also, in the living room, was a piece of art that Mother Goose had made many years ago. It was a charming mobile that she made for Baby Bunting. Little gold musical instruments hung down with crystal beads strung up to attach it altogether. Baby Bunting used to love to lay in her crib, all bundled up in her rabbit skin, and watch the harps and horns, violins and grand piano, gently swaying and she would coooo, when she saw the rainbows created from the crystal beads reflecting off the ceiling and walls. The living room used to be the sleeping area at naptime. The other children also, enjoyed watching the little rainbows as they drifted off to sleep.

The mobile still hung in the same place where Baby Bunting's crib used to be. Mother Goose once offered to let her take it home with her when she got older but she wanted it to stay right where it was. That way, she said, she would know that it was safe and, when she came to visit, she could feel all those warm fuzzy feelings all over again.

Miss Muffet went back into the kitchen where Mother Goose was now telling her geese and her fiddling cat her plans for the next few days.

"Kids," she said, "I am planning to go out and stay with the Old Woman Who Lived Under a Hill. I need to tell her about the Christmas party and you know I always spend a few nights with her at this time of the year. If you'd like to come along, then please go pack whatever you might need so you'll be ready to go when I am."

Of course, they ran off to pack their things. They also loved the Old Woman Who Lived Under a Hill and her pets. They especially loved to play in the forest with them.

Miss Muffet watched this interaction intently. Mother Goose's connection with animals fascinated her and she hoped to have the same ability some, day. Once again, before Miss Muffet left, she looked at her own little painting that hung over the kitchen table. It was a picture of two stick figures; one of herself and the other one of Mother Goose. They were holding hands. In Miss Muffet's other hand she was holding onto Mother Goose's Fine Gander's wing and together they were all standing in Mother Goose's vegetable garden.

They said their "Goodbyes" but, before Miss Muffet left, Mother Goose ran back to her bedroom and got her copy of Maya Angelou's book, *I Know Why the Caged Bird Sings.*

"Here, sweetheart, take this with you. I think you'll really enjoy it. Just be sure you return it to me. Alright?"

"Oh, I will, Mother Goose. I'll be really careful with it, I promise" Miss Muffet said.

She asked Mother Goose for a little bag to put it in and then jogged off into the morning sunrise thanking God for another beautiful winter day. She could hardly wait to get home later that afternoon to read the book.

Every morning, after Miss Muffet finished for her run, she would head over to the college science lab where she was studying to be a veterinarian. Her main study of interest was Arachnida {spiders, scorpions, ticks and fleas etc.} Currently, she was working on a solution of natural ingredients to kill ticks and fleas; one that would not cause brain damage or irritate the skin. She was also learning about spiders and their benefits to humanity and the earth. One thing she learned to respect about spiders was the fact that without them, there would be a mass of flies! Obviously, she got over her fear of spiders. She even got her own pet tarantula and named it Spike.

Chapter Ten

Mother Goose packed her overnight bag with a change of clothes. Then she put on her Redwing leather boots in preparation for a run in the forest, and also a scavenger hunt for wild mushrooms, along with discarded limbs, bark, and moss.

Besides her best friend's famous stuffed mushrooms and mushroom soups, the Old Woman also made the most exquisite wall hangings and baskets using all natural materials, including a variety of different kinds of feathers that she found on the forest floor. Mother Goose and her pets always enjoyed helping her collect these natural treasures.

Mother Goose put her Bible in her overnight bag as well as a few of her new all-natural soaps that she had just made. Sweet-pea, ginger and cantaloupe were just some of the scents. She liked to try out her new creations on the Old Woman That Lived Under a Hill because she knew her best friend would give her an honest opinion. She also packed her a few jars of her homemade roasted walnuts, coated in molasses and some roasted pumpkin and sunflower seeds. She noticed that the last time she visited her friend, she was almost out of them. They were her friend's favorite snack along with the wild berries that she found, in the forest.

Mother Goose and her best friend believed in eating only organic foods, when possible, and they didn't believe in taking over the counter medications or prescription drugs unless absolutely necessary. Mother Goose cheated sometimes because felt the need to use mucinex and nasal sprays for her year-round allergies. The natural remedies she had bought at the coop, she found did not help at all. She also indulged herself every now and then by eating a chemically treated twinkie with a shelf life of a hundred years.

The Old Woman Who Lived Under a Hill thought that she should stop eating them, but Mother Goose just humored her and would say, "Well, whatever is preserving those twinkies might be preserving me too!"

Just about ready to head out, Mother Goose went into her bathroom with her overnight bag and tossed in her toothbrush, lotion, shampoo and a hairbrush. Also, just in case, her little plastic sniffer of Afrin. Almost forgetting, she grabbed her nightgown and robe that were hanging on a hook behind the door. Quickly she rolled them up and stuffed them into her bag.... Now she was set to go.

Her geese and cat were ready and waiting outside for her with their little backpacks filled with snacks and their personal food bowls. Her cat also packed his fiddle and a little stuffed catnip ball for his girlfriend, Poor Little Pussy Cat.

She had once been thrown down a well and left to die! She was very blessed that the Old Woman Who Lived Under a Hill had heard about her story and went to the animal rescue hospital and brought her home along with Three Blind Mice, who had no tails! She just adored them all and she especially liked caring for their special needs. Number one being; the need to be loved.

> *Old Mother Goose*
> *When she wanted to wander,*
> *Would ride through the air*
> *On a very Fine Gander.*

Mother Goose made sure that everything was turned off in the house before she went outside and climbed onto her Fine Gander's back. He loved her more than anything. She was just like a real mother to him and he was so very grateful that she found him while, he was still warm and encased in his protective shell.

> *Intery, mintery, cutery corn,*
> *Apple seed and apple thorn;*
> *Wine, brier, limber lock,*
> *Three geese in a flock.*
> *One flew east, one flew west,*
> *And one flew over the goose's nest.*

What happened was just this. One day, years ago, while Mother Goose was walking through the limber lock, she saw three geese overhead and a nest half hidden in the wine brier. One goose flew west and one goose flew east and one flew right over the goose's nest. She waited until evening, but the goose never came back. Realizing then that the egg had been abandoned, she took it home and put it in a box filled with grass and set a heat lamp over it. The egg soon hatched and would become the finest, grandest gander ever! Besides being a great companion and watchdog, Mother Goose also enjoyed the benefit of free air miles!

The Cat, with his fiddle, jumped aboard Goosey Goosey Gander and then they all headed for the hills. As they flew north over the houses in town, some people were outside picking up their morning papers which had been tossed on their driveways. They looked up and waved to Mother Goose and her pets as they passed overhead, smiling like awe struck children. It was quite a magical sight to see; something akin to having a spiritual awakening. When they got out to the foothills, the geese first circled the Old Woman's hill. With precise strategy, they landed right in front of her home amongst the forest trees.

Chapter Eleven

There was an old woman who lived under a hill,
And if she's not gone she lives there still.

Hearing all of the honking and cackling, the Old Woman came out to welcome her friends.

"Oh what a nice surprise! I get to visit with the whole family," she said. Right away the Fiddling Cat spotted his girlfriend, Poor Little Pussy Cat, over by a tree stump playing with a little snake. He asked Mother Goose if he could go join her. The geese wanted to go play in the creek.

Of course she told them, "Alright, just be sure that you all stay close by so you can hear me call."

"They're just like children," she said to her best friend and they both giggled.

Mother Goose picked up their little backpacks that they had thrown on the ground and then she and her best friend went inside. It was nice and warm inside the little dugout. The Old Woman had a fire burning most of the time. During the winter especially, it could get quite chilly living under a hill.

Mother Goose said "Hello" to the Old Woman's Three Blind

Mice who were all laying on little pillows in front of the fireplace listening to an audio book. Each time the Old Woman went to the library she picked them up a new book to listen to. They just loved that old gal!

The Old Woman motioned for Mother Goose to sit down on a toadstool at the table while she prepared a pot of her reishi tea. While she did this, Mother Goose told her all about her idea for the Christmas party and the fact that she had already invited some people and that Bo Peep was emailing the others.

"I hope you don't mind," said Mother Goose, but I was so excited when the Holy Spirit talked to me and confirmed the idea that I just went ahead with it. Don't worry though, I chose the little abandoned chapel for a place to meet. I didn't want your privacy to be invaded."

The Old Woman got up and hugged Mother Goose.

"I think the idea is a wonderful idea, my friend. It's about time that we share the theophany in the clearing with our friends. Now that I have had time alone out here with the Holy Spirit and my husband's spirit, I feel I am ready to share this sacred ground with our friends. But, I do appreciate you not telling anyone exactly where I live. You know how I cherish my seclusion."

Mother Goose couldn't help herself. She just had to recite one of Einstein's quotes.

"I live in solitude which is painful in youth, but delicious in the years of maturity."

"Oh you and your peppered jerky for the mind!" blurted the Old Woman.

"Peppered jerky!" said Mother Goose with her hand to her chest.

"Yeah, you heard me; peppered jerky. Here gnaw on this awhile," replied the Old Woman. They both guffawed.

Mother Goose and the Old Woman spent the whole day inside, under the hill, just talking. Mother Goose told her friend all about her encounters with The Butcher, The Baker and The Candlestick Maker. She also told her that she had talked to the Blues and a few, of their other friends she had run into the day before.

While Mother Goose was talking, the Old Woman commented that she wished her Old Man had been able to meet all her friends before he passed away.

Mother Goose knew this and also how much her friend missed her husband. She also realized that this day marked the day, twenty-five years ago, that he was killed in a motorcycle accident. She always made it a priority to go out and spend a few days with her dear friend at this time.

Everyday her Old Man had ridden his Harley to work, no matter what the weather was doing. Then one evening, just a week or so before Christmas, he was riding home from work and when he rounded a shaded part in the road, he spun out on a sheet of black ice and slammed right into a tree. He was killed instantly according to the police report.

The Old Woman liked to reminisce about their lives together. She talked about all of the things that her Old Man had taught her and the wondrous blessings that he had brought into her life. Even though he was no longer here in the flesh, she could still feel his spirit all around her under the hill and in the surrounding forest. As she runs along the creek through the forest, she can feel his arms around her encouraging her flight while the gentle breeze presses upon her. She can also hear him laughing and feel his fingers gently tickling her while she bathes in the creek and hear him softly talking to her in the rustle of the leaves, as she returns home after her commune with nature.

On this anniversary of his death she always retold the story of how she and her Old Man first met.

"I'll never forget the first time I saw my Old Man. I was out walking one morning down by the river. It was early and there was still a misty fog hanging over the river's edge. As he approached me I was a little frightened by his attire, all dressed in leathers but, when our paths met, he stopped and smiled as if to have known, of our meeting. His chiseled good looks and his rugged attire set my heart to beating like a skin drum. He bid me some compliments and then we parted ways. I was too overwhelmed by his presence to think of anything to say. But soon after that first encounter, we began to meet spontaneously. I know now that our meeting wasn't just by chance. I'm so grateful that the Lord brought us together. My Old Man's love was the impetus that changed my life."

With misty eyes fogging her vision, Mother Goose said, "I always love to hear how you two met. I don't know that I would have been as brave as you. I probably would have turned and run the other way."

The Old Woman chuckled, "Oh, I don't know about that. At least I don't think you would run the other way if love came knocking at your door. But we'll see; your days a comin.'"

Mother Goose slightly tilted her head downward and looked over her glasses at her best friend with a scrutinizing look.

Soon after their first meeting they were married. The Old Man in Leather bought the Old Woman a pair of leathers of her own for a wedding present. Soon after that they were off traveling all over the countryside on his Old Indian Harley Davidson motorcycle.

The Old Woman loved the feel of her hair blowing in the wind. Listening to the growling purr of the bike's engine, its heartbeat, they moved down a new highway in their lives with each outing. The promise of a new adventure with her safely snuggled up behind her Old Man filled her aching heart. Freedom in motion was what she called it.

Each year during this celebration of her Old Man's life, Mother Goose learned more about their travels together and places that she would like to see for herself someday. The Old Woman and her Old Man went to Sturgis as well as other bike rallies with their friends. But mostly they traveled alone to the wondrous sights her Old Man wanted to share with her.

"He was an intense, fascinating man," the Old Woman said. "He had a respect for our planet Earth and a connection with nature unlike anyone I have ever met before. I wish you had been able to meet him before he passed through the veil."

"So do I," said Mother Goose.

"He took me to see crystal caverns in far off mountains and to see the migration of Monarch butterflies in Mexico."

"Heading south through small towns in the Southwest, we often spotted hundreds of Monarchs resting in trees on their way to the southwest flank of Mexico's transverse neo-volcanic mountains. Sometimes we would see huge caches of torn butterfly bodies camouflaged amongst the fallen leaves. A native told us that at night, especially when the temperature drops, that mice raid the trees and eat the butterflies. This is possible because they travel thousands of miles to get to the mountains and when they become tired, they become very sluggish and when the temperature drops below fifty five degrees, they can't fly at all."

"Oh my, what a dreadful plight," said Mother Goose.

"When we finally got to the mountains where the Monarchs migrate, we were ten thousand feet high engulfed in fifty acres of onyamel pine forest filled with these beautiful graceful creatures. Someday I'll take you there," said the Old Woman.

Mother Goose mostly nodded her head and voiced some vowel sounds as her best friend conjured up her memories. She knew that what she needed most was just someone who cared enough to listen.

"One time, on a trip to the desert, we camped by a river that ran alongside a rock mountain. My Old Man took my hand and we carefully climbed up the side, along a narrow ledge, where he showed me old Indian pictographs still etched in the wall. We both wondered if the artist who left these markings maybe had come from one of our tribes.

The next day, we rode to an area called the Painted Hills. The sublimity of these natural sculptures was absolutely breathtaking; you've never seen anything like them. It's as if someone took a paintbrush and layered the hills with colors of their own design. The varied shades of yellows, blacks, reds, gold's and green tones seemed to change with the light. The colors appeared the most brilliant in the late afternoon. We were told that in late April to early May there was also a spectacular show of wildflowers. We had just missed them by a couple of weeks."

"I've heard of the Painted Hills before," said Mother Goose. "They're not too far east of here, are they?"

"No," said The Old Woman. "Do you want to go?"

"Yes, I'd love to! We can fly over this spring and catch the wildflower show also."

"You got a deal."

"One of my favorite places that we ever went to was the Galapagos Islands in Ecuador. Of course, we couldn't ride the Harley but my Old Man wanted to take me to these enchanted Islands anyway. We flew over on United Airways. It really would have been fun if we had had a Fine Gander like yours to fly us there."

"Oh I doubt there will ever be another Gander as fine as mine," said Mother Goose.

The Old Woman continued her story as there was no reason to debate a fact. "The Islands were first discovered in 1535 by a Spanish bishop named Fray Thomas De Berlanga. He named the Islands Galapogas after the gigantic tortoises that inhabit the islands. Although Berlanga first discovered the Islands, Charles Darwin was the man who made them famous after he went there in 1835. When he returned home to England, he began his theory on evolution. Anyway, we went scuba diving near Florenana Island. My Old Man had told me that it was a spectacular underwater wonderland-and he was right. Beneath the turquoise waters we saw the amazing walking fish, which isn't really a fish but an aquatic salamander. Its real name is Axolotl, a native of Mexico. Our instructor said we had been blessed to see this very rare, endangered species. It's the most adorable little creature you have ever seen, Mother Goose. You should have Bo Peep pull up a picture of it on her computer so you can see it."

Their life together truly had been a colorful spectrum of freedom in motion, adventure, and love. Her Old Man was the one who had shown her the mystical clearing deep in the woods behind their hill. He knew of this place because, at one time, the entire valley had been the land of his native tribe. He had inherited the land, which included their hill and a large part of the surrounding forest, from his great grandfather who had been chief of the tribe. They had planned to move out of town and live under the hill in the forest after he retired, which was to be just another year away. This was their dream and for years they had been going out to the hill and digging it out together.

Sometimes when they were out working on their dream home, they would camp in the mystical clearing out back. At random times, the clearing would become illuminated with light. They knew that it was the Holy Spirit descending upon them, filling them with warmth, peace and joy that was unimaginable.

The Old Woman told Mother Goose that her Old Man said that the clearing had once been a special ceremonial circle and favored place for vision quests.

"The Great Spirit always returns home," her Old Man had said.

After the Old Woman recounted her love for her Old Man and their adventures together, she and Mother Goose talked about how the two of them, had met.

It was on the same day that her Old Man had died. Earlier that day, before the Old Woman got the tragic news about her Old Man, they were both at the library looking through the books in the spiritual section. The Old Woman Who Lived Under a Hill noticed that Mother Goose was glancing through a book entitled, *The Holy Spirit Within.* Being totally out of character for her, she struck up a conversation with Mother Goose. Conversing, they found out that they had a lot in common including their love for Jesus. Neither of them had a special woman friend with whom they could share nor had either of them ever met another woman with whom they had an immediate bond. They both knew in their hearts that their meeting was not a mere coincidence but had been divinely orchestrated. Before parting ways, they exchanged phone numbers.

It was later that evening, when a policeman showed up at her home, that the Old Woman found out that her husband had died. All she could focus on was the Holy Spirit urging her to call Mother Goose.

When she did, Mother Goose came right over and stayed with her for the next few weeks. They prayed together, cried together and even praised the Lord together for all of their blessings and his guidance. Mother Goose helped her in every way that she could and, over the next several weeks, their relationship grew and continued to grow into a deep and lasting friendship.

After the Old Woman and Mother Goose finishing rehashing their first meeting, the Old Woman placed her hands on the table and stood up. "Don't move," she said to Mother Goose. "I have something to show you." She went over to her bed and reached under the mattress and then returned to the table with a yellow, water-stained piece of paper. "Here, read this."

Mother Goose read the letter out loud.

You will not be alone my soul's love. The deer in the woods will run the distance with you. The creek will drown your sorrow. The birds will sing sweet songs to you each day and the wise old owl will tell you to whom you belong. MG, with snow white hair, will be there to comfort you. Your smile will not fade, you will fly on wings of love. I am still here.

Your Old Man

Mother Goose handed back the letter. "That's absolutely beautiful; you never showed that to me before," she said.

"That's because I only just found it the other day when I was out in the clearing communing with God. I saw a little rabbit run into a hollow under an old oak tree and as I was leaving, I went over to say "Hello" and there in her little nest I found this letter."

Mother Goose took a deep breath, "So your husband also referred to the Great Spirit as my God?"

The Old Woman's eyes hazed over with emotion. She shook her head, "No, but he respected my reference to Jesus as my God because I am a half- breed. He wasn't referring to God my dear friend, he was referring to you. MG stands for Mother Goose. Look at the date in the corner."

Mother Goose shivered and chills ran down her spine. It was dated three days before his death.

The Old Woman Who Lived Under a Hill opened her Bible which sat on the table beside her.

"Don't you get it? My Old Man already knew that his time here on earth was almost over and he had a vision of you before he wrote the letter. He knew that the Great Spirit had already made plans for you, and I to meet so that we could share Jesus' love together."

She pointed to St. John 14:16 and read.

> *'And I will pray the Father and he shall give you another Comforter that he may abide with you forever.'*

"Jesus said this to his disciples before he died. Jesus knew, just like my Old Man, that his time was about over."

"Then here it says in John 14:18:"

> *'I will not leave you comfortless: I will come to you.'*
> "And right here it says:"
> *'Peace I leave with you, my peace I give unto you: not as the world giveth give I unto you. Let not your heart be troubled, neither let it be afraid.'*

"Do you understand what I'm saying? The Holy Spirit, that lives in you was there to comfort me in my time of need," said the Old Woman.

Mother Goose got up and hugged her friend and said, "I never looked at our friendship that way before. I always felt I was the one to be comforted and blessed by you."

Chapter Twelve

In the early stages of Mother Goose's relationship with the Old Woman Who Lived Under a Hill, she encouraged her new friend to follow her and her Old Man's dream of the home under the hill. With agreement, she and Mother Goose went out to the hill and finished what she and her Old Man had started.

After they completed digging out the living area under the hill, they dug out portholes for windows and built a fireplace and chimney using rocks that they gathered from the creek out back.

The Old Woman Who Lived Under a Hill insisted on an open fire instead of an insert because she preferred an open flame to cook in. She favored her old cast iron Dutch oven for cooking soups and baked goods. She believed it made food taste much better than anything that came out of a conventional oven. At times, she buried her potatoes in the burning embers, wrapping them in wet leaves, while she slowly cooked her meat or fish above on her homemade rotisserie made out of green limbs.

They installed a door to the dugout, made of tree branches which they bound together with hemp. It was charming with little knots here and there and pieces of moss still attached. They made her furniture the same way. Kitchen table, shelves, a nightstand and her bed. The large workbench, they struggled to make was placed along the back wall for her to make her natural creations on. For seating, they found some beautiful toadstools of different colors and shapes in the forest.

Mother Goose was able to get some burlap bags from a coffee shop in town which she sewed together and stuffed with moss. This made a wonderful mattress, for her new friends bed. And, for a homecoming gift, Mother Goose's geese made her a scrumptious goose down comforter and pillow.

When they completed the dream home under the hill they both knew that if it had not been for the Holy Spirit's intervention and guidance, this amazing accomplishment would never have happened. They stood back in awe of the Creator's creation.

When the dream home under the hill was ready to move into, the Old Woman had no desire to continue living in town so she sold her house. In addition, she sold everything she owned except for a few sentimental items including her husband's Harley and her set of leathers. She had her husband buried in his leathers knowing he wouldn't have wanted it any other way.

Not long before her husband had died, he taught her how to ride his Harley. She resisted learning at first but he told her that she really needed to learn to ride in case of an emergency. The truth was that he was planning to buy her a cute little sportster of her own, but that never happened. She preferred to ride snuggled up behind him.

Now that he was gone she was so grateful that he had taught her to ride and more so, that she hadn't sold his Harley. After everything was settled, for first time since her husband had moved on to the Great Beyond, the Old Woman slipped into her leathers and with Mother Gooses standing by, she mounted the old Indian Harley Davidson. With a turn of the ignition key and a kick to the throttle, *vroom, vroom, vroom,* off she rode, out to her secret sanctuary under the hill leaving Mother Goose behind waving and yelling, "You go, girl!"

Every now and then, you would see the Old Woman cruising through the countryside on her Old Man's Harley or see that old Indian parked outside of the library or the Co-op. To see the Old Woman all decked out in leathers, with her long raven black hair flowing behind her, really was sight to behold.

The Old Woman and Mother Goose had spent the whole day sitting at her kitchen table talking and drinking tea. Time always flew by quickly when they got together. Realizing that neither one of them, nor their pets, had eaten all day, they brought their conversation to a close. Fortunately, the night before, the Old Woman had made a big pot of creamy mushroom soup with chicken and brussel sprouts. That night she didn't feel like cooking so she just put the soup on the fire to warm and then threw together a buttermilk cornbread to go along with it.

Mother Goose went out back to call in their pets while the Old Woman was preparing dinner. She called for them, but like usual on these special outings, they couldn't hear her because they were having so much fun laughing and playing together. Mother Goose could hear them though as their laughter floated up to the hill from down by the creek. She walked out through the forest to get them, along the way she admired the beauty of the forest floor and the intricacies of the trees surrounding her.

Her Fiddling Cat had given his girlfriend, Pussy Cat, her new stuffed catnip ball and they were all using it like a hacky sack. Whenever it fell in the creek, one of the geese would honk and jump in to get it. Mother Goose stood there and watched them for a few minutes. Her pets, just like all children loved being in the spotlight and wanted their parent's attention and praise.

It was especially amusing to watch the cats flipping and twisting in the air trying to hit the ball. Her geese had quite an advantage over them with their wide wingspan and large webbed feet. Before they all headed back to the Old Woman's home, the rambunctious critters engaged Mother Goose in a few moves of her own which landed her smack on the forest floor.

"Ha, ha, ha," she said as she brushed herself off.

Dinner was ready and the table set when they got back. The Old Woman had also sat a toadstool next to herself for her Three Blind Mice. On it was a large spool of thread with three smaller spools around it for them to sit on.

She always said, "At the Lord's supper no one should ever be left out."

Their pets all waited politely while the Old Woman ladled out some soup for herself and Mother Goose. She then put some fresh trout in both of the cats' bowls and poured some of the creamy soup over their chow. It made a nice, thick gravy over their fresh treat. To top it off, she gave them each a small piece of sharp cheddar cheese!

The geese honked with anticipation as she cut them each a piece of her hot, jalapeño cornbread and served them a variety of home grown sprouts. They all agreed that she made the best kickin' cornbread they ever tasted. The Three Blind Mice could hardly contain themselves waiting for their, cornbread and cheese.

"UUUMMMM," they chittered and squeaked, "our favorite!"

"Dear Father, we thank you for this food and for all your mercy and blessings and I thank you, Father, for my best friend here and our precious pets. Thank you for your endless love and guidance, which you have shared with us all. In Jesus' name. Amen." After the Old Woman said grace they all enjoyed their meal.

After dinner, with all the dishes cleaned and put away, the Old Woman got out her laptop for the seeing-impaired. It talked to you, plus it also had a braille keyboard that allowed the Three Blind Mice to search the web on their own. She was always looking for new inventions that would help her mice learn and stay involved with life.

She selected a game which all the pets enjoyed and then sat the computer on the floor. The game was called *Farmland* it was their favorite. If allowed, they would play it for hours on end but the Old Woman limited their playing time because she did not want them to become addicted.

Once their pets were all settled down, the Old Woman and Mother Goose each put on a pair of the Old Woman's running shorts. Mother Goose had forgotten to bring a pair of her own. They then got out their nightgowns and robes and went out back to take a run up the creek through the dense, aromatic forest.

They hung their nightgowns and robes on a tree limb and then took off at a slow jog up the creek. Mother Goose was a bit chilly at first with the winter sun having set and the grey clouds making their stance. But as they ran, they picked up their pace in rhythm with the moving water. Effortlessly, they ran for almost two miles up the creek becoming one with the environment. On their way back, on the other side of the creek, a family of deer joined them.

Mother Goose waved to them and thought to herself, "These must be the deer the Old Woman's husband had mentioned in his letter." Mother Goose had never seen them before but the Old Woman knew the family of deer very well. They often accompanied her on her run in the evenings and, at times, slept next to her hill.

When they got back to the spot where they had hung their nightgowns and robes on the tree, by the creek, they stripped off their clothes and jumped into the exhilarating icy December water. Mother Goose quickly lathered up with some of her new sweet-pea mineral soap and, just as quickly, rinsed herself off and jumped out to put on her nightgown and robe. She tossed the Old Woman the bar of soap and then stood on the bank watching her beautiful friend linger in the water untouched by its frigid maneuvers. After the Old Woman soaped herself down she leaned back to let the water flow over her brown skin and through her raven black hair, relishing every moment.

Mother Goose admired the skillfully done tattoo on the Old Woman's back. It was a realistic looking scene of a flowing waterfall in a rainforest with lots of fiddle-neck ferns and lichen hanging from the tress. A single hummingbird was feeding at a brilliant orange and yellow-colored hibiscus flower by the pooling water. Below the waterfall, resting on a large flat rock, was an Indian peace pipe and a Bible.

Their pets had just finished playing their game when the two of them come back inside. With the moon fully overhead now, the Old Woman gave everyone one of her blueberry-sunflower seed muffins and a little glass of milk and they all went outside to watch the Cow Jump Over the Moon while they ate their desert. The Fiddling Cat played a special serenade for his girlfriend, Pussy Cat, besides his regular gig that he played for the cow and the moon almost every night.

Before they went back inside, the Old Woman pointed to the moon and said to Mother Goose, "You see that ring around the moon."

"Yes," said Mother Goose.

"Well, some people would say that means a change in the weather but I believe it's much more than that. Like, maybe, angels dancing around the moon and the rapid flutter of their wings, like hummingbirds, are casting the moon's light out into the atmosphere. Or maybe, the moon's humming and we can see the vibration of his song. Or maybe, what we're really seeing is the reflection of God's wedding band."

"You know," said Mother Goose, "those are very interesting concepts and you very well may be right. Man's scientific findings are limited to just that. {Man}

The Old Woman smiled, "I love sharing my ideas with you."

The Three Blind Mice got into their little nest under the Old Woman's bed and Pussy Cat and the Fiddling Cat curled up together by the fireplace. The geese lay down on the old rag rug with their wings folded under their heads for pillows. Then Mother Goose, after going outside again to potty, crawled into bed with her best friend. She loved sleeping on her friend's mattress made of moss and had been meaning to make one for herself. The Old Woman Who Lived Under a Hill blew out the candle on her nightstand and they all said goodnight to each other. But, before any-one had a chance to fall asleep, Goosey Goosey Gander politely reminded them all to say their prayers...

Chapter Thirteen

THE NEXT MORNING, EVERYONE was up early and rarin' to go on a scavenger hunt through the forest. Before they headed out, the Old Woman and Mother Goose prepared some avocado, cream-cheese, sprout and tomato sandwiches. They also bagged up some berries and nuts. They would have a picnic later in the day out in the mystical clearing.

Everyone brought along their own backpacks plus Mother Goose and the Old Woman each carried one of the Old Woman's homemade baskets to put wild mushrooms in. They were hoping to find enough for the Old Woman to stuff for the Christmas party along with some extras that she could take to the Co-op to sell.

The Old Woman put her hair up on top of her head in a loose bun and then placed her Three Blind Mice right in the center of it. They loved the excitement and adventure of the hunt. They were especially helpful in locating the wild mushrooms because of their heightened sense of smell and intuition. The cats were especially fond of looking for molted feathers on the forest floor, a task which was right up their alley. The geese were really good at picking moss and getting all of the bugs out of it before they put it in their backpacks. Later, the Old Woman would use the moss in her natural wall hangings and baskets.

They spent the whole morning right up until noon combing the forest for hidden treasures. The cats had a blast! They kept running back to Mother Goose and the Old Woman to show them their multi-colored mustaches of molted feathers before they put them in their backpacks. The geese did a wonderful job of picking moss but Mother Goose had to keep reminding them not to eat all of the bugs they found in it.

"Listen up, my feathered friends, I told you not to eat the bugs. Just spit them out. I don't want you to spoil your lunch."

By the time they got to the mystical clearing, they had found, with the help of the Three Blind Mice, more than enough wild mushrooms for the Old Woman to stuff for the Christmas party- and also enough for her to sell to the Co-op. Her stuffed mushrooms and soups were famous. The Co-op always sold out of them by the end of the month.

Both she and Mother Goose sold their homemade goods to the Co-op mainly just for the fun of sharing their creations.

It was another beautiful, cold, sunny December day. The mystical clearing was mesmerizing with the sun dancing off the creek and the morning dew still glistening all around them. Mother Goose spread out one of her favorite wool blankets that Bo Peep had made for her, and they all sat down and enjoyed their lunch. Afterwards, all of their pets, including the Three Blind Mice, went over to play in the labyrinth that Mother Goose and the Old Woman had built some time ago.

This game was especially fun for the mice. Each of the geese picked a mouse to bet on and then they carried the three of them over to the labyrinth and gently set them down at one of the open ends where the Fiddling Cat stood guard. Pussy Cat placed a piece of cheese at the other end and stood guard to make sure that none of them ran off into the forest by mistake. One of the geese would then honk and off those Three Blind Mice would run with both of the cats and the three geese cheering them on.

While they were playing, Mother Goose and the Old Woman lay back on the blanket to soak in the winter sun. It was at this point that Mother Goose couldn't keep it to herself any longer and said to her best friend, "You know The Baker that has the little shop down on the river front don't you?"

"Yeeeesss."

"Well, the other day when I stopped in to tell him about the Christmas party, he gave me a Big Chocolate kiss on the cheek. I couldn't believe it! He's never done anything like that before. I walked around all day with chocolate on my face and not one of our friends said a word about it! He had some nerve. I don't know what got into him."

As Mother Goose told this story, she experienced all the divine sensations of that moment all over again; Goose bumps and all. Sometime ago the Old Woman had had a premonition of sorts.

Her only response to Mother Goose's frustration with The Baker was, "Huumm, huumm, interesting." Mother Goose didn't press her to say anything more. She knew that her friend would not elaborate even if she did.

They gathered up their things about an hour later and leisurely headed back to the Old Woman's home under the hill. On the way back, they picked up more treasures for the Old Woman to add to her natural wall hangings and baskets. They found knotted sticks and twigs, different types of bark and conks. They even found some rare agates in the creek.

That evening Mother Goose cooked dinner while all of their pets played a game of cards [also marked in braille for her mice} in front of the fireplace. The Old Woman emptied out their backpacks of treasures on her workbench and sorted out the different kinds of mushrooms they found and put them in containers for safe storage.

Mother Goose made her yummy tofu-garbanzo bean-veggie burgers and also what she called a white rabbit salad which included cottage cheese, shredded carrots, apple chunks and raisins with sunflower seeds sprinkled over the top.

The conversation at the dinner table that night was sparked with the day's adventure.

Excitement grew when Mother Goose said, "What does everyone think about flying over to the Coast tomorrow? I'd like to go visit Mary Quite Contrary and take in some ocean air before I knuckle down and get busy with the party. It would be so much fun, don't you think?"

Her geese honked and her Fiddling Cat said to Pussy Cat with a sly smile, "There's all kinds of seafood laying around over there on the docks and tons of scraps in the dumpsters."

"Can we go visit our cousins?" asked one of the Three Blind Mice?"

"Sure we can. If Captain Duck is not out to sea we will be sure to stop in and see them," said Mother Goose.

"You know," said the Old Woman looking at the joy on her mice's little pointy white faces, "that does sound like fun. It's been a long time since we have flown anywhere together and I could probably use some time away from here also."

After dinner, Mother Goose said to her friend, "Why don't you go ahead and take your run up the creek alone while I clean up the dishes and get our kids ready for bed. They can hardly keep their little eyes open."

The Old Woman appreciated the offer for she was feeling the need for some alone time with her Old Man's spirit before they left for a night at the Coast. As she ran along the creek, her husband softly whispered words of love to her and assured her that he was all right and he encouraged her to get out more often.

When she got home, Mother Goose and their pets were already asleep. Mother Goose had thoughtfully left a bowl of yogurt and fruit on the table for her. She slipped into her night- gown and robe and then went back outside to eat her desert. As she watched the Cow Jump Over the Moon, she thought about how the Dish Had Run Away With the Spoon and, like Mother Goose, she still wondered what ever happened to the Little Laughing Dog.

Chapter Fourteen

EVERYONE AWOKE THE NEXT morning excited about going to the Coast. They scurried around to get their things together as quickly as possible. Mother Goose didn't want to have to stop back by her house for something to wear so she just borrowed a change of clothing from her best friend. Mother Goose was bigger boned then the Old Woman but she could still fit into her clothes. Having a great sense of humor, the Old Woman suggested that Mother Goose wear her set of leathers for the trip.

"Wouldn't that give everyone a good hoot and holler?" she said.

"What a fun idea," said Mother Goose. "That would be a hoot. I can just imagine the look on peoples' faces."

They grinned at each other with mischief dancing in their eyes. Mother Goose had never said it before, but she always had wanted to try on her set of leathers; and the Old Woman knew it!

First, she put on a pair of the Old Woman's Levis and a purple V-neck sweater. Then, she slipped into the black leather pants. They had fringe that ran all the way down the side of the legs and zipped from the knee down. Also, spaced down the legs alongside the fringe, were silver Indian head nickels. There was a zippered fly in front and the pants had a buckled waistband that also had Indian head nickels all around it.

She then put on the black leather matching jacket with fringe along each sleeve and zippers halfway to the elbow. There were also zippered pockets on each side of the jacket for her hands as well as pockets above each breast. On the back, between the shoulders, was the Harley Davidson logo with wings and a red, white and green leather rose below.

Mother Goose zipped up the front of the jacket and then put on her Redwing boots and posed for everyone to assess her new look.

The geese honked and the Old Woman exclaimed, "Wow, don't you look hot and sassy!"

Mother Goose shook out her long snow-white hair and said, "Lord have mercy! I feel like a red-hot chili pepper. I didn't realize how just a pair of leathers could make one feel so powerful."

The Old Woman laughed because she knew that Mother Goose was in for a real experience wearing her leathers. She was definitely glad she would be along for the ride because this was going to be fun!

Outside, they climbed aboard the geese. Usually, when the Old Woman went flying with Mother Goose, she sat behind her on her Fine Gander but this time, the Old Woman rode Goosey Goosey Gander with her Three Blind Mice up in her hair. She instructed her Pussy Cat and the Fiddling Cat also to ride sitting behind her. Madame Goose had never liked anyone riding on her. She said that just the thought of it really ruffled her feathers.

The Old Woman wanted Mother Goose to experience all the

glory alone wearing her leathers and flying through the air on her Fine Gander. Although it wouldn't be quite the same as riding a Harley Davidson, she would still get some idea of the exhilaration and freedom. She was hoping that after this experience, Mother Goose would want to get her own bike.

"Oh wouldn't that be fun, two old women out cruising around the countryside?" she thought.

"Whoo! Whoo!" Hollered the Old Woman as they flew through the wild blue yonder headed south of town. Mother Goose felt so giddy and sassy in those leathers she just had to stop by The Baker's shop and let him get a look at her.

The Saturday market would also be in full swing so there would be people all along the riverfront. This would really let her get an idea of what it felt like to stand out in a crowd.

Mother Goose flew straight to The Baker's shop and motioned for Goosey Goosey Gander and Madam Goose to follow her down. Atop Goosey Goosey, the Old Woman was tickled at her dear friend's newfound courage and confidence. They circled the air above the sidewalk in front of The Baker's shop until the people below moved out of the way in order for them to make a safe landing. People all over the place were waving and running up to see them. When The Baker heard all of the commotion, he put down his cookie dough and went outside to see what was going on.

He stepped outside just in time to see Mother Goose dismounting from her Fine Gander all dressed in leathers. His heart skipped a beat and this time, he was the one who got goose bumps all over.

She strut right up to him and said, "Hello you sweet thang! How do I look?"

He looked her straight in the eyes and said, "You look stunning. Absolutely radiant, love. I didn't realize you had such a wild side."

Mother Goose blushed then and said, "Neither did I." At that same moment, she realized that everyone was looking at her and she began to feel very awkward.

Coming to her rescue, the Old Woman stepped up and said, "We just stopped by to pick up some goodies to take with us to the Coast."

Mother Goose quickly added, "That's right. Do you have anything special you would suggest? Not that everything in your shop isn't special, but you know what I mean."

The Baker winked at the Old Woman and took Mother Goose's hand. "Come on in, I think I can hook you up with some treats you will all enjoy."

Mother Goose pretended not to notice that he was staring at her as he packed a box for her and she looked around his shop. She was getting awfully hot, but not because of the leathers, though; it was the fire in The Bakers' eyes consuming her soul.

He packed her a box filled with an assortment of cookies and a loaf of braided cheese bread. Also included was his new creation, chocolate covered cherries injected with peppermint schnapps!

"How much do I owe you?" she asked.

"Not a thing, doll. You just have fun and be careful in that outfit. Please tell our friends hello for me, and also that I hope to see them all at the Christmas party."

Mother Goose didn't argue with him; she just quickly picked up the box before she melted in his presence and then bolted out the door before he had a chance to come around the counter. She jumped on to her Fine Gander like a jockey and took off for the sky with the others right behind her.

Everyone below gawked and cheered as they flew over the riverfront. The tourists had never seen such a sight before and some of the townspeople who knew Mother Goose, didn't know what to make of her leather outfit. It was a rare occasion also to see the Old Woman with mice in her hair along with the two cats flying through the air along with Mother Goose. This was one Saturday no one ever would forget.

Once they got to the Coast Range, Mother Goose finally cooled down. She and the Old Woman were now flying side by side talking and laughing about the expressions on everyone's faces, but nothing was mentioned about The Baker or the Old Woman's little fib. Mother Goose had never, in the entire time of knowing her best friend, ever heard her tell a lie; not even a little fib… but she was sure glad she did this time! Besides coming to her rescue, she had some delicious treats to share with Mary.

Back at The Baker's shop, he was dreaming about riding his Harley again. He, just like the Old Woman's husband, used to love to ride but he hadn't for years. He got tired of riding alone and wanted a special someone to ride with him. After seeing Mother Goose in those leathers and the way she strutted up to him, he now knew that someone was Mother Goose. He had had his eyes on her for a long time. He loved her somewhat shy demeanor, her love for kids, animals and the arts and her homegrown attitude that included growing her own plants and veggies. Most of all, he loved her real down-home spirituality. He also liked the way she always looked so feminine in her long dresses and tights. Before that day, he never would have dreamed of getting her on a Harley, let alone get her into a pair of leathers! She had brought his dream back to life and for once, he felt truly alive and in love.

He could hardly wait to close up shop that night and go home where he still had his old Harley Davidson, Fat Boy, covered up in his garage. He was going to try and start the old boy up again.

Neither Mother Goose, nor anyone else in town, including his close friends the Butcher and the Candlestick Maker, even knew that he owned a Harley. They had only seen him driving around town in his classic old Thunderbird since he moved to their little community.

When the flying menagerie got over the Coast Range, they could see the ocean off in the distance with a few boats dotting the horizon. Off to the right, they could see the bay half enclosed by the jetty. There were a lot more boats in the bay than the ocean, one of which was their friend Captain Ducks.

I saw a ship a sailing,
A sailing on the sea;
And, oh! It was all laden
With pretty things for thee!
There were comforts in the cabin
And apples in the hold!
The sails were made of silk,
And the masts were made of gold.
The four and twenty sailors,
That stood between the decks,
Were four and twenty white mice,
With chains about their necks.
The captain was a duck,
With a packet on his back;
And when the ship began to move,
The captain said, "Quack! Quack!"

Captain Duck was just pulling into the slip where he moored his sailboat. You couldn't miss his boat, the sails were made of silk and the masts were made of gold. It looked like something out of a fairy tale.

Mother Goose motioned for Madame Goose and Goosey Goosey to follow her as she turned to the right and then descended upon the tourists and the coastal locals who were out enjoying the crisp, sunlit winter day.

This little seaside town was also having their weekly Saturday market. The festive atmosphere always livened up the bay front.

Besides the weekly outdoor market, there were all kinds of neat little shops to explore in addition to fresh seafood restaurants to dine in. Open markets also sold freshly caught live crabs and oysters with an array of different kinds of fish.

Mother Goose knew that Mary Quite Contrary wouldn't be home yet because she had her booth set up along with the others for the Saturday Market in order to sell her prized silver bells and cockleshells. This was her favorite day of the week. She loved working her booth and especially meeting the tourists. People, like Mother Goose, who lived inland also made special trips over to the Coast just to buy her flowers. With her outgoing personality and passion, she always did financially very well on the weekends.

Since Mary would be busy all day working, they all decided to go visit Captain Duck and his little sailors before they went to find her. As usual, when they came into view overhead, the people below went crazy yelling and waving to say "hello". Captain Duck could also see them from where he was moored. He quacked hysterically and Mother Goose's three geese all honked back.

They landed on one of the docks where the sea lions came to sunbathe and show off for the tourists.

With the tourists and locals all gathered around to get a closer look at this phenomenal sight.

Mother Goose's cat jumped off of Goosey Goosey Gander and immediately began to play his fiddle for added effect. Like always, when Mother Goose flew anywhere on her Fine Gander, there was quite a stir of excitement. But on this day, with the Old Woman and her Three Blind Mice on top of her head, the two cats, plus

Goosey Goosey Gander and Cackle Cackle Madam Goose along, there was a real frenzy. Not to mention the fact that Mother Goose was dressed in Harley Davidson leather attire.

The tourists speculated about who they were and wondered where in the world they came from. The locals who were accustomed to seeing Mother Goose and her Fine Gander fly to the Coast on occasion weren't so surprised. Though, on this day, even they were very intrigued.

As Mother Goose dismounted from her Fine Gander, she overheard one of the tourists say to her companion, "I wonder if they're all crazy? Good God, that one Old Woman has vermin in her hair. I wonder if that other old woman dressed like a biker chick really thinks she's riding a harley?"

Mother Goose smirked and turned to her best friend. With a flamboyant, two- handed toss of her hair she stated, "My dear, there is nothing like a Saturday drive through the sky on a Harley Davidson!"

She said this loud enough so that everyone could hear her. Then, they all strutted up the dock ramp to the sidewalk leaving the bewildered tourists behind frantically taking pictures of them on their cell phones and disposable cameras. Again, Mother Goose was feeling quite hot and sassy.

Along the bay front there were several bars that catered to some pretty rough characters, men and woman. Mostly, they weren't really rough, they just looked rough; all wrinkled and weathered from working out on the ocean. During the week, but especially on weekends, rain or shine, you could often see a line of Harley Davidsons parked out in front of any given tavern.

One tavern, called *The Dingbats, Derelicts, and Lug Nuts,* was a favorite rendezvous for out of town bikers. There were more than twenty bikes parked out front on this beautiful day.

Just as they were about to pass by this rowdy bar, one of the bikers came outside to check on his bike and his cronies. He was a great big burly guy. The Old Woman had stopped to look at one of the bikes, a new model called a V-Rod, which she thought would be just perfect for her best friend, while Mother Goose continued to walk on not realizing that her friend wasn't beside her. She abruptly turned to see where she was and walked right into a big burly biker's chest!

She stumbled backwards into his arms, and he proceeded to dip her back as if they were dancing and said, "Hey, babe, why don't you come on inside with me and I'll buy you a drink?"

The Old Woman turned and saw what was going on and quickly came to her rescue again, all the while laughing her head off. She knew the big guy; everyone called him Trombone. Her and her Old Man often rode with him and some of their other mutual friends on the way to bike rallies.

She introduced the two of them then said to her friend, Trombone, "In case you're wondering, that's her Harley over there." She pointed to Mother Goose's Fine Gander.

"No gas needed, no tire checks, no lube jobs necessary and no throttles to kick; just free air miles."

He roared with laughter causing his stomach to jiggle like a bowl of jello. He pulled out one of his cards from his jacket pocket that read *Trombone's Eastside Harley Davidson Repair and Detail Shop.* Below was his address and phone number.

He handed it to Mother Goose and said, "Well, young lady, if you ever get serious about riding and need some help picking out a bike or you just want to go for a spin, give me a call. I would be honored to be of service."

Mother Goose, now all frazzled and not feeling so sassy, graciously thanked him for not letting her fall. She took his card and then said in a slightly shaky voice, "Hope you have a blessed safe ride home."

They started to walk toward the mooring when Trombone hollered at his deceased friend's wife and said, "Hey, Old Woman, by the way your hair looks like a rat's nest!"

She turned with her hands on her hips pretending to be insulted and retorted, "Well if you had any sense at all, you would know that these are not rats! They're mice, "Lenny".

"Who the hell's Lenny?" asked Trombone.

The Old Woman snickered, along with Mother Goose, as they turned on their heels and continued on to the mooring to see Captain Duck and his sailors.

The Old Woman couldn't stop laughing. She teased Mother Goose all the way there about running into her friend, "You should have seen the expression on your face; it was just priceless. You would have thought you ran into King Kong!"

"Ha, Ha, Ha," said Mother Goose, "you probably set that whole meeting up."

"Yeah, right," said the Old Woman. "How could I have? I was behind you looking at a new Harley Davidson V-Rod. It be perfect for you."

"Well, after that experience, I think I'll stick to riding my Fine

Gander whenever I want to wander. Just look what you got me into!" The Old Woman doubled over with laughter, extremely amused at Mother Goose's innocence.

When they reached the mooring, Captain Duck and his four and twenty sailors with chains around their necks, were tightening down the hatches of his sailboat.

"Quack, Quack, --- Quack, Quack," said Captain Duck.

His little white mice, his mighty sailors, hollered to their cousins, the Three Blind Mice "Hey cuzz, how you all doin?"

The three of them responded with, "We feel ya. We feel ya."

The Old Woman chortled and put them down on the deck with the little sailors. She knew the little sailors would all keep a close eye on them; they always did.

Before Mother Goose and the Old Woman climbed aboard, her Fiddling Cat asked Mother Goose if he and Pussy Cat could run ahead and go find Mary Quite Contrary's booth to let her know that they were there and would see her later. Mother Goose knew what they really wanted to do and that was to go dumpster diving behind the seafood restaurants and markets.

"Oh sure," she said, "but don't you two spoil your dinner." The two cats looked at her with innocent little eyes and smiled at each other then ran off.

"Come on aboard," said Captain Duck. Being the gentleman that he was, he offered his wing to help Mother Goose and the Old Woman up. Although his sailors had already tightened down the hatches, he decided to set sail again since his friends Mother Goose and the Old Woman Who Lived Under a Hill were there visiting. And besides, he wanted to show off his sailing skills.

"I wasn't expecting a visit from the two most beautiful woman this side of the Pacific Ocean," said Captain Duck. "How would you two lovely creatures like to go for a cruise around the bay?"

"That sounds like a marvelous idea," said Mother Goose. "We have all day. We came over to visit Mary Quite Contrary and she won't be shutting down her booth until this afternoon."

"Quack, Quack, hear that sailors, these two gals want to see what we got. Now unloosen the holds and let's set sail!"

Once they got out in the bay, Captain Duck headed east up the bay to the oyster beds. He thought it would be nice to have a picnic lunch onboard with fresh oysters for the main entrée.

Enjoying the ride, Mother Goose and the Old Woman Who Lived Under a Hill marveled at the way the sunlight played upon the salt water. At times it played hide and seek when another boat passed over and interrupted its dance.

As Captain Duck maneuvered around the rocky oyster beds, Mother Goose and the Old Woman, being very impressed, complemented him on his sailing skills.

"Quack, quack," he said with pride as he anchored his sailboat at a safe distance from one of the beds so as not to scratch his boat.

He tossed a rope across to the bed and secured it tightly to the side of his sailboat before all of his four and twenty little sailors ran across it, like a flash of energy through a telephone wire, to pick a nice fresh oyster for their lunch. Coming back across the rope, they each balanced an oyster on their little shoulders now being more careful of their footing. The hardest part for them was prying the firmly attached oysters out of bed. Captain Duck called them his "little acrobats of the sea."

While they were waiting for all of the little sailors to return, Captain Duck made himself, Mother Goose and the Old Woman, each a salty dog. He poured gin and grapefruit juice into the highball glasses with the finesse of a bartender and then stirred in a pinch of salt.

"Toast!" he said. "Here's to two beautiful women and her majesty, the sea!"

"Aye aye Captain!" said Mother Goose.

"I second that emotion," the Old Woman said.

Soon the little sailors all returned with enough oysters to fill Captain Duck's large steamer.

"You two lovelies just sit back and enjoy yourselves while I go down below to my Captain's quarters to prepare a fabulous lunch."

While he was below cooking, Mother Goose and the Old Woman were entertained watching Mother Goose's geese and their seagull friend's dive bomb for sardines. They also got a kick out of the sea lions frolicking in the bay. All of a sudden, out of nowhere it seemed appeared a pod of dolphins and a lone humpback whale. When they heard from a seagull out at sea that Mother Goose was in the bay, they launched themselves like torpedoes and flew through the water to see her before she disappeared.

"Well, hello, hello, my friends," said Mother Goose reaching over the side to stroke one of the dolphin's snouts. The dolphins invited Mother Goose and the Old Woman to come in and swim with them. The Old Woman jumped at the chance and began to take off her clothes.

"Come on," she said to Mother Goose. "I've never done this before."

Mother Goose looked at her friend, the humpback whale and said, "You go ahead honey and enjoy the ride; it's a blast. I want to talk to my friend here. It has been a long while since we have seen one another."

The Old Woman dove into the water with grace and an animality not unlike the dolphins themselves. The mighty king of the sea raised his head to roar his appreciation and then arched his back and retreated under the water with a spray of saltwater blessings. He reappeared beside the small sailboat in order to talk to Mother Goose.

"I'm so glad to see you, Mother Goose. I have needed to talk to you. You're the only human I know that I can trust."

"What is it, my dear friend? You seem awfully upset. How can I help you?" asked Mother Goose.

The mighty humpback rolled from side to side and then looked Mother Goose straight in the eyes and said, "Did you hear that one of my cousins was captured and put into an aquarium?"

"Yes, I did. I am so sorry about that. I, along with some other animal lovers, tried to get him set free but they wouldn't release him. I hear he's sick now so they're transferring him to Iceland where they say he will have more room to move around and also more qualified people to help him recover."

"That's exactly what happened, Mother Goose. I don't think he will make it being separated from his family here and dumped in the strange cold waters of Iceland," said the whale.

"The whole mess is a crying shame. No animal should ever be captured and taken out of its natural environment. God didn't put any of his creatures here to be exploited or to be a sideshow for human curiosity. It just makes me sick. The only thing I know to do my friend is to pray," said Mother Goose.

"You know what else they have at the aquarium now besides some of my seal friends and fish friends that are trapped in little cages?" asked the humpback whale.

"No, dear, what do they have" asked Mother Goose with concern.

"They have a little salt water pond that people can walk right up beside to gaze at the lost starfish and sea anemones. All day long little kids, and adults too, poke at the starfish trying to get them to move. They especially like to stick their fingers in the sea anemones so they can feel them close around their molesting fingers. I've heard that none of them live very long with all of the abuse, but the people at the aquarium don't seem to care. They just kidnap more from the ocean when the others die. They are more concerned about making money then the welfare of others."

"That's just horrific," said Mother Goose. "There should be a law against such things. I don't understand why people can't be satisfied with watching TV shows and movies about animals in their natural environments. They would learn so much more. I promise you, my friend, that I will do every, thing I can to try and stop this inhumane behavior."

"Thank you, Mother Goose, from the depths of my heart," said the king of the sea, then bowed his mighty head and returned to the ocean.

The Old Woman appeared back in the bay riding high on the back of a dolphin. She hung onto a piece of seaweed that she was using for a bridle. Mother Goose waved and clapped her hands in delight watching her best friend joined in harmony with the blue dolphin.

After the dolphin let her off at the sailboat, she reached over to pet his head and said, "Holy waves of grace, thank you so much for the ride my saltwater brother. I will never forget this experience."

The dolphin playfully backed up in the water by balancing on his tale and chattered a goodbye while nodding his head in agreement. He then dove back under the blue, frothy water and followed the rest of the pod back out to sea.

Captain Duck returned topside carrying a large serving tray with their meals on it. He had cheese and crackers for all of his sailors and the Old Woman's Three Blind Mice. He even chopped up some apples for them. For himself and his two lovely visitors, he had prepared one of his specialties. He had taken the oysters and dipped them in beer batter with some Old Bay seasoning added to it and then fried them up just right and laid them in a bed of lemon pilaf sprinkled with snipped parsley. He wasn't concerned about feeding Mother Goose's geese who were still gorging themselves on sardines. Not only was he an expert at sailing, but he was also an accomplished chef and proud of it.

While enjoying their meal, Mother Goose told him and his sailors all about the upcoming Christmas party. He insisted on bringing his homemade clam dip and crackers. In addition, he added, "I'll also bring some of my delicious shrimp cocktail with my secret sauce."

"Oh my goodness," said Mother Goose, "were going to have enough food to feed the whole community. But that's all right. Like I told the Butcher, whatever we don't eat, I'll take to the local soup kitchen."

They made it back to the mooring just in time for the Saturday market to be closing down.

"Thank you so much for the ride in your sailboat and the wonderful lunch," said Mother Goose.

"Yes, thank you for inviting us," said the Old Woman. I've never ridden in a sailboat before or on the back of a dolphin! I'll treasure this experience."

"Well, you two lovely creatures made my day. Now don't be strangers. You're welcome back any time. Next time you're here, I'll take you out to sea where you can really experience the thrill of sailing." Captain Duck meant every word he said. His favorite thing in life was showing others a good time.

Headed back along the wharf to find Mary Quite Contrary's booth, the Three Blind Mice couldn't quit talking about how much fun they had visiting with their cousins and swinging on the ropes which hung down from the masts. The Old Woman was lit up like a neon tetra after her experience with the dolphins. I'm sure you can imagine.

Chapter Fifteen

THERE WERE STILL A lot of people walking around down along
the bay front. As they passed Morrey's Chowder House, there
was a long line of people waiting outside to get in; there usually
was. Morrey's was famous for its clam chowder and fish and chips.
During the week, people who lived inland often drove over to the
Coast just to eat there. Mother Goose planned on taking everyone
out to dinner at Morrey's later that evening for a special treat.

> *Mary, Mary Quite Contrary,*
> *How does your garden grow?*
> *With silver bells and cockleshells,*
> *And pretty maids all in a row.*

They found Mary's booth clear at the other end of the bay
front. She was still busy selling her flowers and cockleshells when
they arrived. In front of her booth, Mother Goose's cat and Pussy
Cat had their own little set up. The Fiddling Cat had put his fiddle
case open on the ground in front of him and while he fiddled away,
Pussy Cat danced. That afternoon, they made quite a haul.

As they approached Mary's booth, Mother Goose shook her finger at the two cats and said, "You little rascals! I hope you didn't get in any trouble today and asked Mary before you took advantage of her situation." They just grinned and kept on entertaining.

"They were great," said Mary. "Actually, they upped my sales. I did really well today." She gave Mother Goose and the Old Woman each a big hug and then she turned and hugged the geese.

"I love it when all of you come over to visit. You're so much fun to be around. Can you believe it? I was just thinking about all of you this morning! Your Fiddling Cat already told me all about the Christmas party and I can hardly wait. This is really going to be fun. I'll bring some of my silver bells and cockleshells to decorate the tree, o.k. Mother Goose?"

"Sure, honey, that would be wonderful. You know, I really thought that I would be doing most of the catering and decorating myself but everyone has been so generous. They seem to be just as excited as I am about the party. I am so pleased; I can hardly wait for Christmas to get here myself.

Your friend, Jack be Nimble, will be bringing little candlesticks to light the tree donated by the Candlestick Maker. He will also greet everyone out by the little chapel and lead them into the clearing by candle light."

Mary hadn't seen Jack in over a week and knew nothing about these arrangements. Her thoughts shifted into overdrive........ maybe she could help Jack put up the candlesticks. They could decorate the tree together and maybe he could come to the Coast and pick her up along with her decorations and they could go to the party together? Maybe she could also help him greet the guests? And what was she going to wear?

Mother Goose knew that Mary and Jack had had a thing for each other ever since they were young. She was delighted to see that they were taking their time and fulfilling their own goals before rushing into anything serious. She tried to instill self-confidence and a love for God in all the children she had taken care of in hopes that they would be able to take care of themselves and not be dependent on anyone else when they got older. She also wanted them to be independent in case they ended up alone like her or they married and their spouse died.

Mother Goose and the Old Woman could sense Mary's distraction and see that she was getting wound up. They could practically hear the whirlwind going on in her head. They winked at one another and then started to help her pack up for the day.

Mary went across the street to the parking lot to get her old Willy's jeep and then she backed it up to her booth space where they all helped her load everything in.

"Your, going to spend the night with me aren't you?" Said Mary

"Of course we are, sweetheart. Me, and the Old Woman here need a refresher course on what it is like to be young and wild."

The Old Woman growled at Mother Goose and Mary said, "Well, you came to the right source."

Mother Goose and the Old Woman, with her mice now napping in her hair, snuggled up next to Mary in the cab of her jeep. The two cats and geese jumped in the back.

When they reached the top of the hill that descended down to the bay front, they crossed over the main street of town. You could see the ocean less than a mile away displaying her power without restraint. They continued driving west, towards the ocean, past quaint little beach homes and oceanfront hotels until they pull into Mary's gravel driveway in front of her little, weathered grey, shingled cottage that sat right on the cliff overlooking the ocean.

Off to the right they could see the old lighthouse beginning to disappear in the gathering clouds. In the back of Mary's cottage, she had a small yard with a couple of little plastic greenhouses for her plants that couldn't withstand the windy weather. Often she thought about moving back inland where it was much warmer and where she could really expand her variety of flowers. But for now, she was content to stay put. She loved the moist salt air and the ocean. And, her quest to find the meaning of life wasn't over yet. On the coast, she had found a unique group of people to fuel her on her journey.

They all helped Mary unload her jeep and put her things away in the shed by the side of her home. When done, the geese ran around the back of her little cottage to look at the ocean and to say "Hello" to some more of their seagull friends.

Once inside, Mary immediately started a fire in her wood cooking stove and turned on her old kerosene ship lamps to light the place up. Like usual, the fog had rolled in bringing with it a quiet grey.

Mary's cottage was very cozy. It consisted of only three rooms. The main room served as her kitchen and living room and off of it was a small bedroom and bathroom. In the main room, a large bay window looked out over the ocean. The view could almost throw you off balance with the waves, seemingly right under foot. Across from the window was a hideaway couch with a myrtle wood coffee table in front of it. One of Mary's coastal friends made it for her after she found the piece of knotted wood washed up on the beach. He had a shop along the oceanfront where he sold all kinds of myrtle wood creations he had made. Almost all of the tourists that came into his shop bought, if nothing else, a set of his myrtle wood salad bowls along with a large serving spoon and fork to go with it.

Mary built a loft above the couch, not only for extra sleeping accommodations but, also because she had always wanted one. She liked to go up in it to read sometimes or to just lie there and watch the ocean; especially on stormy days.

There's just something about a loft that feels so comforting; like having a special hideaway or being back in the womb where nobody can disturb you. For Mary this really helped keep her moods in check.

Off to one side of the couch she had an overstuffed chair with a little matching footstool and beside it hung one of her old kerosene ship lamps. Next to her woodstove she also had another overstuffed chair, but it wasn't quite as big as the other one.

The kitchen area had a small sink and counter space with an old yellow refrigerator placed snugly between them. Above the sink and counter area and over her little wooden two-winged table, she had old wooden orange crates nailed up on the wall to store her food and other essentials. For some of the homemade cupboards she had made little curtains and for others, she left the shelves open to display her assorted collection of crockery.

Mary's bedroom was barely big enough for her four-poster waterbed, which she just had to have. Beside it was a small nightstand, and on top she kept her book on astrology and other mystic practices. The old captain's trunk at the foot of her bed was where she kept most of her clothes. In the wall, at the foot of her bed, there was also a small, shallow, recessed closet where she hung her other clothes. She put her shoes and extra blankets in the small closet also. In front of this open closet she hung a colorful imported tapestry from India since there were no closet doors. In her bedroom she also had more orange crates nailed up for shelving to display her collection of books and knick knacks which she had gleaned from various ethnic shops and new age retailers.

In her little bathroom there was an old claw foot bathtub, a toilet and a small pedestal sink. Again, she had nailed up more orange crates to store her toiletries and bath towels. Whoever built the little cottage neglected to put up any shelving or cabinets in any of the rooms but Mary didn't mind at all because she liked the orange crate effect. She even placed one of the crates on the floor next to the bathtub where she kept her book, the Bhagavad-Gita, and an assortment of Mother Goose's aromatherapy mineral salts and soaps. On top, she had three beeswax candles of various sizes that the Candlestick Maker gave her. She loved to soak in that old claw foot tub and read by candlelight.

At one point, she completely covered the walls in the bathroom with cedar shingles. They smelled so wonderful and earthy that, a few days later, she also completely shingled her bedroom and main living room. In all three rooms she had carefully placed old oriental rugs which she had picked up at flea markets around the area. These helped to insulate the cabin and covered up the worn out flooring.

"Mary, honey, I was thinking that later this evening I would take everyone out to dinner at Morrey's Chowder House. Afterwards, we could all go down to the beach and build a bonfire and roast marshmallows and indulge in some special treats The Baker sent along with me. What do you say?" asked Mother Goose.

"That sounds great, Mother Goose, how about we take a little nap before we go? It's become part of my Saturday ritual to take a nap when I get home. On Saturdays, I always get up really early, usually at four a.m. so I have time to drink my coffee and eat some breakfast while I read my Bible before I go down to the bay front to set up my booth. Also, being down on the bay front all day, in the fresh ocean air, always makes me tired."

"A nap sounds good, sweetheart. At least laying down a spell wouldn't hurt. We have constantly been on the go the last couple of days. I'll go get my feathered friends and be back in a minute," Mother Goose said.

While Mary uncluttered her hideaway couch so she could pull out the bed for Mother Goose and the Old Woman, the Old Woman went to use her bathroom. While in there she noticed the Bhagavad-Gita resting on the crate by the bathtub. On her way back out to the front room she noticed more books in the wood crates on Mary's bedroom wall and stopped to look them over. *The I Ching, The Art Of Tarot Reading, How to Develop Your Psychic Powers and The Book of Wicca, How to Cast Spells* to name a few of them. She had many more books of occult and new age material all promising enlightenment and special powers. She also had a collection of little idols sitting on top of the crates. This really disturbed the Old Woman to see this. She remembered her own days of searching for answers before she met Jesus.

Coming back into the front room, the Old Woman went over to help Mary pull out the heavy hideaway bed. When she bent over to grab hold of the metal bracing supporting the bed, the little leather pouch she always wore around her neck spilled out of her sweater.

"Wow, cool, is that your medicine bag?' asked Mary.

"No," said the Old Woman.

"Well, what do you keep in it?"

"Bible scriptures; four of my favorite passages."

"Oh," said Mary, "can I see them?"

"No, I'd rather not take them out, but one of them reads, *'Thou shalt love the Lord thy God with all thy heart, and with all thy soul, and with all thy mind.'*

"Jesus said that this is the first and greatest commandment of all. It's St. Matthew 22:37. You can also find this scripture in other places in the Bible."

"I read in the Bible that the Jews back then also kept scripture in little leather pouches. They wore them around their heads like a leather headband and also wore leather armbands with scripture in them, also. I think they were called phylacteries," said Mary.

The Old Woman looked at Mary with surprise of her biblical knowledge and said, "Yes, yes they did."

When Mother Goose came back inside with the three geese she saw that her Fiddling Cat and the Old Woman's Pussy Cat were already curled up together, fast asleep, in front of the woodstove. Her geese went right over and lay down beside them. They too, were also exhausted.

Mother Goose immediately felt some tension in the room.

Her best friend sat down on the hideaway bed and patted the mattress, beside her saying to Mary, "Please sit down, there's something I need to say to you."

Mother Goose knew something was up. She went over and sat down in the overstuffed chair across from them and didn't say a word. The look on the Old Woman's face said 'this is serious.'

"You know, Mary," said the Old Woman, "or rather I should say, you don't know. I used to dabble in the occult and mystic teachings myself when I was a lot younger. I grew up with my mother burning smudge to ward off evil spirits and I remember her talking about the evil spirits all around us; all the time. I never felt them myself but I was curious so I started reading books like you have and practicing different rituals to bring on the spirit world. I had no idea what I was in for. The devil messed with me so bad I became paranoid and confused and I was afraid to go to bed at night. At that time, I wrote a poem for the first time in my life, it read.

> *"Ships a glide on a nightened sky,*
> *Heard the sound of a far off cry.*
> *As they neared they saw the tears of one*
> *Who was lost in all her fears.*
> *They set anchor and prayed with all their might.*
> *But as the day lifted the darkened sky*
> *The pain and fear remained the same*
> *Only slightened by a touch of light,*
> *Then again to unfold at night."*

Mary and Mother Goose both got the chills.

Silently, they listened to the wise Old Woman, "My fear didn't stop me, though, at that point in time. Shortly after I wrote that poem I attended a séance hoping to hear a spirit talk and I got the heebee geebees so bad I ran out of the house and ran straight to Jesus Christ; and I haven't looked back since."

"By reading those books, Mary, and keeping all those little idols around all you're doing is entertaining the devil. This is exactly what he wants you to do so he can distract your attention from Jesus. In fact, I can feel him in here right now." Mary's eyes widened and she shot a look at Mother Goose but Mother Goose didn't respond.

"And," continued the Old Woman, "that cement statue out by your front door of whoever she is with the octopus arms with snakes twining around them; with her eyes bulging out and her forked tongue, has got to be the ugliest, creepiest piece of yard art I have ever seen in my life. I almost turned around and walked home when I saw it."

"My, gosh!" Said Mary, "I didn't mean to offend you or scare you. The books are just fun to read and all the little dolls, well, they're just decorations. I think they're humorous."

"There's nothing fun or funny about them, Mary. Those books are filled with deceit. They are from the Prince of Darkness, himself, and yes, you did offend me but more importantly, you offended Jesus. And no, I am not scared, I'm angry that the devil's messing with you. You're playing with fire, little lady. And with your bipolar disorder you have no room to mess around. Do you mind if I say a little prayer?" the Old Woman asked.

"Sure, go ahead," said Mary now feeling ashamed of herself.

Mother Goose moved over to the hideaway couch and sat

down on the other side of Mary. Together, she, Mary and the Old Woman joined hands in prayer.

"In Jesus' name we rebuke you, Satan. Leave this house now and leave Mary alone!" prayed the Old Woman.

Mother Goose added, "And take the lies you have planted in Mary's head with you. Amen."

"I haven't lied to you, Mother Goose, really I haven't."

"I know that sweetheart. We both do." Mother Goose said this giving a nod to her best friend who, in return, gave her a tight-lipped smile. "I am talking about the lies that the devil has planted in your mind to manipulate your thoughts so that you won't be focused on Jesus."

At that moment, Mary had an earth shaking epiphany. It was as if the ocean flooded her mind and brought her into the guiding light of the Holy Spirit's truth. She trembled uncontrollably while Mother Goose and the Old Woman sat quietly beside her while she shook off the dirty residue of the devil.

When Mary recovered, she jumped up and ran outside to her shed and returned with some empty boxes. She went straight into her bedroom and tore down the books from her shelves along with her so-called decorations.

From the bedroom she called to Mother Goose, "Can I keep the book on how to develop my psychic powers?"

Mother Goose looked at her best friend and rolled her eyes and said, "No Mary, not if your choice is to follow Jesus."

The Old Woman hollered, "Believe me, the closer you get to the Holy Spirit, the more intuitive you will become. That stuff is just a bunch of crap."

Mary continued to pack up all of her hocus-pocus books and little idols; this time, without reservation. She could feel an uncomfortable tug from the devil, himself, still present in her home and tempting her. She now wanted him gone. For good.

After taking all of the packed boxes out to her truck, later to be taken to the dump, she came back inside and went into her bathroom where she remembered she still had the Bhagavad Gita. She picked it up and lightly touched its cover and then went back out to the front room. She held the book up so that Mother Goose and the Old Woman could see it.

"What do you think about this book? It has a lot about getting in touch with God in it." Mother Goose didn't hesitate to say that she thought the Bhagavad Gita was a great philosophical book from ancient India and that Gandhi, along with other great minds, referred to it as a source of spiritual insight. She thought that it was all right for Mary to keep it.

"In fact," she said, "I have read it myself as well as other spiritual teachings written for different cultures. When reading any spiritual teaching, other than the Bible, I first pray that Jesus will give me wisdom to ingest only that which is edifying to the soul and not something that could lead me astray from his divine truths. I also really enjoy books of poetry and other writings by Eastern philosophers. Siddhartha, the story of Buddha, is one of my favorites and I love the poetic wisdom written by Rumi. Confucius also moves my soul," Mother Goose continued.

Mary looked at the Old Woman and asked, "What do you think?"

The Old Woman shrugged her shoulders and said, "Well, personally, I think you ought to stick to the Bible before you go off searching again and get lost. The Bible makes it very clear that there is only one God, and that is Jesus. It also states that you should put no idols before him. I would rather be safe than sorry in the end." Mary hugged the Old Woman, and then she hugged Mother Goose.

"Thank you. I respect your opinions." She went back to her bedroom and put the book away in her trunk at the foot of her bed, burying it deep beneath her sweaters.

Chapter Sixteen

AT THIS POINT, NO one was able to sleep but they did lie down for a while to relax their tensed muscles. Dealing with the devil is never an easy task.

"Mother Goose, can I cuddle with you?" Mary asked.

"Sure you can, sweetheart."

"Oh good," said the Old Woman, "I want to try out the loft." She climbed on up.

Mother Goose still had on the leather pants from her biker ensemble and, as she was taking them off, Mary said, "By the way Mother Goose, what's with the leathers?"

Mother Goose started to answer when her best friend laughed and said from up above, "Let's just say it's a way of two old women amusing themselves."

Mother Goose laughed with her. She filled Mary in on her encounters with The Baker and Trombone, the big biker dude. She also told Mary about the woman, down on the wharf, and her remark about them all being crazy.

Mary cracked up and said, "You never cease to amaze me, Mother Goose, with your lack of inhibitions."

"Oh I wouldn't go as far as to say that; I do have my limits. And really, believe it or not, I am rather shy."

Mary, now snuggled up in Mother Goose's arms, was feeling much better and much safer.

Up above in the loft, the Old Woman was in deep thought, "Mary she said, I notice you have a Bible on your table over there. Do you read it often?"

"Oh yeah, just about every morning. I used to love it when I stayed with Mother Goose as a kid and she read Bible stories to us. I still like to read it but sometimes it's hard to understand because it seems like there are a lot of contradictions."

"That's because you have been contrary to your devotion to the Lord," said the Old Woman. Remember the scripture, the one I keep in my leather pouch that I read to you earlier? Jesus says we are to put him first before all else."

"Yes I remember that and I'm going to start doing that from now on. Maybe people won't call me Mary Quite Contrary then."

Mother Goose and the Old Woman couldn't help but laugh at Mary's revelation and Mother Goose said, "Don't you worry about that Mary. One thing is for sure, there's nothing contradictory about the love in your heart."

From this point in the conversation, Mother Goose jumped at the chance to get the subject off religion. She knew that if she didn't, her best friend might overwhelm Mary with her passionate approach to theology.

"I like using nicknames myself," said Mother Goose, "in terms of endearment."

"How did you get to be called Mother Goose?" asked Mary.

"Well, somebody pinned that name on me a long time ago. I can't remember who it was, but it was after my Fine Gander grew up. Everyone knew that I had raised him from an egg."

"Hmmm, well what's your real name?" Mary asked coyly.

"I'll tell you if you promise not to tell anyone."

"I swear on a stack of Bibles. Really, I promise. Cross my heart and hope to die."

"Well, I don't want you to die, so I guess I better tell you. My given name is Sapphire Blue Soulea."

"Oh, I love that name. It's so cool," said Mary. "How did your mom come up with that?"

"Well, the Sa, in Sapphire, reminded her of Sassafras, which is used to flavor root beer. She loved root beer floats. She said that I also acquired a taste for them early on and that I had a spirit that glowed like the embers in a fire. So together, she had Sapphire. Besides that, I was born in September. I'm sure you know what birthstone that is."

Mary giggled, "Yeah, September has a blue Sapphire. I know all the birthstones, I learned them from my astrology book."

 "I figured you did" said Mother Goose with a smile.

From up above, the Old Woman said, "I used to have another nickname besides the Old Woman Who Lived Under a Hill. My Old Man used to call me, 'Little running doe'. Actually, it was an Indian name he gave me when we got together. He said that I had eyes like a deer and I moved with the swiftness of hinds' feet."

"What are hind's feet? Asked Mary.

Mother Goose thought to herself, "Uh-oh, here we go again."

"A hind is a female deer. They're mentioned several times in the poetical books of the Bible," said the Old Woman.

"For example, in one place it says, *'He maketh my feet like hind's feet,'* in speaking of swiftly escaping from one's enemies."

"My hind's feet sure came in handy when I, ran from the devil."

In a sultry voice, Mother Goose quickly interjected, "Oh how I fawn over your doe eyes, and dem, dare hind's feet make me want to fly."

Mary covered her mouth with her hands trying hard to suppress her laughter and the Old Woman up above said, "That's really scraping the bottom of your poetic talent my friend."

Mother Goose flashed Mary a big white smile and gave her a nudge and then jumped up off the bed and said, "Let's go eat. I'm hungry."

"I'm in," said the Old Woman as she sprang down out of the loft with the agility of a cat. She landed on the hideaway bed below tackling Mary and tickling her until she surrendered.

Before they all got into Mary's old Willy's jeep, the Old Woman pointed to the serpent statue by Mary's front door and said, "Do you think you could do something with that demon sculpture before we leave so we don't have to come back here and see it again?"

Mary immediately went over and picked it up saying, "It is kinda creepy isn't it?" She put it out of sight with the rest of her unwanted books and idol décor.

They went back down to the bay front and were lucky that the line out in front of Morrey's Chowder House was moving quickly. It didn't take them long to be seated. While they were still looking over the menu, Mother Goose noticed a couple come into the restaurant. She thought that they looked a lot like Jack Sprat and his wife. But then again, she thought to herself, "No, that can't be them. He's in way too good of shape to be Mr. Sprat and she's way too thin and trim to be his wife."

That's when Mary said, "Hey, there's the Sprats!

Jack Spratt could eat no fat,
And his wife could eat no lean,
And so, betwixt them both you see,
They licked the platter clean

Mother Goose and the Old Woman could hardly believe it. The Sprats looked terrific! The last time either of them had seen the Sprats, they were both in very sad shape. It seemed that Jack could eat no fat and was just withering away while his wife could eat no lean and had become morbidly obese. They both were terribly depressed. Mother Goose quickly made room for them at their table and asked the couple seated next to her if she could take the extra chairs.

"Of course," said the woman, "it's just the two of us here tonight."

"Thank you so much," said Mother Goose moving the chairs over to their table. She then went out to the lobby to greet the Sprats. When Mrs. Sprat saw Mother Goose, she threw her arms around her and immediately began to explain why she hadn't called her in so long or, come to see her.

Mother Goose just shook her head and said, "There's no need to explain." With a flashy white smile she continued, "But you will have some explaining to do if the two of you don't join us for dinner!"

Once they were all seated at the table, the waiter came right over with complimentary bowls of chowder and little dinner salads for each of them. In addition, he brought a couple more menus for the Sprats and two more tall glasses of ice water with lemon slices.

Mary chattered on and on about how happy she was that Mother Goose and the Old Woman had come to see her, and she talked about her flower business and about her other friends while they ate their chowder and salads. Sometimes with Mary's bipolar disorder she could be all over the board. It wasn't until after the waiter had come back and took their orders and then returned with their main dish that Mrs. Sprat got a chance to share her story.

Mother Goose and the Old Woman wanted to know what brought on this change in the Sprats; not just physically but, spiritually also. They were animated and alive with a vibrancy for life like never before. For Mary Quite Contrary, seeing this change in them wasn't such a big deal since she saw them almost once every month when they came to stay at their own little beach house.

But for Mother Goose and the Old Woman, this dramatic change in their lives was a revelation and they wanted to know what had brought it on.

While still living in the small community where Mother Goose and the Old Woman lived, the Sprats' health increasingly worsened. They began to isolate themselves from others and also felt deserted by God. They couldn't seem to get themselves together. Out of shame, they moved all the way up north to the tip of Alaska hoping to be where nobody would know them and they could start all over again. To their dismay, things only got worse.

Jack became anorexic and Mrs. Sprat was putting on more pounds by the minute. The two of them became increasingly depressed. Mrs. Sprat was even thinking about suicide. They had begun to blame their problems on each another. They went to numerous doctors in search of help but no prescription helped them for long. Also, they were unable to stick to any diet or exercise program suggested by the doctors.

One day, in desperation to save his wife and himself, Jack got down on his knees and began to pray. When his wife saw him doing this, she got down beside him, as hard as that was for her, and prayed with him. She loved her husband and realized that she really didn't want to die either.

After the two of them had finished praying together, Jack got up. He tenderly helped his wife up also and then turned on their favorite oldies station hoping to cheer things up a bit. Instead, of hearing their favorite oldies music coming from the radio, they heard a minister preaching about God.

"Through Jesus Christ all things are possible," said the minister. *"He will not leave you nor forsake you."* They both sat quietly and listened not yet realizing that the Holy Spirit was in total control.

> *Doctor Foster went to Gloster*
> *In a shower of rain.*
> *He stepped in a puddle,*
> *Up to his middle,*
> *And never went there again.*

At the station break, a Christian by the name of Dr. Foster came on and invited anyone in the listening audience to give him a call if they were battling depression or any other type of debilitating condition. He guaranteed that if they followed his advice, they would be healed. What particularly moved the Sprats was that the Dr. offered his help, free of charge.

He told the radio audience that he had, at one time, suffered from depression and self-will himself. But, the Lord intervened and renewed his mind, making him aware that his self-will was the cause of his problems. He was born again, so to speak, and it didn't cost him a dime. All he needed was a sincere desire to be truly happy and to follow Gods word and not his own.

The Sprats could feel the presence of the Holy Spirit in the room. They wanted, more than anything, to be healed and truly happy. So, with hope in their hearts that Dr. Foster's proposal was real and that he was not just another wolf in sheep's clothing, Jack turned off the radio, picked up the phone and called Dr. Foster.

They were amazed and delighted when Dr. Foster picked up the phone and it wasn't some impersonal answering service. He listened with compassion to their stories of ill health, loss and separation from the Lord. After hearing about how the Holy Spirit had interrupted the Sprats' regular radio broadcast, he knew that the Sprats were sincerely ready for help and that he had been summoned by the Lord to do his work. Dr. Foster took down Jack's phone number and address and told him that he would be flying up the next day to meet both of them. He promised that he would stay as long as necessary to diagnose their physical problems and to initiate spiritual healing. Before he hung up, he reassured Jack that help truly was on its way and advised him and his wife to pray without ceasing until he got there.

After Jack hung up the phone, his eyes welled up with tears and he hugged his wife and told her what the doctor had said. She also became flooded with hope. The rest of that day and all evening the Sprats continued to pray for God's healing and to rebuke any negative thoughts that crept in. The Sprats wanted to believe the doctor, more than anything, and hoped that he would actually show up.

Jack tried to tune in the Christian broadcast again after he hung up the phone but all he could get was their regular oldies station. He couldn't find this station on any of the other channels either, so he called the radio station and asked what had happened. The man on the line told Jack that in their area there were no Christian broadcasts and that it would have been impossible to receive one. Jack hung up the phone with his eyes aglow and a big buck-toothed smile.

He pulled his wife into his arms and said, "Don't worry honey, help is truly on its way. In fact it has already been here!"

Mrs. Sprat realized that neither she nor Jack had had anything to eat all day. Feeling quite hungry now, she put a giant pizza in the oven to bake and asked Jack what he would like. As usual, he said he wasn't hungry. Strangely, when she sat down at the table to eat her pizza, she only ate one slice and Jack devoured the rest!

Dr. Foster showed up early the next day, just like he said he would. Enthusiastically, the Sprats invited him into their home. They felt like they had known him for years. And, just like old friends, they sat in their living room comfortably sharing their lives with each other.

During the conversation, Dr. Foster told the Sprats about his own battle with depression and poor health at one time. He had put all his value as a human being in other peoples' hands. His motivation was only sparked by their approval and when he didn't get it he would plummet into self-destruction. His parents always expected more of him and his friends thought his aspirations were too high.

During this period of despair, he heard a little voice keep telling him to read the Bible. The voice assured him that in the Bible he would find truth and all the love and guidance he would ever need to live a healthy and truly happy life. In desperation, he began to read and turned his will and his life completely over to God and accepted Jesus Christ as his personal Savior. From that day forth, his life completely changed.

Dr. Foster had been in practice for several years. Having been to medical school where he learned only traditional western medicine, he hadn't been happy. He, like a lot of doctors, was expected to dole out pills to support the pharmaceutical industry; many of which had vicious side effects. In addition, in order to earn extra money for the medical clinic, he also was required to perform operations-even when the outcome of the operation wasn't really expected to be successful! Whatever quality of life the person may have known would be completely destroyed after having the surgery.

Because Dr. Foster wanted to find real answers to peoples' problems, he closed down his practice and set out on a mission. The Holy Spirit guided him around the world where he learned new ways from other cultures to heal the sick. He also learned new surgical techniques from some of the best surgeons in the world. With this new insight, and the Lord as his guide, he returned home to the States and moved to the desert for his own health. He welcomed the dry climate for he wasn't fond of the continual rain in Gloster where he had been living. He called everyone there, "puddle jumpers".

He re-opened his practice; this time depending totally on the Lord for guidance. He soon became the world's best surgeon; his lifelong dream fulfilled. He also became a leading authority on natural medicine, mental illness and compulsive disorders.

He found that by just adding some essential amino acids and vitamins to a person's daily diet, along with exercise, they almost immediately got well.

He cautioned his patients, "However, if you do not study the Bible daily and pray and meditate focusing on God's word and beautiful things, you will become sick again."

After talking to Jack and his wife, Dr. Foster thoroughly examined each of them and drew some blood for his diagnosis. As he suspected, they were both suffering from thyroid problems. Jack's was way too high and Mrs. Sprat's was way too low. Also, they both had numerous vitamin and essential amino acid deficiencies due to their poor diets. They had almost non-existent levels of vitamin D, the sunshine vitamin, which is essential for fighting off depression. He also discovered, through their conversation, that both of the Sprats harbored past resentments along with a lot of guilt.

Before Dr. Foster left Alaska, he provided both Jack and his wife with enough vitamin D, fish oil, and other supplements to get their health back on track. This was enough to last them for three months. He told them that he would be contacting them again, at the end of this time, to review their progress.

"In the meantime," he said to them, "like I tell all my patients, read the Bible, pray and meditate. I call these the RPMs of healing." Dr. Foster said this with a chuckle and assured them that the rest of their lives would soon fall into place.

Mrs. Sprat was pleased as she could be. She thought that the doctor may have put her on some grasshopper diet and Jack had been concerned that he would be required to eat more fat, which in his mind consisted of food with faces fried in lard. Dr. Foster assured them that after they were naturally chemically in balance and got right with God, they would no longer have the desire to eat unhealthy foods nor would they be mentally distraught. They would also have a desire to be more physically active.

After three months, the Sprats' lives did change drastically just like the doctor had promised if they followed his instructions.

When he contacted them again, he was so pleased with their commitment to his strategic attack on the devil and their love for the Lord that he offered them both a job selling his naturopathic remedies. With this welcome invitation, they moved to the desert where they could also benefit from more sunshine and be close to the good Dr. They have continued to prosper to this day.

Mrs. Sprat also told Mother Goose, and the Old Woman and Mary about how Dr. Foster had also recently traveled to London and put Humpty Dumpty back together again.

> *Humpty-Dumpty sat on a wall,*
> *Humpty-Dumpty had a great fall;*
> *All the king's horses and all the king's men,*
> *Cannot put Humpty-Dumpty together again.*

Apparently, one of the Kings over in Europe had also heard about Dr. Foster. In the same way, he had listened to a mysterious Christian broadcast and then contacted him right away. He told Dr. Foster how all of his horses and all of his men had tried to put Humpty back together again but to no avail. For years, he had lain in a nursing home all broken to pieces.

Again, Dr. Foster knew that he had been called on a mission from the Lord. Immediately he flew to London and put Humpty

Dumpty back together with no thought of payment. Today, Humpty Dumpty is stronger than ever and very proud of his scars. He likes to show them off because before the good doctor left he turned to Humpty and said, "Remember my man, your scars are your stars!"

Mother Goose and the Old Woman were now in tears. "Oh what a testimony," Mother Goose exclaimed. "The two of you look so wonderful. What a blessing! I am so happy for the two of you and for our dear Humpty Dumpty. I would so love to meet this good Dr. Foster."

"That reminds me, I am throwing the biggest, grandest Christmas party ever this year. It will be out in a heavenly clearing in the forest north of town and I would love for the two of you to come. And, if you could persuade him, please bring the good Dr. Foster with you. I would love to hear more about his walk with the Lord and his healing remedies."

"So would I," said the Old Woman. "I would especially like to talk to him about his journey with Jesus and his connection with the Holy Spirit."

The Sprats, as with everyone else Mother Goose had already spoken to, were also very enthusiastic about the party. They said that they would be sure to be there and that they would bring the good Dr. Foster with them if he weren't called out on another mission for the Holy Spirit.

Having finished their meals, Mother Goose's Fiddling Cat and her geese, along with the Old Woman's Pussy Cat were all getting antsy to go down on the beach to roast marshmallows. Mrs. Sprat also appeared to be getting antsy.

The Sprats were out on their weekly date as part of the doctor's prescription for a good marriage. That night they were going out dancing at the Tidal Wave, a favorite hot spot in town for good music, cheap drinks and dancing.

"Come on Jack," said Mrs. Sprat, "we gotta run, the band is just about ready to start."

Mrs. Sprat was already standing as Jack casually pulled out his wallet and found the card he was looking for.

It read:

> *'And be not conformed to this world: but be ye transformed by the renewing of your mind, that ye may prove what is that good, and acceptable, and perfect, will of God.'*
> *Romans 12:2*

Handing it to Mother Goose he said, "It all boils down to the way we think and the way we perceive ourselves. He pushed back his chair from the table and reached over and picked up the tab for all of them. Arm in arm, he and Mrs. Sprat headed for the bar.

Chapter Seventeen

Before they went down to the beach, they stopped back at Mary's little cottage so she could get her large green blanket from her closet; the one that she liked to take down to the beach. She then put some bottled water for each of them in her backpack along with a bag of marshmallows. Mother Goose made sure to include in her backpack the treats from The Baker. She could hardly wait to taste the chocolate-covered strawberries injected with peppermint schnapps!

Instead of walking down the steep, rickety old steps that led down to the beach behind Mary's cottage, they flew down. Mary had the geese fly to a little alcove she knew of that blocked the wind.

After they all helped gather driftwood and made a big bonfire, Mother Goose's Fine Gander flew back up the steep cliff, overlooking the ocean to break off some limbs, of a whether beaten tree to use for roasting their marshmallows. He returned quickly, ready for the sweet treats.

Mary laid out her old wool army blanket and passed out the bottled water. She handed Mother Goose's Fine Gander the bag of marshmallows; putting him in charge. Once the geese and the two cats positioned themselves around the sparking flames, they tried to see who could roast their marshmallow the longest and then get the gooey little burnt puff into their mouth before it fell off the stick.

The Three Blind Mice were thoroughly enjoying The Baker's braided cheese- bread and assortment of cookies. Meanwhile, the three women indulged themselves eating The Baker's sinfully delicious chocolate-covered strawberries. He must have given them at least thirty of those little devils.

Mary popped another chocolate in her mouth, and with an awkward twist, she rose up on one hip to brush some sand from beneath her off the blanket. "OW!" She yelped.

"Are you alright, hon?" asked the Old Woman.

"Yeah, I'm fine, thanks. My back has just been bothering me some lately. I think I whacked it out of place last weekend while I was taking down my booth at the market. I went to a chiropractor earlier this week, one that a friend of mine here on the Coast had suggested, and that was nothing but a big joke! You wouldn't believe what he did. He had me sit down on the back-cracking table then he told me to hold my left arm straight out in front of me and told me that when he pushed down on it, not to move. He said he was checking first to find any diseases and or vitamin deficiencies that I may have before he adjusted my back. Any way He placed one hand on top of my arm near my elbow and, with his other hand, he poked me in the chest with his stubby fat finger while pushing down on my arm. Nothing happened. He did this again but this time he poked me in the stomach, and quickly shifted his hand just a bit further below my elbow. This time my arm collapsed."

"I see you have colon problems," he said and continued.

"This next time he poked me near my lung and again, no movement. But then, down sank my arm again when he poked me in the liver and kidneys. Just then his receptionist lightly tapped on the door."

"Sorry to bother you doctor, but she forgot to fill out this questionnaire."

"A couple of days before I went into see him I had received in the mail a welcome wagon packet telling me about his practice which also included the questionnaire asking about my past and present health conditions. There was another form about health insurance coverage and another form covering consent for him to work on my back. Anyway, on the health sheet I included that I had a chronic problem with diverticulitis, allergies and a fatty liver."

"To make a long story short, I stood up and looked the receptionist right in the eye and said, 'You know darn well I filled that paper out already; it was stapled to the other two forms I handed you today when I came in.'"

"Boy, did she flush. Then, I turned to the doctor and said, 'You're nothing but a quack! I saw a show the other night on Sixty Minutes about this new age chiropractic horse crap. You already knew before you came in here that I had colon issues and a fatty liver. Why not just throw in the kidneys also, so when I leave you can try to get me to buy some of your kidney support concoctions along with something for my liver and colon also? That would be nice, huh, tack on another three hundred bucks to the bill. Your little magic trick is only a matter of leverage."

"You should have seen them, you guys, they both stood there stunned and looking at me as if they'd seen a ghost.

I grabbed my tote bag and said, 'You're nothing but a quasi, feng shui, phony ass wannabe!' Then I stormed out of his stinky, eucalyptus -smelling, pseudo-spiritual healing suite."

"Whew!" said Mother Goose handing Mary another chocolate, "I'm sure glad I wasn't him or his receptionist"

The Old Woman patted the blanket, "Here, Mary, lie down on your stomach."

She straddled her and put her hands, palms down, on either side of Mary's spine. With a few quick thrusts she went pop, pop, pop all the way down her back. Mary rolled over on her back and lay there a moment and then sat up.

"Oh, my God! I can breath."

She rolled her head around and said, "No crunching."

Standing up she touched her toes, "Wow! My back feels great. Thank you. Where'd you learn how to do that?"

"From an old medicine man," said the Old Woman.

"Too cool," said Mary.

Mother Goose and the Old Woman chuckled. "Well, let's see how it feels tomorrow. I'm no miracle worker; sometimes I just get lucky."

As they continued to sit on the blanket, next to the warm fire, licking chocolate off their fingers they all began to feel a bit muzzy. Mary laid back on the blanket and stared at the moon.

"I wonder what it would be like," she said, "to pole dance on the moon and then sit, on his face?"

"Mary!" spouted the Old Woman, but said no more. She and Mother Goose couldn't help but be amused. With the pull of the moon raising the tide, Mary jumped up and stripped off her clothes.

With her hands in the air she proclaimed, "Glory to the moon!"

"Come on you guys," she yelled as she ran out into the ocean.

Mother Goose and the Old Woman looked at one another and in unison said, "Why not?"

They played in the chilly water and splashed one another in the teasing waves yelling like little children over the wave's loud threats to engulf them. When they returned to the blanket beside the bonfire, they danced around till they were dry and watched the Cow Jump Over the Moon.

Mary stayed in the front room that night. She didn't want to sleep in her bedroom, which was still tingling with negative energy. She felt safe as she snuggled in with Mother Goose on the hideaway bed and it wasn't long before she was out like a light.

Before falling asleep, Mother Goose commented to her best friend above in the loft, "I need to have a little talk with that Baker, he needs to put caution labels on those chocolate strawberries!"

They both giggled.

Chapter Eighteen

The next morning, Mother Goose was the first one up. Quietly, she eased herself out of bed and went outside to get some wood to start the wood stove. She wanted the cottage to be nice and warm when Mary woke up-which she didn't expect would be much before noon. She wasn't accustomed to drinking in any fashion; the spiked strawberries really did her in.

After Mother Goose zipped herself into the Old Woman's leathers, she wrote Mary a thank you note for her hospitality while the others quietly got ready to go also. They slipped out of the house, locking the door behind them.

Outside and saddled up on the geese, the Old Woman looked at Mother Goose and said, "I prayed for that child all night. Lord, have mercy, pole dancing on the moon!"

"I know," said Mother Goose, "I did too. I prayed that the good Lord would bring her a friend her own age to sort of mentor her. She really has been doing well lately though, since she got off those Molotov cocktails for the brain that her dr. prescribed for her. It says in all of the literature I've read on bipolar disorder, that medications often times can make the mood swings worse and more severe. Now that she isn't taking any of those drugs and has her own business I have seen a big change in her."

"I think your right," said the Old Woman. "If Mary had a good friend that was stable it would help her a lot. Just getting rid of all that hocus pocus crap she was reading I think will help her even more."

To Mary's surprise, she woke up to a knock at her door. She noticed that Mother Goose and the others were gone and thought maybe they had just gone out to breakfast down the street at the neighborhood café and had locked themselves out. But when she opened the door, there stood Jack Be Nimble! She didn't know what to say. She knew that she looked a mess and she wasn't feeling all that good either.

"Well," Jack said, "aren't you going to invite me in?"

"Oh yeah, yeah come in."

Jack smiled at her with raised eyebrows and shook his head like one of those bobble head dolls. Mary was so flustered that she flushed bright red with embarrassment. She looked like something the cat had dragged in. Her breath smelled like peppermint schnapps and, to top it off, she had seaweed in her hair!

"Sit down," she said to Jack pushing him toward a chair at her kitchen table.

"I'll put some water on the wood stove for coffee. Mother Goose and the Old Woman Who Lived Under a Hill are over visiting; I'm sure they'll be back soon. They probably just went out for an early breakfast.

Jack noticed the note on the table and read it aloud.

Good afternoon, sweetheart. Thank you so much for the wonderful visit. Last night on the beach was a hoot! I hope you're not feeling too bad. I am going to have a little talk with The Baker about his alcoholic strawberries! Maybe we all should have smoked some of your pot instead. JUST, KIDDING, We all love you. See you again soon. XXX OOO

Jack placed the letter back on the table and thought to himself, "Hmm, I didn't know she smoked pot."

Mary looked at the clock and blurted out, "Oh My Gosh, it is afternoon! I can't believe I slept in this late. They should have woken me up!"

"Well, you probably needed the extra sleep. Why don't you get dressed now and I'll take you out to lunch, my little party girl?"

When Mary went into the bathroom to take a quick shower, she looked in the mirror and saw the seaweed in her hair. She smiled wryly as she pulled the long piece of green slime out of her matted curls. She had to admit that even though she wasn't feeling so sharp, she did have a blast the night before.

Mary dressed in her usual attire of tight, faded Levis fringed at the bottom, a blouse made of silk and delicately embroidered from India, and on her feet, a pair of Birkenstocks with wool socks. Before she went back into her kitchen area, she also put on a pair of dangly Indian earrings along with her crystal pendant necklace.

Jack was reading her Bible at the kitchen table when she came back out.

"Ready to go?" he asked as he closed the Bible and looked into her blue-green eyes. He admired her long blond curly hair as he was trying very hard to avoid looking at her voluptuous curves.

"Yeah, I'm ready," she said while grabbing her fleece-lined, blue jean jacket and woven tote bag from Peru.

Jack took Mary up the Coastline a few miles to his favorite little café overlooking the ocean. It was a perfect place to sit and enjoy a meal while watching the whales rub their barnacles off on the jagged rocks protruding from the ocean below.

"This sounds good," Jack said pointing to the menu. The special of the day included a crab omelet served with home, made pan fried potatoes with melted cheese on top and a side of dense whole wheat toast.

"I think I'll have that," Jack said.

"Umm, yeah, that does sound good," said Mary. "I'll have that too"

While waiting for their meals, Jack couldn't help but notice Mary's pensive mood as she played around with her napkin and made an origami swan. This didn't bother Jack, as he'd seen her like this before and he wasn't one to take it personally. He allowed other people the right to their emotions without questioning them.

Jack had a calming effect on Mary. She felt secure while she was with him and also in control of herself. Amongst her friends who lived on the Coast she always seem to be in flight or fight mode. These emotions overrode her true spirit.

"Jack," she said looking up at him, "why do you like me?"

"Well, I like you because you're kind and thoughtful of others. I admire your strength and how you stuck to your dream of starting your own business. I like your style and your smile and I like the fact that you're an anomaly and a querist. Above all, I love your love for Jesus."

Mary shook out her linen swan of thoughts and put it on her lap while the waitress placed her meal in front of her.

"Thank you," Mary said, as she reached for the little bottle of Tabasco.

"Can I get you two anything else?' asked the waitress.

"Not right now, ever thing looks great. Thank you," said Jack.

"So, where were we?" Jack continued.

"That's enough." said Mary. "Thank you for your confidence in me. I'm glad to know that you know that I love Jesus although, it may seem like I'm off chasing rainbows at times.

Jack smiled his one and only "Jack smile".

"Well, my little pot-smoking, rainbow-chasing friend, I know where the pot of gold is. It's, right there," he said pointing to her heart.

Changing the subject, Mary asked, "How is everyone out in Babaylon? Caveman, Lizard, the little Peyout and Corndog.... are they all still camping out under the bridge in this cold weather?"

"Not Caveman," said Jack. "Get this. The Lord laid some divine intervention on him and he's been sober for two months now and he also has his own apartment.

"You're kidding me," said Mary

"No, he finally got on disability after the state reconsidered his mental and physical problems. He's doing great! He even reads his Bible every day. When I get enough money together for my Christian housing project, I'm going to ask him to work for me.

He's quite an example for the other guys of what life could be if they only gave up their free will."

"That's not all that easy, Jack," said Mary.

"I know Mare," said Jack. The Lord allows each of us to make our own choices. Fortunately for Caveman, God saw that spark of faith in him and intervened. God renewed his mind and gave him the desire, to stop drinking. Sometimes this kind of intervention from God is the only way these people can turn their lives around because their brains are so pickled they can't think straight.

A lot of the homeless guys have chosen to tough it out in the cold rather than go stay in the winter shelter because they can't drink there. I've seen too many of these guys die holding on to what they call freedom. I intend to have a section in my housing facility where the diehards can still drink while they're getting the attention and nourishment they need to make the change. Vitamins, in particular, shots of B12, can really make a difference in the way an addict thinks. A lot of people think these guys are all mentally ill but they're not. Addiction often mimics mental illness."

"Do you think I could also help you when the housing is built," asked Mary.

"Of course, Mary. Your love for the Lord and your personal experience would be a big help. You know the guys already love and respect you and I'm sure you would be a blessing to the women on the street. Your empathy and non-judgmental personality would probably allow them to open up to you. You know, they don't do that very often with strangers. And you know Jewels, The wild woman, she like yourself has a real love for Jesus yet keeps going in and out of treatment centers. I really think she could benefit from having a strong woman role model."

"I have just one question for you. How would you be able to help me if you continued living here on the Coast?"

"Well, I don't know. I'll have to think about this some more. Maybe I'll move back to the valley; I do kind of miss the warm weather and my plants would definitely be a lot happier. It hardly ever gets warm enough to wear shorts over here."

Jack held his tongue as he didn't want to persuade Mary in any way. He wanted her to make the decision herself. He wanted her to be through wandering and searching for purpose in life. And, most of all, he wanted her to want him.

This time, Jack changed the subject.

"Mother Goose told me how to get to the mystical clearing from the little chapel, so I'm going to guide the people into the clearing on Christmas day. Would you like to help me? Before we do that, you could help me put the little candles on the tree. Mother Goose told me that there is a big old fir tree that stands alone, right in the middle of the clearing"

"I'd love too," said Mary, delighted that he asked.

"I'll bring some of my silver bells and cockle shells to help decorate too.

Although Jack and Mary had strong feelings for one another, and as you already know, Jack was planning to propose to Mary someday, they both kept their feelings of love to themselves. Jack did this to guard his heart and Mary wasn't sure that she could be committed to a man like Jack. She thought the freewheeling, macho-type guys whom she regularly dated were more fun.

She did know one thing for sure though; she wanted to spend this Christmas together with Jack.

After brunch, Jack took Mary straight home. He could tell that she still needed some more rest.

"Come in" said Mary opening her front door.

"No, I better not. I want to hit the road for home before the tourists head back to the valley," he said.

The temptation to just lay down with her and hold her was way too strong. He had never been that intimate with Mary before and he didn't want to start now.

After he gave Mary a friendly peck on the cheek he said, "I'll come pick you up Christmas Eve around nine in the morning. That way we'll have time to get back to the valley and get out to the clearing and decorate the tree, without rushing before the Christmas party. And, we will have all Christmas Eve night to do whatever we want. How does that sound?"

"Great," said Mary, "I can hardly wait. This is going to be so much fun. I haven't been to a "real" party in a long time."

"I'll reserve a room for you at the new Hilton," Jack said.

"Jack, I can't afford that. Why don't I just stay at your place?" Mary asked.

"No, that wouldn't work," Jack said.

"Why not?" asked Mary.

"I have too much to do before the party. And, besides, it would be more fun for you to stay at the hotel. My treat."

"Jack is always so thoughtful and generous," thought Mary.

Chapter Nineteen

Mother Goose, the Old Woman Who Lived Under a Hill and all their pets got back to the valley before noon. They stopped, on their way back into town, to see Little Tommy Lin and Little Tommy Stout who now owned an animal shelter.

> *Ding, dong, bell,*
> *Pussy's in the well!*
> *Who put her in?*
> *Little Tommy Lin.*
> *Who pulled her out?*
> *Little Tommy Stout.*
> *What a naughty boy was that*
> *To drown poor pussy cat,*
> *Who ne'er did any harm,*
> *But killed the mice in Father's barn.*

Little Tommy Lin, who had once put Pussy down the well, {the Old Woman's cat} and Little Tommy Stout became partners awhile back, after Tommy Stout had convinced Tommy Lin to attend anger management classes and also to go to a Bible study with him.

They then bought a big old farmhouse with a large barn set on several acres of land along the highway leading to the Coast, just outside of town. Here on this property they prepared to open an animal shelter.

They renovated the old barn, or I should say, Tommy Linn did. He installed condos for the cats and private suites for the dogs. Each of which had its own door leading outside to an enclosed forty-acre playground. The playground was well-equipped with an agility course for the dogs and plenty of trees, and shrubs and an array of wild grasses for the cats to play in. There was also a pond that the wild birds flocked to and the dogs liked to take a swim in.

The inside of their home was a collage of art deco, antiques and a touch of ultra-modern. Tommy Stout, with his vivacious personality and flamboyant style, had a real passion for decorating. Keeping house, taking care of the animals, and entertaining were also right up there with his love for design and spending time with others.

Tommy Lin, on the other hand, was more refined and masculine. He had a rather austere air about him. He did enjoy company, though also. In his spare time, he enjoyed cooking; especially barbecue. He made his own sauces and also liked to make his own sausage.

Tommy Lin came to love animals, along with Tommy Stout, after he had dealt with his pent-up emotions. He had enjoyed building the accommodations for the animals and even enjoyed keeping their homestead in tip-top condition. Their shelter was noted as being the cleanest and most exceptional animal care facility in the whole country. The two of them even wrote articles for pet magazines and taught special training techniques to people that were about ready to give up on their pets.

When Mother Goose rang the doorbell, they could all hear Tommy Stout holler in his sing-song way, "Come in-in, the doors al-ways open and you know how I looo-ve a party."

They stepped inside the house to the smell of eggs frying and they could hear clattering in the kitchen.

Tommy Stout peeked around the kitchen doorway and threw his arms up in the air. With his best inflection of a surprised woman's voice, he screamed, "Oh! Heavens to Betsy, it's my beloved Mother Goose and my favorite young woman that lives under a hill."

He ran over to them on his twinkle toes and smothered each of them with kisses. "You're just in time for Sunday brunch. You will stay, won't you?"

Before they could answer, he turned on his toes and twirled his way back into the kitchen like a human swizzle stick. He poured them each a glass of champagne.

"While I throw together some strawberry crepes, why don't you two Goddesses take your cocktails on out back and say hello to the "man" of the house. He would just kill me if I didn't let him know you were here right away!"

"Is there anything I can do to help, honey?" asked Mother Goose.

"Now you know better than to ask that, Mother Goose. The only woman I like helping me in the kitchen is Betty Crocker or sometimes that sweet chocolate treat, Aunt Jemima."

Mother Goose and the Old Woman chuckled and went out back to the extravagantly decorated, covered deck complete with overhead heat lamps. Palm trees lined the perimeter of the deck and luxurious padded wicker lounge chairs were randomly placed with a few cozied up to the enormous steaming hot tub.

Tommy Lin stood at his grill with tongs in one hand and a paintbrush, dripping with barbecue sauce, in the other. He looked as much like Adonis as ever. He was an aphrodisiac for the eyes in his skin-tight blue jeans, bare feet and his Joe Boxer t-shirt. Muscles rippled up and down his body like a quiet stream whispering to be touched. Pussy Cat went right up to him and did crazy eights between his legs rubbing her scent all over him.

He gave her a little nudge with his bare foot and with a slight smile on his face, in his gravelly voice said, "Go on Pussy, why don't you go out and play in the street?"

She purred and moved in for the kill stretching her body up his leg begging to be held. Tommy put down his tools and picked her up. He scratched her behind the ears and under the chin, like all cats love.

"Hello, Mother Goose, good to see you," he said eyeing her leathers. "And nice to see you, too," he said nodding at the Old Woman Who Lived Under a Hill. He rarely saw her, but when he did, he was grateful that she never brought up the incident with the well. Pussy squirmed out of his arms and she and the Fiddling Cat ran off to the shelter to see if they knew anyone out there.

"Why don't you all fly out back and check out the pond? I just stocked it fresh trout," he said to the geese as he resumed his position at the barbecue with paintbrush in hand.

Mother Goose couldn't help herself and grasped Tommy Lin's brawny bicep as he nonchalantly gave it a flex.

"My, my, my," said Mother Goose still holding on, "something sure smells good."

"I'm just trying out a new sauce I made on these turkey sausage patties. It has hickory and tangerine with a hint of cayenne in it. I'm glad you two stopped in. You can let me know what you think."

The cats hadn't been gone more than five minutes when the Fiddling Cat came running back to Mother Goose all excited, "Come quickly! You won't believe who's here, it's my Little Laughing Dog friend!" Mother Goose and the Old Woman took off in a sprint right behind him.

Sure enough, it was the Little Laughing Dog! He told them that for the past few years he had been all over the country looking for his dish and spoon but, had never found them. He survived off of scraps that he found in garbage cans. Every once in a while, he would hook up with some homeless guy who would feed him. To his surprise, one of these guys hopped a train with him tucked under his arm and took him all the way across the state. He then abandoned him in the middle of nowhere. The Little Laughing Dog waited for the next train then climbed aboard an empty boxcar and finally made it back to town.

"Oh! My goodness what an ordeal," said Mother Goose taking him in her arms.

The Old Woman patted him on the head and said, "We missed you terribly and prayed that you would return home safely."

Tommy Stout rang the iron triangle dinner bell which hung from a beam over their deck and sung out over the land, "Brunch is ready, ladies."

Putting the Little Laughing Dog down, Mother Goose said,

"Now don't you worry little one, everything's going to be alright now."

The Old Woman reassured the Little Laughing Dog also by saying, "God didn't bring you home for nothing."

While they went back inside to have brunch, the Fiddling Cat and Pussy Cat stayed out in the shelter to visit with the Little Laughing Dog. They told him all about what they had been doing and also how much the moon and the cow had missed him, also.

The dining room table was set explicitly. A finely crocheted white tablecloth catered too, vintage, mint green plastic place settings with sterling silver utensils and blue crystal champagne glasses. In the center of the table sat a brilliant bouquet of tiger lilies, purple orchids, white lilacs and vibrant hibiscus flowers.

Tommy Stout ordered at least one, new arrangement each week from Hawaii; sometimes even more. If he was feeling especially tropical, he would order one for each room in the house. During these periods, he would also wear his collection of Hawaiian shirts and shorts and play music by Hawaiian artists.

On this day, in the background, they could hear Donna Summer croon, *"Ooooo, I love to love you baby. Mmmm, love to love you baby...*

Tommy Stout said grace then popped the cork on another bottle of champagne and poured everyone another glass. "Toast!" he said. "Here's to the two most beautiful, real women I know and to best friends lost and found!"

After filling one another in on the latest events in their lives, they discussed the fate of the Little Laughing Dog. The guys weren't too concerned about this because, they were always entertaining and they could usually talk one of their new guests, into taking one of the animals home. Besides, they had a phenomenal placement record.

Mother Goose couldn't stand the thought of their little friend being cast away to strangers and neither could the Old Woman. She really wanted to keep the Little Laughing Dog but first she tried to convince Mother Goose to take him home with her.

"You should take him home. Your Fiddling Cat and he were best friends," she said.

Mother Goose countered her remark, "So what? You and I our best friends and I don't live with you! Besides, I already have three guard dogs; my geese."

Tommy Stout laughed and Tommy Linn, in his low authoritative voice, said, "She's got a point. A good looking woman like yourself should have a guard dog." Unlike the Old Woman, she blushed.

After brunch, they all went out to the enclosed acreage behind the kennels. Tommy Lin wanted to show Mother Goose and the Old Woman the new wildlife rescue addition that he was building to house raccoons, bunnies, squirrels, turtles and maybe even monkeys. The anger management classes he had participated in, along with the Bible study that he and Tommy Stout continued to attend, really turned his heart around. Not to mention his partner, Tommy Stout, who had the patience, of Job. Mother Goose motioned to her geese, who were over at the pond, that it was time to go. She then called for her Fiddling Cat and Pussy Cat who were still inside the kennel.

When the Little Laughing Dog heard Mother Goose call his best friend, the Fiddling Cat, and Pussy Cat and he saw them run out to her, his heart sank. He lay his little head down on his paws and began to cry. With the rush of the Holy Spirit, in came Tommy Lin with the Old Woman right behind him. The Little Laughing

Dog's eyes lit up and he began to wag his tail.

"Get your gear together, buddy," said Tommy Lin. "You're going home!" The Old Woman opened her arms and the Little Laughing Dog jumped right in. She tenderly rubbed her cheek on his head.

After they all got situated on the geese for the ride home Mother Goose said, "Now, you two will be sure and come to the Christmas party won't you? A party just isn't a party without you."

Tommy Stout said, "You know how I just love any gay event. Of course, I'll be there"

"Yeah, I'll be there, too" said Tommy Lin. "If I don't escort her to the party she'll take away my membership to the YMCA."

"Oh, heaven forbid! Like you don't already get in enough weight lifting around here," said Tommy Stout. Mother Goose and the Old Woman laughed at their queer exchange.

Tommy Lin then said, "I really do have to say Mother Goose, you look quite butch in those leathers." The Old Woman about fell off Goosey Goosey Gander she laughed so hard.

"That's it! That's it!" Said Mother Goose. "I'm through playing the biker chick." And with that announcement, she took off for the sky blowing kisses behind her.

Chapter Twenty

When they got back to the Old Woman's home under the hill, Mother Goose said to her pets, "You kids stick nearby. I'm just going to run inside and change back into my own clothes. I can hardly wait to get out of these Levis and leathers."

The Old Woman laughed and said, "Being a biker is not something you can easily fake."

"Obviously, said Mother Goose. Thanks a lot for the lesson, you old bat."

The Old Woman cracked up and said, "Well how about next time you wear my Indian powwow outfit? Maybe you can pull that off."

"Oh you're just full of it aren't you? You really do need to get out more often," said Mother Goose.

The Old Woman had to admit that although she had hopes that Mother Goose would be riding a bike alongside her, the idea had been far-fetched. It just didn't fit her personality.

They both thanked each other for the fun adventure and gave each other a hug goodbye. Mother Goose also gave the Little Laughing Dog another hug and told him that they would all be back in a few days to watch the Cow Jump Over the Moon together. The Little Laughing Dog gave a big bow wow to that.

On the way home, Mother Goose decided to stop in and see the Butcher's wife, Old Mother Hubbard, and son, Simple Simon and, her dog. Several years ago, Old Mother Hubbard had started going to the soup kitchen at the local church for her meals and also, in hopes of picking up a bone or two for her dog.

Old Mother Hubbard
Went to the cupboard
To fetch her poor dog a bone.
But when she came there
The cupboard was bare,
And so the poor dog had none.

She had always lived alone and after she retired from being a waitress, she had a hard time making ends meet. Soon she became a volunteer at the soup kitchen. This suited her well because she was able to eat all of her meals for free and she was able to give back to the community at the same time. This not only helped her out a lot but it gave her something to do.

While working at the soup kitchen, she met the Butcher who was also working as a volunteer. He did most of the cooking there and also generously donated meat for the meals, when needed. After meeting for the first time, they were immediately smitten with each other. From that day forward, he wanted to be with Old Mother Hubbard all the time. He saw it as his calling in life to take care of her and her little dog. Old Mother Hubbard was head over heels for him and before long, the two of them were married.

Simple Simon was another volunteer at the soup kitchen. He would do whatever was needed as long as it was a simple task. The Butcher and Old Mother Hubbard just adored him and took him under their wings. They included him whenever possible in what they were doing and gave him more complicated tasks than just washing dishes or busing the tables. He really enjoyed peeling the potatoes and putting them in the magic genie slicing machine then seeing them turn into French fries.

He just lived down the street from the church in a home for mentally challenged adults. The proximity to the church easily allowed him to walk to work by himself. He loved the opportunity to get out of the house on his own. This made him feel like he was really a part of society. He especially loved seeing the Butcher and his wife every day and prayed that maybe someday they would adopt him.

Simple Simon had never experienced kindness and love like they showed him. His own parents had given him up at the age of four because they just couldn't cope with his disabilities. Besides being mentally challenged he also had a deformity called prognathism. This is a deformity which causes the jaws to project beyond the upper part of the face. When he spoke, the proglottis {tip of his tongue} got stuck behind his upper teeth, which made it very hard to understand what he is saying at times.

He was also born with quite a mesomorphic physique, which the doctor said could make him quite strong and hard to handle when he got older. At three years old, he was already very strong and muscular.

When he hit, his five year old sister and then wouldn't let go of her hair, his mother was fit to be tied. With Simon's ever increasing size and strength and all of this highbrow terminology thrown their way, along with no hope in sight, Simple Simon's parents simply gave him up.

Sadly, he became lost in the system, going from one institution to another, until finally he ended up at the adult care facility in town. There, he learned much more than he had anywhere else. He even learned how to count money and opened his own bank account. With help from one of the staff members, he was able to deposit and withdraw his small amount of money.

One evening while relaxing at home, with the old dog in front of the fireplace chewing his bone, the Butcher and Old Mother Hubbard snuggled up on the couch together. They discussed the possibility of adopting Simple Simon. Neither one of them could stand the thought of him living out the rest of his life in the care facility. They saw how much he loved to get out and how much he craved their attention. They also knew that with constant love and personal attention, he would really thrive. Though they were both old enough to be his grandparents, they believed that he would be better off having a family of his own that loved him than none at all. So, after having this discussion the next day they got hold of the facility where Simple Simon lived and put in a request to adopt him.

The director of the care facility told them that he would do everything in his power to make this possible seeing as that ever since Simon had met the two of them, his learning abilities had grown tremendously and all he could do was talk about them. Also, the caregivers at the home often caught Simon alone in his room praying out loud for the Butcher and his wife to adopt him. To the Butcher's and Old Mother Hubbard's surprise, the arrangements to adopt Simon were quickly and easily arranged.

Simon had now lived with the Butcher and Old Mother Hubbard for several years and continued to grow in his abilities. Together as a family they still volunteered at the soup kitchen each week and also attended the church's Sunday service. Simon especially liked to hear everyone sing.

Besides volunteering at the soup kitchen, Simon also worked with his dad at his butcher shop on the riverfront. He loved squishing the ground round through his fingers to make hamburger patties and working at the counter where he got to talk to the customers.

Mother Goose rang the doorbell, but no one answered. She had forgotten that it was Sunday and that they always went to church and then out for breakfast and a drive afterwards. It was just as well. She really didn't have a lot of time to visit because she had plenty yet to do before the Christmas party.

Flying the rest of the way home, Mother Goose recalled a special moment with Simon. She and Old Mother Hubbard had been sitting on her porch swing in her backyard visiting one day and Simon was sitting under Mother Goose's big maple tree watching the various birds come and go. He got really excited at one sighting and motioned for Mother Goose and his mother to come see. They crouched down beside him and looked up into the tree branches where they saw a brightly colored green and yellow pine warbler.

"Hmm", said Mother Goose, "he must be on migration. Pine warblers usually stick to pine woods like a cocklebur to a pant leg."

Their presence didn't faze the little bird and he began to sing with a loose sweet twirl.

Simon pointed at the little bird and said, "Zatz,za, purdy burdy, I yikez itz ittle zong. Id ikez ta be a burdy zen Id zing pazzaz toda ord."

Old Mother Hubbard smiled joyfully to hear her son say that he would like to sing praises to the Lord. She was so grateful that his jaw deformity did not keep Simon from trying to express himself.

Mother Goose unpacked her things as soon as she got home then made herself a strong cup of coffee and sat down at her kitchen table to drink it. Although she had just dropped her best friend off at home a short time ago, Mother Goose knew she was probably, already preparing her stuffed mushrooms and getting ready to make her gifts for their guests to take home. For some she was making baskets and for others, her unique wall hangings. Mother Goose thought about making everyone a collection of her aromatherapy bath salts and natural soaps, but they already had plenty she thought. She was always giving these away to her friends.

"What else can I make?" she thought. She traipsed around her house like a person impatiently waiting for a return phone call while, racking her brain for a new idea.

Finally, she threw her hands up in the air and said, "Thank you Holy Spirit. Thank you."

What a great idea! She would make each of her friends their own personal book filled with pictures she had taken of them over the years. She would also include the rhymes she had written about each of them.

"Well, I guess I had better get a move on if I want to have these done by Christmas. Jesus, you sure are putting me on a tight schedule Lord. But, like the bible says, with you all things are possible."

Mother Goose had taken a class some time ago at the crafts store where they taught you how to make your own little books. On display they had all the materials you would need to buy after the class to do so; including a little binding machine.

There was also a book for sale, filled with all kinds of creative ideas to make your book unique. After the class, Mother Goose did buy the design book. But instead of buying all of the other materials, she just bought a blank scrapbook. She took it home, and filled it with her collection of photographs she had taken of all her friends and the children that she had cared of over the years. She also included other memorabilia and all of the rhymes she had written. For Christmas, she wanted to make the books for her friends herself, and incorporate some of the creative ideas shown in the design book she had purchased.

While sitting at her kitchen table, she grabbed her notepad and pen that was always in reach and made out a list of supplies she would need to buy.

1. Binding machine
2. Coils for the backbone
3. Special grade cardboard for the fronts and backs
4. All different colors and textures of paper to reprint her rhymes on
5. Photo paper
6. Different kinds of fabric to cover fronts and backs

7. An assortment of ribbon, cording, twine and leather
    strips to decorate the backbones

"Oh this is going to be fun," she thought to herself.

It was still early and another beautiful December day. She knew that it was only a matter of time before the snow would begin to fall from watching the squirrels in her yard frantically hiding nuts beneath the bushes and the blue jays stashing their finds in her gutters. With her pets outside in her backyard playing, she decided to walk into town and enjoy the sunshine and get some exercise along the way. She put her empty coffee cup on the drain board then put on her coat and backpack. She grabbed a couple of her tote bags also; just in case she needed them. Along the way, she tried not to think about The Baker as she fought the impulse to stop in and see him.

Mother Goose loved to go to the crafts store. They had everything one needed to make their own unique creations. They even had a frame shop that ran weekly specials. The crafts store was where she took her favorite paintings and drawings, from the children, to be matted and framed.

Before Mother Goose entered the store she first looked over the posting taped to the window with upcoming classes listed on it. A class on how to make sculptures out of wool caught her eye. It was entitled "Needle Felting in the Raw". She stepped through the entrance and got a cart and then off she went up and down every aisle. As she gathered up all the supplies needed to make her books, she thought about telling the Old Woman about her project but then she decided against it. She wanted the books to be a surprise for her, also. While looking at the large selection of fabrics, she felt overwhelmed and had a hard time making any choices so she took a moment and asked the Holy Spirit for guidance. She wanted just the right fabric to match each person's personality. It didn't take long after her inquiry before she had an assortment of different kinds of fabric: batiks, ginghams, tweeds, silks, flannel, and even some tapestry. Of course, she also got some black leather to cover her best friend's book.

By the time Mother Goose got up to the register, she had an entire shopping cart filled to the brim. This used to happen all the time when she went shopping for art supplies to make projects with the kids.

As the cashier was scanning her items, Mother Goose glanced up at the clock and gasped, "Oh my goodness I have been in here over three hours!"

The checker laughed and said, "It's easy to get carried away in here isn't it? I have to be careful when I get paid not to spend all my check before I walk out the door."

After everything was bagged up, Mother Goose realized she had way more than she could carry herself. "Do you mind if I take a cart home with me?" she asked the cashier.

"Oh sure," the little gal said, "we know you'll bring it back; you always do."

When Mother Goose got home, she unpacked the shopping cart and put everything back in her spare bedroom, which she also used as an art room. The walls were lined with shelves containing clear plastic boxes filled with her dried flowers, sea salts, sewing necessities, clay, beads, rite dyes, different mediums for drawing and painting, and many other useful items. She even had a box of feathers which her geese gave her to keep for them in case they wanted to make a special quill pen for someone. In the closet she had several bags of their down also, in case they got ambitious and wanted to make a comforter or some pillows.

Mother Goose fed her pets an early dinner and heated up a bowl of soup and some sourdough bread for herself. She was very anxious to get to work on her project. After sopping up her dinner, she went back to her bedroom and got her scrapbook- photo album out of the trunk at the foot of the bed. She sat down at the large mahogany table in her dining room where she had plenty of space and, began to sort things out. She put all of the photos she intended to use in one pile and all of the rhymes in another. She decided to make a third pile for the special notes and little drawings that the children and her other friends had given her over the years also, just in case she wanted to include them at the last minute. She planned on taking everything to the print shop to have copied the next day. With the Holy Spirit's help, she hoped to get them all back within a few days. Christmas was right around the corner.

She spent the entire evening making her selections. This ended up being a much more tedious task than she had anticipated. It was especially difficult to pull back the thin magnetic plastic, take out her memorabilia and photos and then smooth the plastic back in place without wrinkles.

Frustrated, Mother Goose stood up and went into her kitchen. She looked out on her back yard through the window above her sink. The moon was peeking at her over her large maple tree. He was almost ready to rise into full view for his nightly show as whispers of snow fell to the ground and then disappeared.

"I sure hope we don't get enough snow to close down the print shop," she thought to herself and took a few deep breaths.

She went into the living room where her pets were now playing scrabble and told them it was time to get into their pajamas. Once this was done, they would all go out and watch the Cow Jump Over the Moon.

She went to her bedroom and also got ready for bed. Before they all went outside she got each of them a chocolate ice cream bar from the refrigerator.

Mother Goose and her pets all knew that the Old Woman and her new pet, the Little Laughing Dog, and Pussy Cat were all outside too watching the Cow Jump Over the Moon. They could hear the Little Dog laughing all the way across town with his voice echoing off the surrounding hills. Mother Goose's Fiddling Cat jumped with joy when he heard him for he imagined that his long lost friend could also hear him fiddling away. The Cow Jumped Over the Moon, especially frisky that night with his favorite audience member back in town.

After the moonlight show, Mother Goose went back to work on her project while her pets settled down in front of the television to watch their favorite T.V. show. Every Sunday night, they got to stay up late to watch Animal Planet. Mother Goose was very selective about what she or her pets viewed on T.V. The cable company was always sending her extra mail and calling her trying to get her to upgrade. They said they had a package where you could "bundle" your services. She was sick and tired of telling them that she was quite satisfied with what she had and that she did not own a computer or a cell phone. Plus, she owned an old console T.V. that still worked just fine and she had no intentions of buying a new flat screen T.V. with HD. Basic cable was all she wanted.

One day, after the salesperson finished his spiel, she told him, "Like I have said before, I am quite satisfied with what I already pay for and the only thing that's getting "bundled" around this home are my bloomers!"

Fortunately, this stopped the soliciting. But, she did receive one more piece of mail from the cable company, other than her regular bill. It was from the salesperson she had spoken to on the phone.

He wrote:

Dear Mother Goose I am just writing to apologize for disturbing you. I admire your spunk and your willpower. My mother used to say the fewer choices you have, the better off you are and, I believe she was right. You remind me of her. I had a hard time working the rest of the day after speaking with you because every time I talked to another customer on the phone and mentioned the word "bundle", I would visualize their panties getting in a wad and I would crack up laughing. Needless to say, I didn't make much of a commission that day but, I did have a lot of fun. Sincerely, Commodore Comcaster.

Mother Goose stayed up until after midnight to finish making her selections of photos and other memorabilia. She just had to get it done if she was to have any chance of getting her books completed by Christmas. Before she went to bed, she put each of the piles in separated tote bags so they would be ready to go to the copy shop in the morning. With a sense of accomplishment she went to bed and said her prayers. Again, she thanked the Holy Spirit for the inspiration and all of his guidance.

Chapter Twenty-One

MOTHER GOOSE GOT UP the next day raring to go. Right after breakfast, she flew into town on her Fine Gander. She didn't want to waste any time getting to the copy shop. She showed the clerk how she wanted to lay things out and he gave her a couple of helpful suggestions.

"I'll have these ready for you tomorrow," said the young man.

"That would be wonderful," said Mother Goose, "but aren't you extremely busy with Christmas right around the corner?"

"No, with all the students already done with their term papers and leaving town for Christmas break we don't have much to do."

"Well, don't you print out a lot of Christmas cards?" Mother Goose asked.

"No, not many these days, a lot of people have their own copy and printing machines so they have no need for our services. A lot of people, now send eCards instead."

Mother Goose graciously thanked the young man and then went straight home to work on her project. She began by cutting out the fabric to fit the fronts and backs of the books. While cutting the fabric, she could envision to whom each book would go to. She chose a colorful calico print to cover the Old Woman Who Lived in a Shoe's book; a sweet flannel print covered with moons and stars and dancing sheep for Little Bo Peep; a forest green wool for the Butcher's; a fire engine red, orange, blue and yellow batik for the Candlestick Maker; naturally, velvets and silks for all of the queens and assorted plaids for the kings. Of course, for her best friend, she would use the black leather.

Mother Goose was very engrossed in her project when she heard the doorbell chime, just before noon. She thought about not answering it, but that wasn't in her character and she was glad that is wasn't, when she answered the door.

"Hi, Mother Goose," said Bo Peep with a big smile. I came over to show you the emails I got back about the Christmas party- check it out!" She said this waving the papers she held in her hand. "One is from the Queen of Hearts!"

Mother Goose smiled, "Come in sweetheart. Why don't you stay for lunch, you can read them to me while I make a spinach lasagna."

"You don't need to make anything special for me," said Bo Peep."

"Oh I'm not, I was getting ready to make it before you showed up. I intend to have it for dinner tonight, also so I don't have to cook later on. I have way too much to do."

Subject: Mother Goose

Date: December 12, 1977

From: The Queen of Hearts < @www.HeartTarts.Eng

To: Bo Peep (Blue) Sheepish@.com.yahoo

My dear Bo Peep, thank you so much for the email. The king and I would have been just heartbroken if we were to have missed this grand event. I have already made reservations at the new Hilton Hotel there in town. We expect to arrive there on Christmas Eve, in time to recover from jet lag, before the party the next evening.

It's been such a long time, hasn't it my dear child since the king and I were there to visit and got to meet you and some of Mother Goose's other friends. I am so looking forward to seeing you again and our dear beloved Mother Goose. Please give her a big hug from the king and I; you know, she has always had a heart of gold.

With much love,

In God we trust,

The Queen of Hearts

Subject: Mother Goose

Date: December 13, 1977

From: Old King Cole < @.WWW.Soulmerry.Eng

To: Bo Peep (Blue) Sheepish@.com,.yahoo

Dear Mrs. Blue,

In reply to your email, please tell Mother Goose that we, the queen and I, merrily accept her invitation to the Christmas party. You can also tell your husband, Boy Blue, that my Fiddlers Three and the rest of the band welcome the chance to play with him. They are already fiddling around with some new blues and jazz riffs. Earlier today, my lovely queen talked to the Queen of Hearts and found out that she had already reserved a room at the new Hilton Hotel there in town so, my lovely queen called and reserved all of the rest of the rooms for the other royalty who will be traveling with us, including some of our knights and knaves. I talked to the King of Hearts and Good King Arthur, who used to rule this land, and also the King of Spain and Humpty Dumpty. I told them that I would provide the transportation. We will all be flying over together in my private Leer jet; that way, we will all be sure to arrive together, on time. Oh my dear, my dear, this is going to be one merry ole Christmas indeed!

We shall all see you soon.

Twee Tweedle Dee Tweedle Dee!

Old King Cole

Subject: Mother Goose
Date: December 14, 1977
From: Humpty Dumpty
To: Bo Peep (Blue) Sheepish@com.yahoo

Dear Bo Peep,

Thank you so much for including me in your emails. I don't know if Mother Goose has heard the news yet, but I am a new man. A miracle happened to me a few months ago when the Lord sent me a Doctor Foster, who once lived in Gloster, to heal me. The king with all the horses, who tried to put me back together again, heard about this magnificent doctor mysteriously over the radio. He flew him over here to England and he put me back together. I am stronger than ever! I can hardly wait to show Mother Goose my new body. She never gave up hope that one day I would be healed. I always admired her faith. She continued to write to me over the years and always had an encouraging word. If not for her faith and what little rubbed off on me, I don't think I would have survived long enough for this miracle to have taken place. Although I am well now, I didn't think at first that I was going to be able to make it to the Christmas party. Have you seen on the news over there, that the London Bridge is broken down? For me and a few of our other friends, there is no way to get to the airport without crossing the bridge. They say it will take more than a year to rebuild it. Some of the contractors wanted to rebuild the bridge with silver and gold but it could be stolen away. Then they thought about wood and clay; but then it would just wash away. Another contractor suggested iron and steel but everyone agreed that it would just bend and bow. Finally, they decided to build it up again with stone so strong that it would last for ages to come. To make a long story short, I found out just an hour or so ago that I will be able to make it after all. I received a call from Old King Cole and he said that he would gladly pick me up in his private leer jet, along with our other friends that live in this neck of the woods. We have plenty of open space here for him to land.

Well, I have talked long enough. Please tell Mother Goose that I love her and thank her again for not forgetting about me.

In Jesus' name,
God bless us all,
Love from Humpty

Subject: Mother Goose

Date: December 13, 1977

From: The King Of Spain < @WWW.SpainDangle.com. Net

To: Bo Peep (Blue) Sheepish@yahoo.com

Dear Bo Peep,

The queen and I, along with our precious princess, thank you for contacting us on behalf of our dear friend, Mother Goose. Please let her know that we will be attending this grand event. Also, the queen would like you to apologize for her, for not writing Mother Goose in the last several months. We have been having a lot of problems with our little princess lately. She went to visit a boy, whom she heard 'had a little nut tree and nothing would it bear but a single silver nutmeg and a golden pear.' When our precious princess returned home, all she could talk about was that boy and his little nut tree and she kept running away to be with him. We have really had to keep a close eye on her and have even been to some counseling sessions. I think this trip will be good for all of us.

Signed,
The King of Spain

Subject: Mother Goose

Date: December 14, 1977

From: Bryan O Lin< @WeeFriends.IRE.Net

To: Bo Peep (Blue) Sheepish@.com.yahoo

Hello me little lassie! Tis a pleasure to hear from you as it has been quite a wee bit of time since we last spoke. Please tell our Mother Goose that I wouldn't miss this party for anything, even if it were Saint Paddy's day and they were giving away free green beer all night at my favorite town pub!

Gee wiz Bo, it's been a long time since I have talked to you or to your husband, Boy Blue. I hope everything has been going well for the two of you.

Remember when I had no breeches to wear so I bought me a sheepskin and I made me a pair? Well, I now make several pairs of breeches a week, along with sheepskin jackets with deer horn buttons. I also make leather purses and wallets. Since me, family and me, moved back here to Ireland, I have been doing much better. When Bonny Lass turned down me proposal for marriage, she broke me Irish heart. Moving home has been good for me because I now have me concentration back and me zest for life. I work for a company called the Sheepskin Merchants. One day, while I was walking through town, I went into the shop and showed the merchant me pair of breeches. He was quite impressed but he wanted to know what else I could make and I had nothing to show him. I bought me one of his sheepskins and went home and made a sheepskin jacket and, for an extra touch, I added some deer horn buttons. The next day when I took it in to show him, he hired me on the spot and I have been working for him ever since.

I am very excited about seeing you and Boy Blue again and, of course, our one and only Mother Goose. Please give her a hug and a kiss from me.
Until we meet again.

Sincerely,
Bryan O Lin

Subject: Mother Goose
Date: December 12, 1977
From: Tommy Tucker < @.www.Songbirds, Cal.com
To: Bo Peep (Blue) < Sheepish@.com.yahoo

Knock, knock. Who's there?
Pucker.
Pucker who?
Pucker up!
It's Tommy Tucker. Ha, Ha, Ha!
Yes, Bo, I still have my sense of humor. Wow, it's been a long time since we've talked. Besides having a sense of humor, as silly as it may be, I also now have Jesus in my life and a beautiful wife! Yes you heard me right. I can hardly wait for you and Boy Blue to meet her-as well as everyone else.

Please tell Mother Goose that she should be receiving a letter from me within the next few days. Right after I got your email last night, I sat down and wrote her a letter. Sorry to cut this short but I have a concert I have to get to.

See you soon,
God bless you!
Your friend,
Tommy

Subject: Mother Goose
Date: December 13, 1977
From: Margaret Miller < @.Minebiz.com.yahoo
To: Bo Peep (Blue) < @.Sheepish.com.yahoo

Dear Bo Peep and Boy Blue,
I am so glad to hear that the two of you are doing well.
Dusty and I our doing well, also. We have been meaning to drive over there for a visit but since the mill closed
down, we have been really busy mining in the hills east
of here. This Christmas is going to be so much fun. What
a great idea Mother Goose had to have a big party. I have
so much to tell you Bo, but I'll wait until I see you. I know
you have more emails to send out so I'll let you go.
See you soon, Bo

I love you!
Your friend always,
Margaret

P.S. I have a surprise to tell you Bo, but I want to tell
Mother Goose first. No offense. Please tell her to check
her mailbox

After Bo Peep read all of the emails she jumped up and hugged Mother Goose, "That was from the Queen and King of Hearts and these are from your other friends."

Hug, hug, hug; kiss, kiss, kiss.

They both laughed and Mother Goose proclaimed, "Well, I sure got my share of love for the day! As they ate their lunch, they talked about the emails. Bo Peep was so pleased that the Queen of Hearts remembered her and even addressed her as "My dear child"

"I kinda feel sorry for the King of Spain's precious princess not being able to go see the boy with the little nut tree," said Bo Peep, to Mother Goose.

> *I had a little nut tree, nothing would it bear*
> *But a silver nutmeg and a golden pear;*
> *The King of Spain's daughter came to visit me,*
> *And all for the sake of my little nut tree.*
> *I skipped over water, I danced over sea,*
> *And all the birds in the air couldn't catch me.*

"It must be hard living up to royal standards."

Mother Goose interrupted Bo's train of thought by saying, "You know what, Bo? You do come from royalty. You also, are a precious princess and so am I and all the other woman alive who believe in Christ Jesus."

"What do you mean? I don't get it," said Bo Peep.

"Well, said Mother Goose, "look at it this way. You know that our Lord God, Jesus Christ, is the real king and our father. And, we are all heirs to his kingdom…. so that makes us women all princesses and, all boys, princes."

"Wow! I never thought about it that way. I guess the King of Spain just has his precious princess's best interests at heart."

"Yes, I would say that," said Mother Goose.

Bo was also thinking about Bryan O Lin's email and said, "I wonder how Bryan's going to react when he comes to the party and finds out that Bonny Lass is a lesbian. What do you think, Mother Goose?"

"Well," she paused a moment and thought about it. "I think he will probably react just fine. In fact, he may even be somewhat relieved.

> *Bryan O'Lin had no breeches to wear,*
> *So he bought him a sheepskin and made him a pair.*
> *With the skinny side out and the woolly side in,*
> *Ah, Ha! That is warm! Said Bryan O'Lin.*

Over the years, I suspect that he has probably questioned his own sexuality. You know, he was the one who taught Bonny Lass how to sew. He may have felt that she rejected him because he wasn't masculine enough. With the truth out on the table, I think both of them will find some relief. It's been hard on Bonny Lass, coming out of the closet so to speak, and I don't think the two of them ever felt any real closure to their relationship. I wouldn't doubt it, at all if they picked up their old friendship and maybe even collaborated on some sewing projects."

"You know, Mother Goose," said Bo Peep, "I just love visiting with you. I always come away feeling enlightened. I just love you!"

"I love you, too, sweetheart. Thank you so much for sending the emails out for me. I think everyone I wanted to contact, now knows about the party. You made it happen, Bo."

"Knowing your relationship with the Holy Spirit, Mother Goose, I'm sure you would have found some other way to contact everyone if I hadn't. I was glad to help."

Mother Goose went on to say, "You probably won't receive an email back from the Sprats because I already invited them and they accepted the invitation. My friend, you know, the Old Woman Who Lived Under a Hill and I flew over to the Coast over the weekend to visit Mary Quite Contrary.

"Oh, how's Mary doing? She's so much fun to be around; I wish she would move back here."

"She's doing fine, Bo. We all had a lot of fun together. We went out to dinner Saturday night at Morrey's Chowder House and there is where we ran into the Sprats. They look amazing and the change in their personalities was something to behold. The Holy Spirit really did an overhaul on them. You'll see what I mean at the Christmas party."

"I always liked the Sprats," Bo said. "But, they always seemed so unhappy. It was always so depressing to be around them. I hate to say it, but I kinda, quashed our friendship because of their sour mood. I hope they will forgive me."

"Oh I'm sure they will, honey. They've been born again and there's no room for grudges when you're living for the Lord. They now have a lilt to their walk. It is such a joy to see the two of them smiling. It's really obvious now that they have the Holy Spirit in them."

"What? You're telling me that the Sprats now believe in Jesus?"

"Yes, Bo, they always have. But like a lot of Christians, they missed the mark by not really turning their will over to God so that the Holy Spirit could and would reveal himself to them. Now that they know the Holy Spirit and choose do his will and not their own, they're living in peace and happiness. Remember Dr. Foster, the one who put Humpty Dumpty back together? Humpty mentioned him in his email?"

"Yes," said Bo.

"Well, the same Dr. Foster was also sent to heal the Sprats by the Holy Spirit."

Bo listened in awe and asked, "What can I do to have an experience like theirs Mother Goose?"

"I'm sure there's nothing you can do to have an experience like the Sprats or Humpty Dumpty. God sees us each individually and he knows our hearts and our individual needs. I believe you have already been experiencing the Holy Spirit at work in your life, Bo, just in a more subtle way. You have a wonderful husband, a prosperous business, good friends and your health. God only knows what else he has in store for you and in what way he will manifest his love for you."

"I guess I sound pretty ungrateful, huh, Mother Goose?"

"I wouldn't go as far as to say that, sweetheart. A lot of people question whether God's working in their lives because they haven't had a dramatic experience like the Sprats or Humpty Dumpy. Some people question his presence saying that they can't feel God. I think it's really important to sit back and count our blessings when we question whether God's working in our lives or not.

The Old Woman Who Lived Under a Hill says, If you want to feel God, do something nice for someone else. Just because. Or hug a tree and play with your pets long enough to see them smile. If your, really feeling desperate, put your hand in front of your mouth and breath.

"Wow, I never would have thought of that," said Bo. "How simple is that. The breath of life?"

"That's right," said Mother Goose. "She's a very wise old woman."

Bo looked at the clock above Mother Goose's stove and jumped up, "Oh no! I told Boy I would be home an hour ago. We have a big yarn order to fill and I was supposed to be home helping him sheer the sheep. Oh, also, I almost forgot to ask you. When you get Margaret's letter will you please call me and let me know what the big secret is?"

Mother Goose chortled and gave her a big hug. "Of course I will, sweetheart. I love you"

"I love you, too. Bye, Bye."

Mother Goose covered up the rest of the spinach lasagna with a piece of foil and put it away in the refrigerator for dinner.

Back to work, she got an efficient system going. As she cut out the material for the covers, she would then place it between two pieces of the hard cardboard covers, ready to be glued. Then, she placed a post it note on top saying who it was for.

She was back to work for less than an hour when her Fine Gander came into the house carrying the usual junk mail and bills. Included also, were the letters from Tommy Tucker and Margaret Miller.

Her Fine Gander loved to greet the mailman. He would always tell him what a good boy he was and give him a little colored milk bone. Mother Goose asked him to please put the letters on her nightstand and told him that she would read them later that night; but for now, she wanted to concentrate on her project.

Her Fine Gander eyed her workbench and then strutted off to her bedroom with the mail. Mother Goose didn't even attempt to start back in on her books because, like she expected, back in came her Fine Gander along with Goosey Goosey Gander and Madame Goose. They couldn't stand it when she worked on a project without them. They were just like little kids; they always wanted to know what she was doing and help if they could. She told them all about the books and had them, promise not to tell anyone; not even her best friend.

"Can we make some books?" asked Madame Goose

"Thank you for asking" Madame Goose. Right now I don't need any help, but I might later. For now, why don't I get down your box of feathers and some ink pen inserts and all of you can go out in the kitchen and make everyone, one of your beautiful quill pens? This will be something special just from you."

The geese all liked that idea so, she handed them their supplies and they started to head off to the other room.

"Oh by the way," said Mother Goose, "do any of you know where my little Fiddling Cat is?"

Madame Goose sheepishly said, "I do. After you left this morning to go to the copy shop, he high-tailed it out to the hills to see his long lost friend the Little Laughing Dog. I thought he'd be home by now."

They all stopped in their tracks waiting to see if she was going to get upset, but she didn't. She just waved them off to the kitchen and went back to work.

"No need to get upset," she thought. "He had, at least let Madame Goose know where he was going." She also realized how much he had missed his little friend.

Mother Goose worked the rest of the day, until well past dinnertime, cutting and stacking. When she went into the kitchen to check on her geese and to see if her Fiddling Cat was home yet…. He wasn't.

The geese had already fed themselves and were just finishing up making their quill pens. Mother Goose fixed herself a plate of the lasagna, and sat down at the table with them to eat. No one said a word.

After she finished eating her dinner, she put her plate in the sink and went to her bedroom to get ready for bed.

There, she got down on her knees and began to feverishly pray, "Dear God, in Jesus' name, please bring my Fiddling Cat home safely now. He never stays out after dark. I love him dearly, Lord. Please oh, please."

Her Fine Gander came running into her bedroom "Honk, honk, honk! Come on, Mother Goose, come on!"

She quickly jumped up and ran outside with him where the other two geese were honking and cackling away. Off in the distance, they could hear the Little Dog laughing just a howling away and her cat was fiddling like crazy. The moon overhead was brighter than ever with the cow jumping around it like a hamster caught on a spinning wheel. The geese all laughed hysterically. Even Mother Goose couldn't contain herself. At times the cow tripped over his own feet because he was trying so hard to keep up with the music.

It wasn't five minutes later that her Fiddling Cat came squealing on to the back porch on all fours and almost slammed into the side of the house.

Mother Goose waited until he caught his breath and then said,

"I haven't seen you run that fast since that old coon dog that used to live across town, chased you and threatened to pull your toenails out!"

The little Fiddling Cat grinned, "I'm sorry I didn't ask you first if I could go but I didn't think you'd let me stay out after dark."

"Come here, you little rascal," she said and picked him up giving him a big hug. "The next time you want to go visit your friend just let me know ahead of time and we will arrange it so you can spend the night out under the hill."

"Alright-puuuurrrrfect," the Fiddling Cat said.

"Now everyone, it's time to go to bed. Get on in the house." Mother Goose was going to stay up and work some more on the books but instead she just got into bed and read the letters from Margaret Miller and Tommy Tucker before going to sleep.

Little Tom Tucker
Sings for his supper;
What shall I eat?
White bread and butter.
How shall he cut it
Without e'er a knife?
How will he be married
Without e'er a wife?

Dear Mother Goose,

I got the email from Bo Peep, a few days ago, telling me about your Christmas party. I'm so excited, I can hardly wait to see you and all my friends again and to be there in my hometown for Christmas. I have so much to tell you about. I can't wait for you to meet my wife.

I'm sorry I haven't kept in touch but I have been so busy since my parents and I moved down here to Hollywood. Remember how my mom always made me sing for my supper? Well, after we moved here, she got stars in her eyes and signed me up for voice lessons. She made me sing in all of the school musicals and even made me sing whenever she and my father had company. She had seen a show on television one night called, *Americans Got Guts*, and it spurred her on.

Anyone who thinks they have some kind of talent can try out for the show. If you win, you receive one million dollars. This became her dream for me, or should I say, her dream. Needless to say, I was soon performing for the whole world to see. I didn't win the million dollars but I did get recognized by a top record producer for having some singing talent and they signed me on. I recorded several albums along the likes of Frank Sinatra, Dean Martin and Sammy Davis Jr. I even got to meet those guys after they heard my albums and got to go on tour with Frank.

After I returned home from the tour, I had enough money to buy my parents a new home. Mother was especially thrilled. I, too, now have my own home which I share with my lovely wife. Even with all the money and fame, I felt somewhat empty so I started reading my Bible and going to church. I remembered how you always had us kids say our prayers at naptime and how you would tell us about God, his son Jesus, and the Holy Spirit.

After church surfing for a while, I finally found a great church filled with the true spirit of Christ. I started attending regularly and singing in the choir. Also, I joined a Bible study; that's where I met my beautiful wife.

I know you're just going to love her and she will definitely love you. Who wouldn't? I now write my own Christian songs of praise and worship and record on a Christian label. I feel much more fulfilled now and, for once, I am truly happy. I have so much more to share with you Mother Goose and I can't wait to hear what's been going on in your life. I know one thing for sure; whatever it is, it's been blessed. For now I'll let you go. I'm sure you're busy getting ready for the party. We'll see you then.

Love to you,
(I Miss You! XXOO}
Tommy Tucker
P.S. My wife says hello

Margaret wrote a letter,
Sealed it with her finger.
Threw it in the dam
For the dusty miller.
Dusty was his coat,
Dusty was his siller,
Dusty was the kiss
I'd from the dusty miller.
If I had my pockets
Full of gold and siller,
I would give it all
To my dusty miller.

Dear Mother Goose,

I just finished reading Bo's email about the Xmas party and emailed her back but I wanted to write you a letter personally to let you know that my Dusty Miller and I will definitely be there. Thanks for the invitation. Sorry I haven't written to you in such a long time. I guess, like a lot of other people, I have kinda gotten caught up in these new electronic gadgets, I'm even texting on my cell phone. To be honest, I'm ashamed of myself. Especially, for not taking the time to write to you! I know you would never own a computer or a cell phone. Let me tell you, they really can be demanding and addictive. You wouldn't think that living clear over here in this little old mill town, in our little log cabin out in the big sticks, that I'd get caught up with such things would you? Well, I didn't either.

I moved away from the hustle and bustle of town when I married My Dusty Miller and looked forward to the simple life, communing with nature. But, before I knew it, I was caught up in it all the new technology too. I couldn't resist when the big wigs came in and opened an electronics store in our little town. They had all kinds of demonstrations and promotions for us "hicks out here in the sticks." Ha, ha.

It's really sad to see the area around here growing in leaps and bounds. I don't know if you heard it on the news or not but a year ago, the mill closed down. My Dusty Miller started mining in the hills above a beautiful lake, east of here, just for something to do to keep his mind off his worries and to his surprise and mine, he actually started finding gold. At first, Dusty kept his findings a secret from the townspeople but one morning after I made him a big breakfast of sowbelly bacon, cackle berries, flap jacks and home fried potatoes, he announced over his fourth cup of blackjack that he thought it best to let everyone know there was gold in them thar hills. He didn't want his friends and family to worry about having to move elsewhere to find work, which wouldn't be easy for them seeing as most of them only had a high school education; if that. All they had ever been is a bunch of axe-men and wood hicks dressed in dashboard overalls and red long johns.

When the brass hats, who owned the mill, first let every-one know that they would soon be out of work, some of his friends just bunched it, and up and quit. A lot of the guys took to drinking bald -faced whiskey and many a night got arrested by the town clown and got thrown in the calaboose for disturbing the peace. Dusty's best friend Cork-eyed Bobby, went yaps. He was brushed crazy out of his mind from drinking and fear of losing his job. He even took to beating his wife and kids.

Anyway, Dusty and I agreed that it would be in the best interest of the whole town to know about the gold. That night, Dusty put on his best boiled collar and the only good pair of jeans he had with his new pair of braces to hold them up. He put some lick- a- dob on his boots 'til they shined and then he went to the town meeting, down at the grange hall, and told everyone the good news.

Everyone was really excited. Just like us. We were all able to stake claims on the mines before the government got involved. Remember when I wrote you last, Mother Goose, and told you that if I had a pocket full of gold and siller I'd give it to My Dusty Miller? Well, he now has his own pocket full of gold and so do I! We just mine enough to get by and then sell the gold to a buyer who comes through town every few months.

Some of the people here depleted their mines within a few months and sold their homes and property to some outfits who are planning to come in and build more houses and commercial properties. They got gold fever and moved on to look for more.

I'm sure glad that didn't happen to Dusty and me. Wow! Sorry, Mother Goose, I just read what I've written so far. I hope I didn't depress you.

On a happier note, guess what? I'm pregnant! "With Adams, fruit", as the locals say around here. Yes, you heard me right. We just found out a few weeks ago.
We don't know if it's a boy or a girl; we want it to
be a surprise.

Dusty has already begun building an addition on to our little cabin for the baby's room. He felled a bunch of trees out on our back forty while yelling like a banshee; like the ole axe-man he was born to be. He has even been carving out a crib for the baby out of an old oak stump. It's going to be so much fun having a little one running around here and I know Dusty is going to be a great father. I'm afraid that after this one gets here, I'll be barefoot and pregnant for the next six years. Ha, ha, ha!

My doctor is located in the next town over from us, where they have a hospital. I have only seen him one time. I went Just to make sure the baby's health was good and that everything was going well. He told me that I was in tip-top shape and that he didn't expect me to have any problems. Although where he works has the latest in birthing facilities, we have decided to have the baby here at home.

Shortly after we moved here, I met a woman in town who everyone refers to as "the medicine woman." She reminds me a lot of you. Actually, a mix between you and your best friend, the Old Woman Who Lived Under a Hill. She is a full-blooded Shoshone Indian. Since she was a little girl she had practiced medicine with her father, who used to be a medicine man. He taught her everything he knew before he went to join the Great Spirit in the sky. She now looks after the people here in town and has been midwife for almost all of the woman here in town with children. Her technique for giving birth is to squat rather than lay down. She says that it is much easier on the baby and the mother. Before the birth, she instructs the mother to practice her breathing and chanting techniques. Plus, she has the women do a lot of exercises, particularly deep knee bends, to strengthen their legs and ankles for the birth. She says that our legs need extra strength so they don't give out while carrying our little papoose.

When she's not caring for someone in need of her services, she works at the local trading post where she sells her handmade beaded moccasins and beaded earrings with porcupine quills. She also sells little beaded leather pouches; they sell like crazy. People pretend they're medicine bags. She does really well since the trading post is the main attraction for anyone passing through town. Out in front of the trading post stands a larger-than-life-sized carved wooden Indian and also a totem pole which her great grandfather carved years ago. Anyone passing through town can't help but stop in and take a look around.

Since we met, we have become pretty good friends. While the mill was still running, I used to stay home alone all day while Dusty was working. I tried to get on at the mill but, they wouldn't allow women so, I looked around in town but the few other jobs that had been available were already taken.

Out of boredom, I started walking into town everyday just for something to do and to get some exercise. Sometimes I would stop into the trading post to pick up something we needed. One day the medicine woman invited me to sit down beside her on an extra stool at the counter. This soon became a regular routine.

 As I watched her work on her beading projects, I became really interested in beading myself. She would tell me all kinds of stories about her tribe, their ways of living long ago and their spiritual beliefs. A lot of the people from her tribe, who live her, still follow the old ways, including her. Eventually, she taught me how to do bead work also, after she got to know my spirit. She now even puts some of my work on consignment there at the trading post.

Right now, I am working on a little pair of moccasins for my own little papoose. Anyway, to make a long story short, I am planning to have the medicine woman deliver our baby.

I have so much to tell you, Mother Goose! You know what? As soon as I get through writing this letter, I am going to go right in the other room and put a block on my computer so I can't send any more emails, only receive them and I'm going to get rid of my cell phone too so I quit texting. It's all so impersonal {I know Dusty will be glad to know I quit}. Writing you this letter has been the best thing that I have done for myself in a long time. Thank you, Mother Goose. After the Christmas party, believe me, I will be writing you more often and also will be coming over to visit you more.

We will see you soon.

With all my love,
XXO0
Margaret

P.S. maybe I will keep my cell phone just for emergencies, but I will quit subscribing to the texting part

Before Mother Goose turned out her nightlight to go to sleep, she got back up and went into the kitchen to call Bo Peep, just like she said she would. She knew that Bo Peep was just dying to know what Margaret's secret was.

"Hello, sweetheart. I hope I'm not calling too late."

"No, no we're still up, Mother Goose. What's up?"

"Margaret is with Adams fruit."

"What?"

"She's pregnant!"

Bo Peep screamed, "You're kidding me! Is she really? I need to email her right now. Thanks for calling, Mother Goose. Bye."

Chapter Twenty-Two

MOTHER GOOSE WENT DIRECTLY, back to work on her books after her usual morning routine. She wanted to get all of the fabric cut out for the covers before she went into town to pick up her copies. All she would have left to do then would be to assemble the books and she'd be done.

After she cut out the last two pieces of black and white checkered sack cloth for The Baker's book, {just like the material his pants were made of that he wore to work) she threw her blistered fingers up in the air and sighed, "Whoo-eee, I am sure glad that part's done. Thank you, Jesus."

She set out the little binding machine along with the other supplies on her worktable ready for assembly. While dumping out a little bag of trinkets she had also purchased from the craft store, out fell an appliqué of a piece of chocolate with a bite taken out of its side. It was overflowing with a pink creamy filling and had a cherry on top.

She picked it up and thought to herself, "Where in the world did this come from? I don't remember buying this."

Giggling, she waved it in the air and said to the Holy Spirit, "You sure have an amusing way of entertaining yourself." She than placed the appliqué on top of The Baker's soon-to-be book so she would be sure to attach it to the cover later on. Who else would the Holy Spirit have had in mind?

Just as she was about to get some lunch for herself the phone rang. It was the young man from the copy shop calling to let her know that all of her copies were completed and ready to go.

"Oh thank you so much, honey. I will be right in to pick them up. See you in a bit." She didn't want to waste any time so she just grabbed a bagel out of the breadbox and held it in her mouth while she slipped on her wool coat. As she headed out the door, she grabbed her tote bags and off to town she went.

On the way, she couldn't stop thinking about The Baker. After seeing that chocolate appliqué she again got goose bumps as it reminded her of his Big Chocolate Kiss. This time she didn't fight the feeling. She thought about how sweet he was; not just to her but to everyone.

She wondered, "Why, isn't he married? Surely in his line of work he meets plenty of sweet woman." To her surprise, she imagined what it would be like to be married to him and wondered what their home would like.

"Oh for heaven's sakes," she said to herself, "the man hasn't even asked you out on a date. Maybe he just likes being alone or maybe he's gay. Stop it!" She said aloud. Mother Goose rationalized that since she had just finished her last bagel she would stop in at the bakery and buy some more. And besides, she was almost out of bread also.

She glanced over the treats in the window, not taking the time to calm her emotions like usual before she went into the, bakery. Feeling quite self-conscious, she repeated over and over again in her head, "Just be yourself. Just be yourself."

The Baker was very busy that afternoon. When he heard the little bell ring that hung above his doorway he looked over from the counter where he was taking an order from a customer. His eyes lit upon Mother Goose like a satellite orbiting her space. When he raised his hand to wave "Hello" he knocked over a candy dish on the counter filled with chocolate samples. The Baker was so flustered that he tripped on the floor mat as he came around the counter to pick things up and fell flat on the floor. Mother Goose quickly ran over to him and dropped to her knees slipping her hand under his black curly head of hair.

With concern in her eyes she asked, "Are you alright? Do you need a doctor?"

He pretended to be confused, like something you would see in a movie, "Who are you? Where am I?"

With a concern growing out of control on Mother Goose's face, The Baker looked her in the eyes and said, "Doll baby, just calm down. Believe it or not I have never felt more grounded in my life." It was at that moment that Mother Goose saw the love in his eyes and he could see the true love in hers as well.

She shook her finger at him and said, "Have you been into some of those dangerous peppermint schnapps strawberries of yours?"

He gave her a sly smile and they both laughed as he got up from the floor. While he was finishing up taking orders from his waiting customers, Mother Goose looked around his shop at all of the delicious new treats.

While she was doing this, she pondered what she thought she had seen in The Baker's eyes, "Maybe I am just projecting my own emotions? I am too old to be fantasizing about love. What do you think God?"

> *Georgey Porgey pudding and pie,*
> *Kissed the girls and made them cry;*
> *When the girls come out to play,*
> *Georgey, Porgey ran away.*

She wasn't paying much attention as she was wandered around the shop listening for an answer from God. As she came around a table she bumped right into Georgey Porgey by a selection of pudding pies.

"Excuse me," said Georgey turning to see who ran into him. He couldn't help but notice the bedazzled look on Mother Goose's face.

"Oh! Hello Mother Goose, {big hug} it's good to see you. Thank you for the invitation to the Christmas party. I just read your email from Bo Peep on my laptop this morning and haven't had time to respond to it. I have been out of town on business and just stopped in here on my way home to pick up some special treat for my wife. She always cries when I go out of town; even when I kiss her good-bye. Maybe a pie will put me in her good graces. I know she will be thrilled about the Christmas party."

He picked up a vanilla and kiwi pudding pie covered with slices of strawberries, "What do you think, Mother Goose? With the good news of your upcoming Christmas party and this pie, do you think I will have a welcome homecoming?"

Mother Goose chuckled, "I think that will do the trick. You always did have a way with the ladies, young man."

Mother Goose picked out an assortment of bagels and took them up to the counter. She was having a very difficult time concentrating. The way The Baker kept looking at her with such intensity wasn't helping any. His eyes were shining like white diamonds in a bed of coal. She had never seen this before.

"Is there anything else I can get for you, love?" The Baker asked.

"Oh, yes! I need to get some more bread and I think I'll pick out some croissants also." While Mother Goose was picking out the other items, The Baker put the bagels in a box and also slipped in another little box with a round bottom and a clear dome top. Inside it was, a chocolate truffle with a rich creamy pink filling, topped with a maraschino cherry. He placed a layer of wax paper on top so she wouldn't see his surprise. Returning to the counter with some croissants and a loaf of bread Mother Goose set them on the counter before The Baker.

He carefully placed the croissants in the box, on top of the waxed paper, as if he were gently placing baby birds back in their nest. Mother could feel the goose bumps rising all over again. The heat in her cheeks gave color to her emotions so that all could see.

"How much do I owe you?" she asked.

"Hmmm, well let's see," said The Baker as he took out his calculator. We have a dozen bagels, seven croissants and a loaf of bread. I'll write it down for you."

The Baker picked up his order pad and wrote, "I would be very pleased if you would have dinner with me tomorrow night. If not, the cost will double."

Mother Goose read his note and with a bit of a stutter replied, "Are you asking me out on a date?"

"Well, yes, I guess you could call it that. Don't you think it's about time, my love?"

Mother Goose didn't know what to say.

"Here," said The Baker handing her his pen, "just write your phone number down there."

Mother Goose re-read his invitation and then wrote down her phone number with the giddiness of a young woman, and handed the note back to him.

His long, slender, brown fingers feathered across hers as he took the note back. "I will call you tomorrow morning with an expectation of an acceptance," he said coming around the counter to give her a hug and a little kiss on the cheek.

He reached up on the counter and took hold of her box of goodies and put them in one of her tote bags then walked her to the door.

As she headed to the copy shop she felt as if she was walking on air. She couldn't even tap dance. Everything seemed surreal. Although her thoughts were scattered, she also had a very strong sense of well-being. Before she knew it, she was standing at the counter in the copy shop and the young man behind the counter was looking at her with an inquisitive look on his face.

"Are you o.k. Ma'am?" he asked.

Mother Goose pulled herself together the best she could and answered, "Oh yes, yes I'm fine. I'm here to pick up my copies and the originals. I dropped them off to you yesterday."

"Yes I remember you," he said. "I couldn't help myself and

I read some of your rhymes. They're really funky. Did you write them yourself?"

"Yes I did….you think they're funky?"

"Yeah man. I really dug that one about the blackbirds pecking off the maid's nose and that other one about the fat dude who fell off the wall. I'll be right back; let me get'em for you."

Mother Goose giggled to herself, "Funky. I'll take that as a compliment."

The young man went into the back room, where his boss was working and grabbed her order, "Hey boss! Man, you got to come out front and see this old woman she's gotta, kinda aura around her and her eyes are dilated and glassy. They're twinkling like they're studded with stars. I think she's high on something. She's the one who wrote all of those funky poems or rhymes or whatever they're called. She must get loaded before she sits down to write."

The young man's boss put down what he was doing and took Mother Goose's order from his employee and said, "You stay back here, son. I'll take them out to her."

Mother Goose paid the gentleman and said, "Thank you for such prompt service. That young man of yours has been so polite and personable-we could us more like him in the work place."

As soon as Mother Goose was out the door, the owner of the copy shop hollered at his employee to come back out front.

"Wow, man, did you see that? She looked high didn't she?" said the young man.

His boss looked at him and said, "Son, that's what we old folk call true love. She's been bitten by the love bug."

"Wow, man, that's some crazy kinda love!

When Mother Goose got home, she went straight into her bathroom to look in the mirror. She thought that maybe the young man at the copy shop was looking at her funny because she had another Big Chocolate Kiss on her cheek from The Baker. Instead, she saw an image of herself that looked much younger. Her eyes, just like the Baker's, were lit up like firecrackers. She looked immortal. Mother Goose told herself that she had no time right now to think about The Baker, at least not until after Christmas. She just had way too much to do.

She reminded herself of what she always told others, "Don't rush into anything!"

Back in her craft room, she once again regained her focus. While emptying out her tote bags, she realized that if she were to get the books done by Christmas she would have to enlist the help of her pets. She laid everything out in an assembly line fashion. She would have Madame Goose help her glue the material to the covers, her Fine Gander punch holes in the pages, Goosey Goosey Gander set the coils and her Fiddling Cat, who was very good with his paws, decorate the backbones with the different lacings. Lastly, she would personally sign each book and add a special blessing and then, she would be finished.

Before they got started on the books, Mother Goose fixed them all a big tuna salad for lunch. When she opened the box of croissants and bagels, to go along with the salad, she found the little round box with the truffle inside. She couldn't believe her eyes. She carefully removed the little dome top and just stared at the chocolate with the cherry on top. Gently, she picked it up and took a little bite out of the side. The rich, pink, creamy filling spilled into her mouth and over her lip. It was just like the chocolate appliqué she had mysteriously found in her bag of trinkets!

She giggled and said, "My, my, my, Holy Spirit, you sure have been working overtime these last several days. I can hardly wait to see what other surprises you have in store."

She called in her pets who were still playing outside in the snow, which had begun to fall and told them that after lunch she would like them to help her with her project. They were thrilled. Like I mentioned before, they loved working on projects with Mother Goose; especially because she always made it so much fun.

As they worked, they sang rounds of Old MacDonald and made up their own imaginary animals and lyrics.

> *With a blue stripped goose here,*
> *And a cat with wings there,*
> *Here a pink giraffe*
> *And an octopus there…..*

They all roared with laughter until their little sides hurt. They worked all afternoon, right up until dinner.

After dinner, with still a lot of work to be done, Mother Goose decided to give her pets a break for the day as she felt the need for some time alone. She suggested to her pets that they all relax for the rest of the evening in front of the fireplace and told them that she would put their favorite movie *Dr. Dolittle on.* They all agreed to this idea, so she tossed down some throw pillows in front of the T.V. and made them a big bowl of popcorn sprinkled with cheese.

As Mother Goose continued to work on the books alone, she mulled over whether or not to accept The Baker's invitation for dinner. She felt that she just had too much left to do before the party and, even more, she was concerned that her emotions might go astray and she would embarrass herself or, worst of all, she would be disappointed with their encounter. Finally, she just let it go and turned it over to God.

Chapter Twenty-Three

When the phone rang the next morning Mother Goose hesitated to pick it up because she knew it was The Baker. She still didn't know how to respond to his invitation. She hadn't had her morning coffee either and wasn't quite awake. Unable to resist, she picked the receiver up anyway.

"Good morning, my love. I hope you will forgive me but some things have come up and I am going to have to cancel dinner tonight. I hope you understand."

Mother Goose bit her lip, "Oooh, no, that's quite alright. I have way too much to do before the party anyway."

A pregnant silence hung in the air and then Mother Goose asked shyly, "Will you still be able to make it to the Christmas party?"

"Yes, my love, of course I'll be there. Remember, I'm bringing the desserts! I hate to cut this conversation short but I have some very important business to take care of. I'll see you then, doll."

Mother Goose felt disappointed but, on the other hand, somewhat relieved and a little foolish. Maybe she had made way more out of everything than she should have. After hanging up, she took a nice, hot shower hoping to wash off the residual disappointment. Before she went back to work on the books, she went into her kitchen to make herself a good strong cup of coffee only to find that she was all out.

That wasn't going to work at all. She never felt ready for a new day without her cup of morning brew and her day was already going topsey, turvy. Usually, she had her cup of strong brew first thing in the morning and then she took her shower. Not vice versa with added emotions thrown in.

She slipped into her warm wool winter coat and put her narrow little feet into her rubber boots, then she walked down to the neighborhood Co-op in the lightly falling December snow and marveled at its cleansing beauty.

"Please God, Jesus," she prayed, "let the rest of this day go well."

After Mother Goose dispensed her favorite blend of dark, full-bodied French roast coffee into a tall, brown, recyclable bag, she walked through the aisles to see what was new on the shelves.

She couldn't resist. The Co-op's rustic old wooden floors and the carefully displayed array of natural products invited her to linger. She picked out a new luffa with a long wooden handle so she could reach the middle of her back while showering. She then spied a new product on the shelf beside the hanging fruit skeletons; Authentic African Black Soap.

"Hmmm," she hummed as she read the label "many cultures in West Africa use charcoal to detoxify and purify the skin."

She opened the lid and took a sniff. "Mmmmm," it had a fresh tangerine scent. She just, had to have it.

"Now, that's enough," she said to herself and headed to the

cash register diverting her eyes from the neon green and orange NEW signs. Mother Goose almost made it to the checkout stand, just past the circular where all of the latest books were on show, when the Holy Spirit urged her to stop and take a look.

She wanted to argue with him and say, "I get all my reading material at the library. I need to get home and back to work on our books, Lord." But instead, she stopped.

> *Lady bird, lady bird, fly away home;*
> *Thy house is on fire, thy children all gone.*
> *All but one, and her name is Anne,*
> *And she crept under the pudding pan.*

One of the books caught her eye. On the cover was a beautiful young woman whom she thought she recognized. The title of the book was, *On Fire for the Lord,* by Anne Lee Horner. She picked it up and felt as if she were holding the transcendent soul of this woman in her hands. Goose bumps covered her body as she read the back cover.

> *This is the true story of a young woman who was*
> *abandoned as a child by her own family after a house*
> *fire. Authorities found her hiding under a pudding*
> *pan. They held her in child protective custody for*
> *over two months hoping that her family would return*
> *for her but to no avail. They were then going to put*
> *her in the children's shelter but it was overcrowded*
> *so they transferred her to an orphanage in another*
> *state. Anne was too young at the time to fully express*

herself, but she prayed that a woman named Mother Goose would find her. This is more than a testimonial; this is a book of prayer.

#1 Pulitzer Prize Winning Book of the Year. A Must Read.

Trembling, Mother Goose opened the book and again saw a photo of the young woman on the back inside cover with a young man at her side. Below the photo it read:

Anne Lee Horner and her husband, Jack Horner now live in Africa and are happily married. They both are missionaries there and also attend a small church regularly where Jack is the junior pastor.
To contact Anne and her husband Jack:
Call 1 800-777-LORD [5673]

Mother Goose stood there in the aisle with the book pressed to her bosom and tears of joy streaming down her face.

"My merciful God; thank you Jesus; thank you Holy Spirit. Thank you. Thank you. Thank you."

After Mother Goose paid for the book, along with her other items, she quickly returned home. She made herself that strong cup of coffee she had been yearning for then sat down in her living room in front of the glowing fire and began to read:

This book is dedicated to the only real mother
I have ever known: my momma, Mother Goose.

Mother Goose wiped the moist droplets of joy off her cheeks and continued to read. She learned that Little Anne had spent her entire pre-teen and teenage years living in the orphanage. As soon as she was able to read, a visiting nun gave her a Bible. She studied it fervently and continued to pray without ceasing that she would be reunited with Mother Goose. She was an inspiration to the other children at the orphanage as she was constantly reassuring them that they were loved and that, some day, they all would have families of their own. Above all, she taught them that their father in heaven would never abandon them and that his son, Jesus Christ, and his Holy Spirit were already making arrangements for their futures. While here on earth, he would always be there to protect and comfort them along the way. When Anne turned eighteen and was able to leave the orphanage, she did just that and joined a convent.

> *Little Jack Horner*
> *Sat in a corner,*
> *Eating a Christmas pie;*
> *He put in his thumb,*
> *And pulled out a plum,*
> *And said, "What a good boy am I!"*

While studying at the convent for her initiation into nun ship, Anne and all of the other young women went on a missionary trip to an orphanage in Africa. There, in a small rural village, is where she met Jack Horner. He was preaching at a little rural church, actually it was a grass hut. They fell in love and, not long after they met, Anne dismissed herself from the convent and they were married. They have lived in Africa now for many years spreading God's word and sharing the gift of hope. Often Little Anne talks to her husband, Jack, about her Mother Goose. Whenever she does, Jack always gets the feeling of déjà vu and envisions a little boy sitting in a corner with a plum on his thumb with several other children sitting around him by a glowing fireplace.

The story went on to tell some about Jack's family stating that they had been missionaries and had moved around a lot.

Mother Goose was so caught up in the rapture of Little Anne's story that it didn't take her long to read the book and she was finished by mid-afternoon. When she closed the book, she promptly picked up the phone and dialed: 1 800 777-LORD

"Hello?"

"Hello"

"Is this Anne Horner?"

"Yes, it is. May I ask who's, calling?"

"My dear, dear Little Anne, this is your Mother Goose."

"Oh my God! Oh my God! Thank you, Jesus, thank you! Is this really you Mother Goose?"

"It is, baby girl. My sweet Little Anne. I just finished reading your phenomenal book, *On Fire for the Lord.*"

"You did — where'd you find it? I didn't think it would be available in the States for another year or more."

"I went down to the neighborhood Co-op this morning for some coffee and was led to the bookrack by the Holy Spirit. While I was looking at the books, I thought I saw your beautiful face on one of the covers. Your photo looked familiar and I got goose bumps all over my body. Then, when I turned it over and read the back cover, I knew it was you. Oh honey, over the years you have no idea how often I have thought about you. So many people here have continued to pray for you and your well-being. What happened to you and your family was such a tragedy; I'm so sorry you had to go through all of that. Over the years I have also thought about and prayed for your husband, Little Jack Horner, and wondered whatever became of him. Now I know. My prayers have been answered."

"What? You know my husband Jack also, Mother Goose?"

"Yes, honey, I do. He also used to be left in my care whenever his family was back in town from one of their mission trips"

"This is so unreal, Mother Goose. Now, I have goose bumps!" They both giggled.

"I have missed you terribly, Mother Goose. You know if it were not for your love and the spiritual teachings you shared with all of us children long ago, I would not be who I am today. I can't thank you enough."

"No need to thank me, Anne. It was your faith in Christ that saved you, not me. Anne, honey, you know we could talk for hours but for now I have a lot to do. Number one being, to get out to the airport right away, before all of the flights are booked for the Christmas holidays, and purchase round trip tickets for you and Jack to come over here and spend Christmas with me. Do you think you can make it?"

"Well, I need to ask Jack. I'm not sure what his plans are and if he has to work on Christmas or not."

"Oh, sweetheart, you just have to come over here. I have planned a big Christmas party this year. Well, I should say, the Holy Spirit did and he has provided everything to make it a wondrous occasion. All of you children, who were once in my care have all been invited. I know the others would be thrilled to see you and to hear your testimony. What a great gift that would be for everyone to hear your story on Christmas day."

"Please, hold on a minute, Mother Goose, Jack just walked in."

"Jack! Jack, honey, you're not going to believe who's on the phone; it's my Mother Goose!"

"Great God almighty! Praise the Lord. How did you find her?"

"I didn't. The Holy Spirit did it for me. Mother Goose wants to make arrangements for us to go spend Christmas with her. Can we go?"

"Yes we can, babe," Jack said wrapping Anne in his arms. "I'm sure I can get the senior pastor to fill in for me. I wouldn't want you to miss this opportunity for the world."

"I love you! Thank you!" said Anne.

"Yes! Yes! Mother Goose, we will be there. I'm so excited I'm going to go pack as soon as we get off the phone and when I'm done, I'm going to go for a walk up and down the streets and go to the orphanage here and tell everyone how faithful our Lord is!"

Mother Goose chuckled, "You do that, honey, but don't get so caught up witnessing that you forget your flight."

Anne giggled, "Don't you worry; that won't happen."

"May I speak to Jack a moment, sweetheart?" "Yes, here he is."

"Hello, Mother Goose," Jack said in a deep manly voice. "I had been anticipating your call, but I wasn't expecting it so soon. I had a feeling that once Anne's book was published and broadcast worldwide on the wings of the Holy Spirit you, and her, would be reunited."

"What a beautiful way to state matters, Jack. The Holy Spirit brought you back to me also. You were also in my care over the years. You probably don't remember too well because you were not here very often. I still have pictures of you as a little boy. I can hardly wait for you to see them when you get here. Anne is also in the pictures."

"I'll be darned. No wonder I always felt a connection with you when Anne brought your name up," said Jack. "This being a Christian is one phenomenal ride. It's a small world, like they say, huh Mother Goose? Oceans apart but the merciful journey with the Lord knows no boundaries."

"Yes it is, Jack, we never know when a blessing is about to land in our laps. God truly does work in mysterious ways. Well, it's all settled then. I will make the flight arrangements so you can arrive on Christmas Eve. I can hardly wait to see you both again. May I please speak to Anne again, honey?"

"Sure, here she is and thank you, Mother Goose."

"Anne, baby, this is going to be the most spirit-filled magical Christmas ever. I can hardly wait for you to get here. If you have any problems with your flight, please give me a call. My number is 1-541- 707-GOOSE. I love you, baby girl. See you soon."

"Bye, mama, I love you too," Anne said.

After hanging up the phone, Mother Goose thought about how little Anne had called her mama although she was not her mother. She was tickled that Anne felt she could take the liberty to address her in this way. After all, what harm could it do? The child never had a real mother.

She went to her craft room to see if, by chance, she had included Anne and Jack in her project. It wasn't a total surprise, not with the way the Holy Spirit had been orchestrating things, to see that indeed she had. There on the table, along with the other books, was a book for each of them ready to be assembled. Like Little Anne's husband, Jack, Mother Goose thought to herself, "Yes this being a Christian is one phenomenal ride."

For extra warmth, Mother Goose put on a pair of wool leggings over her tights then put on her heavy wool coat and a hat. While she and her Fine Gander flew out to the airport, she praised the Lord and tried to catch the falling snowflakes on her tongue. They reminded her of the precious manna, the food God had provided for the Hebrews during their exodus from Egypt.

The airport was clamorous. People were rushing here and there in search of their departure gates. Angry remarks filled the air while people waited in the long lines; some with small children crying in response to the chaotic atmosphere.

"Oh my goodness, what a mad house," Mother Goose mumbled.

She got in line and bowed her head focusing on her breathing with patience in mind. Her mediation was interrupted when a handsome dark-skinned man with a white turban upon his head lightly tapped her on the shoulder.

"Namasté," he said with his hands pressed together before him.

"Namasté," replied Mother Goose.

His mystifying eyes bored into her soul and he spoke again with a warm hush saying, "*I will keep still and wait like the night with a starry vigil and head bent low in patience*"

"Ahh, you know the works of Rabindranath Tagore, he is one of my favorite poets," said Mother Goose.

"Mmm," hummed the mysterious visitor and motioned for her to come with him saying, "Mere sagth a geeye." The two of them went straight to the head of the long line where they stopped next to a honorable looking, woman. She was dressed in a colorful wrap, like an unopened present, the dot in the middle of her forehead being the bow.

The man spoke to the woman quickly in his native, agile tongue. She nodded in compliance and then pulled Mother Goose by the hand so that she stood in front of her.

"My husband says that you have the patience of the night, one who waits for Gods light, we would like you to take our place in line," the woman said.

"Are you sure?"

"Yes, yes. Go ahead."

"Aap bahut dayaloo hain," said Mother Goose hoping that her stagnant Hindi wouldn't embarrass her.

The man and woman both smiled. "You speak our language?" asked the woman.

"Mujey Hindi Ka. I need to practice," said Mother Goose.

"You do well," she said as she tipped her head forward letting Mother Goose know it was her turn in line.

The flight arrangements were made without any problem. The ticket agent even went so far as to call the airport over in Africa to make sure that everything was lined up on their end. The agent in Africa confirmed the reservations and said that she would give the Horners a call and let them know that their tickets would be waiting for them at the counter.

When Mother Goose stepped away from the ticket booth her new acquaintances both bowed again and wished her "Christmas Kee badhagee yann."

"Merry Christmas to you, also. Thank you very much," said Mother Goose overflowing with joy.

"No. Shukriyaa," said the mystery man. In unison, he and his wife said, "Alvida."

Mother Goose tap-danced her way out of the airport. "Shukriyaa Alvida," she sang as she passed by the waiting, spectators.

{Thank you very much; goodbye.}

When Mother Goose got home, she felt the same as Anne. She was so excited about seeing her and Jack again that she wanted to tell everyone how the Holy Spirit had reunited her with her beloved children. She decided that she would try to keep the news a secret until Christmas. Of course, with one exception; she would tell her best friend, right away.

Mother Goose had spent the whole day focused on Little Anne, reading her book, talking to her on the phone, and making the flight arrangements. What was left of the evening she used to finish gluing the fabric to the book covers. She planned to enlist her pets to help her the next day and they would work until the project was completed.

Chapter Twenty-Four

MOTHER GOOSE WAS UP and at 'em before five a.m. the next morning. Although she didn't sleep much the night before, thinking about Little Anne's story and the other events that had taken place over the last several days, she did have a renewed sense of energy. She and her Fine Gander ate a quick breakfast and then flew right out to see her best friend.

The Old Woman was already up, also, and busy working on her baskets and wall hangings.

"My, my you're out early this morning. Come in."

"I just couldn't wait any longer to come out and see you. I almost flew out here late last night, but I made myself stay in bed and rest. You're not going to believe what happened yesterday."

"What? What? Tell me," the Old Woman said.

Mother Goose pulled Little Anne's book out of her coat pocket and handed it to her.

"Hmm, *On Fire For The Lord*," the Old Woman looked at the young woman's picture on the cover and her eyes welled up with tears. "I think I know this young woman. It's Little Anne isn't it?"

"What? How did you know?"

"Lately I have been having visions of this young woman," she said while lightly tapping Anne's face on the cover with her index finger.

"The vision is interrupted at times with a vision of her as a young girl; the Little Anne I used to know."

Mother Goose didn't question her. She knew from years of experience that the Old Woman Who Lived Under a Hill was, without question, a very gifted seer. She was continually amazed by her gift.

"Read the back," Mother Goose said with misty eyes.

The Old Woman read the back and the inside cover and then, placed the book on her table. Standing, she raised her arms in the air with her hands bent out to the sides like the wings of a bird in flight and recited Psalms 95:1

> *'O come let us sing unto the Lord;*
> *Let us make a joyful noise to the rock of our salvation.'*

"Alleluia!" shouted Mother Goose.

Her best friend put a Diana Ross cassette in her player and together they sang:

> *Ain't no mountain high enough—*
> *Aint no valley low enough—*
> *Ain't no river wide enough,*
> *Nothing can keep us — keep us from you Lord.*

They sang loudly while doing a little cakewalk around the Old Woman's earth-enclosed home all the while rejoicing in the mightiness of God.

Mother Goose told her how she had come across the book at the Co-op the day before and that she had also talked to Little Anne and Jack on the phone. Her smile, lit up her face, as she shared the good news that they would be flying out to spend a couple of nights with her over the holidays.

The Old Woman had, at one time, had a strong connection with Little Anne also. Throughout the years, she had prayed for her and continued to wonder whatever became of her.

When the Old Woman Who Lived Under a Hill's Old Man was still alive, they had met Little Anne's family, who lived just a few houses down from them. Often, Little Anne and her brothers and sisters would be left alone at night. The Old Woman and her husband did not feel good about this and would go check on them. Although Anne's oldest sister was left in charge to watch over the others, the Old Woman and her husband didn't feel that a twelve year old should be given that kind of responsibility, nor be staying home alone either.

The Old Woman, on occasion, would make them a pan of vanilla pudding with bananas on top for a treat. When she realized that they were really hungry, she also started making them casseroles. Often, when she went over to their home at night, she would find Little Anne locked in her bedroom alone. She and her Old Man talked to the twelve year old about this and the young girl said it was easier to keep an eye on her if she stayed in her room and wasn't running around the house. She said that this was what her parents did when they were home.

The Old Woman and her husband, the Old Man Dressed in Leather, tried to talk to the children's parents when they got home one evening but were met with extreme hostility for interfering in their lives. The next day, their house burnt down and they were never to be seen again. A newspaper article at the time stated that Anne had been found hiding under a pudding pan but did not say what became of her. When the Old Woman and her husband contacted the authorities, they would not release any more information.

Mother Goose went on to tell the Old Woman about Jack Horner, Annie's husband, and how he also had once been in her care.

"I am so looking forward to this Christmas," said the Old Woman. "I have never felt the Holy Spirit's presence so intensely this time of year. It always amazes me how Jesus seems to bless this worldly holiday to celebrate his birth, although he was born rather, sometime around the middle of spring or summer. I'm almost afraid to go to sleep at night because I don't want to miss a thing."

"I know how you feel, my dear friend. Believe me, I know how you feel."

The Old Woman showed Mother Goose the projects that she was working on. They were beyond any earthbound ideas.

"These are spectacular," Mother Goose told her. "How do you come up with such creative works of art?"

The Old Woman looked at her longtime friend and said, "Now, we both know the answer to that."

"True, true," said Mother Goose. "I'm working on a special project too. I didn't want to give my usual gift of mineral salts and soaps again this year. I almost wore my carpet out pacing up and down trying to think of something special. The Holy Spirit finally stepped up and gave me an awesome new idea. It's going to be a big surprise." The Old Woman pestered her, like a child, trying to get her to tell her what it was.

They laughed and Mother Goose said firmly, "No! This is a surprise for you too. As a matter of fact, I've got to get going because I still have a lot to get done. I'll be back in a few days to help you stuff the mushrooms, if you're not already done. We can also set up the tables in the mystical clearing then, too."

As soon as Mother Goose left, the Old Woman made herself a nice hot cup of mushroom tea and sat down to read Little Anne's book, *On Fire for the Lord.*

After she came home, Mother Goose, along with her pets, went straight to work on the books.

"Kids," she said, "I really want to have all of these done by Christmas Eve before Anne and Jack arrive. You're all going to have to really concentrate and work hard so we can get this done. All right? No playing around."

Her Fiddling Cat laced a piece of ribbon through the backbone of one of the books and said looking with squinted eyes at his feathered sister, "No problem. We got your back, mom. Don't we?"

"Don't worry, we'll get them done," said Madame Goose. "I'll make sure furball here doesn't run off to play somewhere."

Around two in the afternoon, Mother Goose was somewhat relieved to hear the phone ring because she needed a break.

"Hi, Mother Goose, it's me Bonny Lass. I've got your dress done. I'm so excited for you to see it. Can I bring it over to you right now?"

"Oh, that's wonderful, honey. I can hardly wait to see it. How about I walk over there. I have been working on a project all day and I could really use a walk to stretch my legs,"

"Sure! Come on over, Mother Goose. I know everyone would

love to see you open your package. I put your dress in a box and wrapped it up like a Christmas present since I thought I would be bringing it over to you. They're as excited about your dress as I am."

"O.k., then. I'll be over there in about twenty minutes."

Mother Goose thought about walking down along the riverfront past The Baker's shop but she decided against it. She would wait to see him at the Christmas party. After all, he had told her that he was busy.

When Mother Goose arrived at the "Women's Retreat" she was glad that she had taken the time to walk over. The gals always decorated their yard and the big Old Historical Old Gingerbread House with an elaborate display of lights and animated figures. Their house was the main attraction in town for holiday light seekers. The yard was all lit up with animal figures of every kind along with children of all different races. These lifelike children were playing in manmade snow along with the snow from above that was beginning to accumulate on the ground. Some of them were ice-skating on a fake little pond and others were throwing fake snowballs at one another. A little Chinese boy and a little black girl were building a snowman together. On the huge wraparound porch were seven life-sized animated people singing Christmas carols and on the roof a neon sign beckoned "JUST BELEIVE" with an angel attached to a wire that flew around the sign. From the street, this all looked very real. It was absolutely the most magnificent display you have ever seen.

Before Mother Goose had a chance to knock, Bonny Lass opened the door and threw her arms around her, "Come in, come in, Mother Goose. I can't wait for you to see your new dress." The house was abuzz with all of the gals getting ready for the upcoming Christmas weekend.

"Make yourself at home," said Bonny Lass. "I'll go get your dress-it's in my sewing room."

Mother Goose went into the kitchen where she could hear the joyful noise of a lot of chattering going on and pots and pans clattering. Cross Patch and the Fair Maid were making Christmas cookies and Sukey and Polly were cooking up homemade noodles and deep fried shrimp. They were preparing the food ahead of time for a Chinese-themed dinner party they were having that evening.

"Hi, Mother Goose!" they all chimed.

"Wait until you see your dress, its gorgeous!" said the Fair Maid handing her a gingerbread man. At the same time, Sukey handed her one of the jumbo fried shrimp which had been draining on a paper towel.

"What do you think, Mother Goose?" Sukey asked.

"Oh, this shrimp is delicious, Sukey. This batter is so light and crisp."

"The secret is to use rice flour and just the right amount of seasoning," Sukey revealed. "My mom sent me her recipe, from China."

Mother Goose finished the succulent piece of shrimp and then bit the head off of her gingerbread man, "Mmmm. Yum, yum, yum spicy!" she said.

Bonny Lass came back out of her sewing room with her partner, Pretty Maid, who had been in there wrapping Christmas presents.

"Come on, you guys," hollered Bonny Lass from the living room. "I'm ready for Mother Goose to open her package." Mother

Goose and the other gals all went in to the living room where Bonny Lass was anxiously waiting.

"Here, Mother Goose. Sit over here," Bonny Lass said pointing to the big overstuffed chair. Bonny Lass placed the box in Mother Goose's lap and then plopped down on the ottoman in front of her, waiting with anticipation, along with the other gals. Just as Mother Goose was about to open the package, the doorbell rang. Sukey quickly jumped up to get it.

"Who could that be?" she said shaking her head. "Our dinner party doesn't start till seven," she growled.

"Hi, Sukey," said Little Bo Peep. "Is Mother Goose here yet? I talked to Bonny Lass awhile, ago and she said that she would be coming over to pick up her dress so, I thought I would come over and give her my present also."

"Yes, yes she's here. Come in. She is just about to open the package. Sorry, I'm a little stressed out. Come on in," she said as she took Bo Peep's hand.

Bo Peep followed Sukey, or rather, she was dragged into the living room. She sat down on the couch next to Sukey and Polly. She placed her large, boxed gift for Mother Goose on the floor in front of her.

"Go ahead, Mother Goose. I can't wait any longer said," Bonny Lass.

Mother Goose carefully tried to open the package, like some people do, without tearing the paper.

"Just tear it open!" squawked Bonny Lass trying to control the impulse to rip it open for her.

"But this is such beautiful paper. I hate to tear it up," Mother Goose said.

"Yeah, yeah, yeah. Just rip it open."

Amused at Bonny Lass, Mother Goose tore into the package like a child. But gently, savoring the moment, she carefully removed the tissue paper covering the dress.

"Goodness gracious. What in the world?" she said as she lifted the dress up out of the box and held it out in front of her. All of the gals watched as the tears welled up in Mother Goose's eyes.

"No, this is not of this world. This is absolutely heavenly. Bonny Lass, this is the most exquisite, most elegant dressI have ever seen in my life!"

All of the gals clapped and laughed at Mother Goose's astonishment. She held the dress up to herself eyeing the fit and then ran into the sewing room to try it on. Gazing at herself in the full-length mirror, she realized that she had never felt so beautiful in her life. And, to her surprise, sexy also. She sashayed her way back into the living room with regal poise.

The dress was made of sheer white gossamer and lined with a light golden silk. It fit snuggly around Mother Goose's breasts and through the torso. At the waist was a scalloped bodice covered in white rhinestones, which sparkled like the stars. It flowed over her slender hips to the ground like feathers. Bonny Lass had cut strips out of the sheer gossamer and had layered them over the skirt of the dress. She used the same design for the sleeves. The effect was quite ethereal.

Mother Goose gave Bonny Lass a big hug and then coyly asked her and the others, "Do you think maybe this is just a little too sexy for an old woman like me?"

"No! No!" they all shouted.

"Heavens no! Said Bonny Lass You look exotic and beautiful, Mother Goose, and you are. No woman should ever feel she's too old to look her best."

Cross Patch piped up and said, "No it's not too sexy at all. You look like a well preserved angel."

Mother Goose and the gals all got a good laugh out of that.

Mother Goose slowly waved her arms and circled the room in front of them. She then started to head back to the sewing room to change.

"Wait a minute, Mother Goose, I have something for you too," said Bo Peep. Mother Goose sat back down in her appointed chair.

Bo Peep opened the box on the floor in front of her and said to Mother Goose, "O.K., now stand up and turn around."

Bo, pulled from the box a luxurious crimson-colored cashmere cape, which she had made, and draped it over Mother Goose's shoulders. She then turned her around and fastened the white rhinestone clasp she had added at the neck.

Mother Goose reached down and grasped the sides of the cape and pulled it around her. "This is just gorgeous, Bo." She lifted one side of the cape to her cheek and said, "Its soooo soft. You know what, gals, I don't think I have ever seen anyone outfitted in such divine spender before. Not even one of the queens."

Both, Bo Peep and Bonny Lass blushed with unselfish pride in response to Mother Goose's compliment. They were so pleased that she liked their gifts of love for her. After giving each of the gals a hug, Mother Goose picked up the box for the dress and the one for the cape, and went back to the sewing room to change back into her clothes.

She looked at herself once more in the mirror. "I hope the Queens aren't jealous," she thought as she smiled appraisingly at her new outfit.

After changing back into the dress she had been wearing, she neatly folded up her new dress and cape and put them back in their respective boxes.

With one box under one arm and another under her other arm, Mother Goose said her goodbye's and headed for home. On the way, all she could think about was The Baker and how he was going to react when he saw her in her new dress, "I sure hope he likes it," she thought as she imagined the look on his face.

Mother Goose got home after dark. With the winter sun setting early, the darkness often took the day by surprise without any warning. She walked into a nice, warm, cozy home. The fire was popping and spiting in her living room as someone had recently put fresh logs on it. From the kitchen, she could smell a wonderful aroma drifting her way. She set her gifts on the dining room table and then went into the kitchen to see what was cooking.

On the stove, a pot of stew was simmering and a plate of Christmas cookies sat on the counter beside her stove with a note attached.

Hello my friend. Simple Simon and I just stopped by to drop off a little something for you. Simon and I have been making cookies for the past week and, this evening, we have been out delivering them to our friends. My husband, the Butcher that he is, wanted to share a quart of his scrumptious lamb stew with you. I hope you don't mind that I took the liberty of putting it on the stove to simmer for you. Madame Goose told me that she thought you would be home soon. She said that you have been extremely busy so I thought it might be nice to have dinner already for you. We're all very excited about the Christmas party this weekend. We'll see you there, dear.

Love from us all,
Your friend Mother Hubbard

"Well, how nice," Mother Goose said to herself while taking a peak at the Butcher's lamb stew simmering on the stove. He always had the best cuts of meat in town and he really knew how to cook them.

After hanging up her beautiful new dress and cape, Mother Goose went into her craft room to check on her pets.

Madame Goose pointed to the stack of books sitting on the edge of the table and said, "Look, Mother Goose, we're almost done. I made sure that these guys didn't slack off while you were gone."

Her Fine Gander, Goosey, Goosey and her Fiddling Cat just mumbled quietly and let Madame Goose think that she had been in charge. Sometimes she could get a little bossy.

"You're all such wonderful little helpers, said Mother Goose. I can't believe you have almost half of the books completed." She figured that if she stayed home and helped them, without any more interruptions, they could have all of the books done by the 23rd. This would give her enough time to go out to the Old Woman Who Lived Under a Hill's home and help her set up the tables in the mystical clearing. And also, to get ready for Little, Anne and her husband Jack's arrival.

Before Mother Goose went to bed that night, she prepared enough meals to last them for the next few days so there would be no need for her to stop working on the rest of the books and cook.

Chapter Twenty-Five

THEY MADE IT! DECEMBER 23, just two days before Christmas and all of the books were done. Bless their little hearts. Her pets worked non-stop with her on the books, only stopping to take a potty break or to stretch their little legs before they were at it again. They were so pleased with themselves for the work they had done and so was Mother Goose.

She said to them at breakfast, "You know what kids? You have been so good and so helpful these last several days. What do you say we all go into town, *right now*, to Animal Crackers and each of you can pick out three things that you would like to have. Anything at all, your choice."

The geese honked and cackled and her cat picked up his fiddle and played jingle bells. Mother Goose giggled at their joyful displays of enthusiasm.

"When we get home, we can decorate the house. After that we'll go out to the hill--- oh, that reminds me, don't let me forget to pick something up for the Three Blind Mice, Pussy Cat and the Little Laughing Dog.

"We won't!" they all said at once.

When they got to the pet store, Mother Goose told her pets to all meet her back at the cash register in half an hour.

"Don't forget…" her Fiddling Cat started to say.

"I remember," said Mother Goose. And off they ran. While her pets were shopping, Mother Goose picked out a beautiful purple rhinestone collar for Pussy Cat, and for the Old Woman's Three Blind Mice, she got them each their own little exercise balls. Although they already had a wheel, Mother Goose thought with the clear plastic balls they could go outside and move around on their own without supervision. For the Little Laughing Dog she found a cute new food dish and spoon with little paw prints all over them. It didn't take Mother Goose long at all to pick out their gifts so she went back up to the cash register where there was an assortment of treats and filled a bag of goodies for each of her pets and also for her best friend's. She picked out a few other little items also that caught her eye for stocking stuffers. Quickly then, she made her purchases before her little rascals could see them.

Mother Goose's geese and Fiddling Cat showed up at the register right on time all excited with their new items. Both Goosey Goosey and her Fine Gander picked out new riding blankets for themselves as well as some nice new saddlebags. Her Fine Gander also, picked out a red silk bow tie to wear to the party and Goosey Goosey Gander got himself a green beret. Madame Goose also picked out some nice new pink saddlebags even though the guys usually did all the carrying.

She also found herself an eye-catching purple and yellow neck ruffle and some feather shine with sparkles in it. She wanted to look especially nice for the Christmas party because it wasn't often that she and her mate went out.

Instead of getting things all for himself, her Fiddling Cat got them all a new Frisbee and a real hacky sack to play with. He was tired of losing his catnip toys to hacky sack games. He did get himself a little tuxedo. Although it was made for a small dog, it fit him perfectly and he wanted to look exceptionally good since he was going to be fiddling with the king's Fiddler's Three. Mother Goose paid for their gifts. Then, together, they romped in the snow all the way home and sang Christmas carols.

As soon as they got home, Mother Goose went up in the attic and brought down all of her Christmas decorations. Some years she only brought down a few, but with Anne and Jack coming, she wanted the house to look especially festive.

Handing her Fine Gander a box of colorful lights for the house she said, "Here, you take these and go outside and string them along the eves."

Next, she gave Goosey Goosey a box with some more lights, which were smaller and white. She used these to decorate the old fir tree in the front yard. She didn't see the need to cut down a tree for the inside of the house when she had one right outside her front window.

Giving Madame Goose a box filled with large plastic icicles and huge red and gold bows, she said to both her and Goosey Goosey, "You two are in charge of decorating our Christmas tree."

Inside, Mother Goose and her Fiddling Cat decorated all of the rooms with fallen tree boughs and sprigs of holly. Amongst the holly they placed candles and unique decorations which she had collected over the years. Her favorite decoration of all was a beautiful animated angel that her mother had given her years ago. The angel's face was the most beautiful, realistic face, she had ever seen on a doll. Her molded wings moved back and forth slowly, as did her arms. In her left hand she held a golden harp, and in her right hand she held a lighted candle that flickered as she moved. Mother Goose named her *Gardenia*. She always placed her on the mantle over the fireplace facing her picture window so all who passed by could see her radiance. Between the five of them they got the house decorated in record time. Mother Goose was pleased that this left the whole, rest of the day open for her to go out and help her best friend set up for the party in the mystical clearing.

When they landed under the hill, at the Old Woman's home they could hear the most beautiful music coming from within. Included in the Old Woman's soulful choice of music she loved to listen to the old black gospel choirs. The music was extraordinary with its praise and uplifting beat. You couldn't help yourself, but to raise your hands to the Lord and dance whenever you heard this music. When Mother Goose opened the door, that's exactly what they saw the Old Woman doing. She'd stuff a mushroom and then throw her hands in the air and dance across the room before she stuffed another one.

"Lord, have mercy," she said turning to see Mother Goose and her menagerie standing in her doorway. "Haven't you heard of knocking? You about gave me a heart attack!"

"Don't get all bent out of shape. I did knock-you just couldn't hear me over the music."

"Where's Pussy Cat?" the Fiddling Cat asked the Old Woman.

"She and the Little Laughing Dog are out back in the forest playing down by the creek. Why don't you all go down there and play while we finish stuffing these mushrooms? Be back in an hour or so and you can help us move the tables into the clearing."

Mother Goose and the Old Woman continued to stuff mushrooms while they sang and danced. They both wished that there were more black people in their community along with a real gospel church and choir that really moved the Holy Spirit. They had been to a few churches like this on their travels together and, growing up in the south, Mother Goose had been exposed to many soul-stirring churches. They both loved the joy and enthusiasm they felt there. When the black people prayed and praised the Lord they didn't hold nothing back! And the music, oh the music, cut right to the soul.

When their pets got back from playing down by the creek Mother Goose, the Old Woman and all of their pets walked over to the north side of the forest where the little abandoned chapel still stood on God's little acre. The little chapel had remained the same over the years with the exception of the fallen church bell that Mother Goose now had. Inside, the pews and altar, and even the stained glass windows, were still intact. In the little kitchen there were even some utensils still in the drawers with a stack of folding tables and chairs leaning up against the wall.

"How unfortunate," Mother Goose said to her best friend looking around inside. "With a little tender, loving care and a good paint job this could be a lovely little church again."

"Well maybe it will be someday. It's stood here vacant a long time and is still intact like it's just been waiting to be reborn. It's really amazing some hoodlums haven't come out here and trashed this place."

They all pitched in and began moving the tables into the mystical clearing. But before setting the tables up, they couldn't help but stand in awe of nature's canvas. The snow gracefully waved its way over fallen debris, ebbing back in the presence of overgrowth. The creek whisked its way around the clearing in an arc of frothy blue and green. The whole scene looked like an inviting, textured quilt made up of earth tones and splotched with white stardust. The pattern, being a mandala with the wise old fir in the middle spreading its arms out wide to protect its children from the elements; symbolic of the tree of life.

The Old Woman pointed out to Mother Goose the soft white rays of light dispersed amongst the forest trees.

"See the light?" she said. "That's the internal spirit of the trees showing off their energy. You can only really see it well when it's overcast and there's snow on the ground to reflect off of."

Mother Goose didn't question this phenomenon because, after all, this was the mystical clearing. While Mother Goose was unfolding the legs on her table, she noticed something twinkling at her from the forest floor hidden beneath a layer of shed leaves and needles. Quickly she bent over, picked it up and put it in her pocket. She was not entirely sure why she was being so secretive. The others were ready to go back to the little chapel to get some more tables.

"Go ahead," Mother Goose told them. "I want to walk through the labyrinth and say a little prayer. I'll be right there."

Once they were gone, she went over to the maze of blessings

and pulled the small shiny object from her pocket. It was her best friend's Harley pin; a gift from her husband which he had given her shortly before his unexpected death. The Old Woman had told Mother Goose about it several times and relayed how much it meant to her, but she had given up hope of ever finding it. She thought she had probably lost it while out riding somewhere. Mother Goose looked down at the pin caressing it with her thumb. The design of the pin was the renowned Harley Davidson logo with little wings stretched out to either side. This pin was unique though; down from the wings dangled a heart shaped locket suspended from little chains. She opened the locket and inscribed on one side read, '*You will always be the ride of my life*' and on the other side, was a picture of the Old Woman and her Old Man cheek to cheek. Mother Goose closed the locket and with tears in her eyes read the back, '*Love always, your Old Man.*'

Mother Goose thanked the Holy Spirit for guiding her to the pin and praised the Lord as she hurried back to the little chapel.

Mother Goose was very accustomed to the supernatural workings of the Holy Spirit but never in her life could she remember a time filled with so many miraculous events, one after the other: the material she had envisioned for her dress there on Bonny Lass's table, the chocolate appliqué with the cherry on top, finding Little Anne and the Little Laughing Dog, and now her best friend's special memory of her husband....not to mention all of the other events which had taken place over the last couple of weeks. Mother Goose walked into the chapel and found her best friend kneeling at the altar saying a prayer of her own.

When she stood up she turned to Mother Goose and said,

"While I was praying I had a vision. The Lord spoke to me and said, "Soon this will be a place of worship again filled with my Holy Spirit. Jack will be empowered as my guide to bring the lost back to me and other Christians even closer."

Mother Goose and the Old Woman beamed with delight, as their skin tingled. They could feel the Holy Spirit moving all around them. At that moment, Mother Goose was tempted to tell her friend about finding her Harley pin but she bridled her tongue and kept quiet.

She thought about the book she had made for her which was filled only with pictures of the Old Woman and her Old Man's beloved memories of their life together. After her Old Man had died, she gave Mother Goose a special box in which she had kept these pictures. The Old Woman wanted Mother Goose to save them until the time came when she would be ready to look at them again without falling all to pieces. Up until finding the pin, Mother Goose had been hesitant to give her the book at Christmas. But now, she had no doubts. She would attach the symbolic Harley pin to the front of her best friend's leather bound book.

After they finished setting up all of the tables and chairs in the clearing, they went back to the Old Woman's home and had a cup of reshi tea.

"Why don't you come over tomorrow, Christmas Eve, and go out to the airport with me to pick up Little Anne and Jack? I know how much Little Anne meant to you also. I don't want you to miss her arrival," Mother Goose said.

"I don't know. What about my pets?" asked, the Old Woman.

"They'll be just fine. Remember, you have the Little Laughing Dog now to take care of them."

"Well, alright. I'll ride in tomorrow morning. I really would love to greet her and her husband at the airport with you."

Before Mother Goose left, she took the presents, the ones she had purchased for the Old Woman's pets, out of her backpack and gave them to her.

"I figured you had been too busy to go shopping yourself so I picked out a few things at Animal Crackers for your pets, this morning. Up until today, I hadn't had time out to go shopping either. So, this morning right after breakfast, I took all my "kids" into town and let them pick out their own gifts."

"Oh thank you, you're a jewel," said the Old Woman and gave her a hug.

As soon as Mother Goose got home, she went straight into her craft/spare bedroom and pinned the Harley pin, with its little locket, to the front cover of her best friends' book. Then, she opened the front cover and added an extra note,

'Under his wings you will find refuge,' from Psalms 91:4

"Now!" She said to herself, "all of the books are completed and ready to go."

Mother Goose wanted to make her spare bedroom look especially nice for Anne and Jack. She gathered up all of the books and put them in the geese's new saddle bags so they would be ready to go on there, flight to the mystical clearing on Christmas day. At this moment, she was glad Madame Goose also got herself some saddlebags. She put away all of her craft supplies and got out a couple of her delicate hand-crocheted tablecloths to cover the craft tables.

As she stood there looking at the open shelves covered with containers holding her art supplies, she thought, "That looks messy!"

Wondering what she could do to fix the problem, the thought occurred to her how Mary Quite Contrary had hung a tapestry in front of her open closet. Hoping to find something nice, she went to her linen closet to see what she could use. She found two sets of velvet burgundy curtains that used to hang in her living room.

"Perfect," she said taking them back in the room where she tacked them in place. Strategically, she placed a bowl of fruit on one table and an electric tea kettle with a couple of cups and saucers next to it. In her kitchen she found an assortment of herbal teas and decided to put out some bagels and cream cheese too.

On the other table, she placed a beautiful wreath with a beeswax candle in the center. To one side of it, she added a couple of bottles of fine wine and long-stemmed crystal glasses. On the other side of the wreath, she placed an assortment of specialty crackers and cheeses.

On the dresser facing the bed she already had a small television with a built in VCR, so she placed some videos, which she thought Anne and Jack might like to watch, next to it. For the finishing touches, she remade the bed using a set of cream-colored satin sheets in a package that she had never opened. Finally, she covered the bed with a cream colored, satin and gold comforter with matching throw pillows. She had been saving these for a special occasion, also. She hoped she wasn't over doing it but she just wanted them to feel comfortable. Besides, this was an extremely special reunion!

In the guest bathroom, she set out a pile of plush bath towels and washcloths along with some of her aromatherapy bath salts and natural soaps. For an added touch of ambience, she placed a candle in each corner of the bathtub.

"There! Too bad I don't have a couple of his and her bath-robes," she said to herself and chuckled.

The rest of the evening Mother Goose and her pets played board games and watched movies in front of the fireplace. For dinner she ordered a giant pizza and had it delivered. This was a rare treat. And you know how "kids" love pizza.

Chapter Twenty-Six

MOTHER GOOSE WOKE UP the next morning filled with anticipation. After pouring herself a cup of coffee, she called the airport to see if Little Anne and Jack's flight was still scheduled to arrive on time. It had been snowing quite heavily throughout the night and was still coming down at a steady pace. She also asked what time Old King Cole's private leer jet would be arriving.

The airport attendant told her that all flights had been arriving on time and that they didn't foresee any delays at the time. The King's jet was scheduled to arrive late that night around ten o'clock. Mother Goose wasn't surprised that the Old King Cole would be arriving late because she knew he had a lot of stops to make along the way, to pick up the other royalty along with Bryan O'Lin and Humpty Dumpty. Knowing them, she figured they would all retire to their rooms for the night once they arrived so that they would be well rested for Christmas day.

With this in mind, Mother Goose felt more at ease knowing she would have all day and evening to spend with Little Anne and Jack. With only a couple of hours until the plane from Africa arrived, Mother Goose quickly downed her coffee and ran back to her room to shower and get dressed.

She stood, passing time, looking out her front picture window at the falling snow and day dreamed. Suddenly, the Holy Spirit gave her another wonderful idea. During the Christmas holidays, when there was enough snow on the ground, Yankee Doodle hitched up his team of horses to a most magnificent sleigh which he had imported from the South Pole. He loved to give sleigh rides to anyone who requested his services. With his Fair Lady sitting beside him, they would ride through town and anyone could flag him down for a ride-just like a taxi. He never accepted any payment, for the Doodles just loved sharing the nostalgic fun of it all.

"Good morning, Yankee, I was wondering if possibly you could give me a ride out to the airport in your sleigh. I need to be there in about an hour and a half to meet some guests, who I am expecting to arrive from Africa. I thought it would be especially fun for them to ride home in your magnificent sleigh with your beautiful team of horses. I know they would love it."

"Of course, Mother Goose, I would be honored to carry you to the airport. I was just getting ready to go out and hitch up the team. It will take me awhile, but don't worry I'll be there in time to pick you up and get to the airport before they arrive. You'll hear me when I get to your place. My Fair Lady has decked out the horses and sleigh with enough bells to drown out the town fire bell."

"Oh thank you so much, Yankee, this is really going to be a special treat."

Mother Goose gazed upon the snow again, this time out her kitchen window facing the forested hills north of town. The white fluffy puffs were growing larger and falling at a faster pace. She thought about her friend riding into town on her Harley. Not in favor of the idea at all, she called for her Fine Gander.

"Come on," she said, "we need to fly out to the hills and pick up my best friend. I don't want her to chance riding her bike in this weather"

The Old Woman was all dressed in her leathers and ready to go when Mother Goose arrived.

"Oh I'm so glad you flew out here to get me, I really don't like the idea of riding in these conditions after what happened to my husband."

"I know, honey. I should have told you yesterday that we'd come and get you. I wasn't thinking. Since you're coming with us, why don't you just spend the night so we can all visit? I am sure Little Anne would love that and this way you will get a chance to get to know Little Jack Horner also and tell him about the vision you had at the chapel. Wouldn't that be something if they really did move back here?"

"Well, what about my pets?" the Old Woman asked.

"We already went over this," said Mother Goose. "Remember, you now have the Little Laughing Dog. He took good care of them the last time you came with me and I am sure he will do the same this time."

"You're right. I really don't want to miss this; just let me grab a few of my things and let my critters know what's going on and I'll be right out," the Old Woman said.

They got back to Mother Goose's house just shortly before Yankee Doodle arrived. Mother Goose turned on all of her outdoor Christmas lights and got a fire going in the fireplace. The Old

Woman Who Lived Under a Hill turned on her animated angel above the mantelpiece.

"Oh it looks so lovely and Christmassy in here," said the Old Woman. "Your angel is so lifelike. She seems to beckon her protection with every move of her head and wings."

"She does, doesn't she?" said Mother Goose. "I have always loved her. I don't know if I told you before, but my mother gave her to me years ago. I was about twenty at the time. I named her Gardenia."

"No, I don't think you told me that before. Nice name. What a blessed keepsake."

Mother Goose and her best friend heard Yankee Doodle's horses and sleigh approaching. Excited, Mother Goose dropped their conversation and tap danced over to her front window.

"What are you so giddy about?" asked the Old Woman. "I know that can't be Santa Claus and his reindeer it's way too early for them"

Yankee pulled up in front of Mother Goose's house where they could clearly see him out her front window.

"Oh for heaven's sakes, you didn't tell… …" Mother Goose grabbed her best friend's hand yanking her away from the rest of her thought.

"Come on!" she said, "We gotta go. The plane will be arriving soon. As she pulled her best friend out the door she grabbed their coats hanging on the coat tree by her front door.

Yankee Doodle, always the gentleman, helped them both aboard and covered them with a heavy wool blanket.

Noticing that Yankee's wife was not with him, Mother Goose asked, "Where's your Fair Lady?"

"She's at home still getting ready for the Christmas party tomorrow night and for our rides through town later today. She's really anxious about seeing our friends from overseas tomorrow night. I told her to stay home while I took you out to the airport. Hopefully, she'll be relaxed by the time I get back. I think, she.…

"Oh no!" Mother Goose blurted out. "Sorry to interrupt you but I completely forgot something. Can we stop back by your place? I forgot to ask you to bring Ladybird along with you."

"Why do you want to bring Ladybird?" asked Yankee.

"Because one of my guests is Little Anne. Ladybird used to be Little Anne's pet when she was little. When their house burned down, Ladybird found her way out to your place. It's a long story, Yankee. I'm sure Ladybird's told you some about it."

"Yes, she has, but just briefly. This is amazing. How did you find Little Anne?" Yankee asked.

"Let's just get to your house, Yankee, and I'll tell both you and Ladybird all about it on the way to the airport. I don't want Little Anne to step off that plane without me standing there."

Yankee pulled up right in front of his barn and whistled for Ladybird. She flew right out and landed on his shoulder. On the way to the airport Mother Goose told them how she had come across Little Anne's book, *On Fire for the Lord,* at the Co-op and then how she had been able to contact her and her husband over in Africa.

Ladybird flew round and round the sleigh singing, "I knew God had something special in mind for her. I just knew it."

They arrived at the airport just in time to see the big yellow jet with Air Africa written on its side, sliding in to home base.

Yankee pulled up right in front of the main entrance and

yelled as Mother Goose and the Old Woman jumped out of the sleigh, "Better get movin' ladies. I'll be waiting for you right here."

They ran into the airport and inquired as to what gate Little Anne and Jack Horner would be coming through. The attendant directed them to go clear to the south end of the airport. They ran like they were trying out for the Olympics with Ladybird flying above. As people entered the terminal, Ladybird flew around trying to spot Little Anne.

"There she is! There she is!" sang Ladybird.

Anne yelled back, "Ladybird! Ladybird! My precious Ladybird!"

Mother Goose threw her arms around Anne squeezing her to her body while rocking her from side to side. Her tears of joy landed softly on top of Anne's head.

"Welcome home, sweetheart. Welcome home."

Everyone was overwhelmed with emotion. When Mother Goose finally released her embrace, Little Anne looked at the Old Woman Who Lived Under a Hill who now also had droplets of love streaming down her own face.

"Are you the wo-woman?" Anne stammered. "Aren't you the woman who used to live down the street who brought our family pudding pies and tried to help me?"

"Yes, my dear Little Anne, it's me," the Old Woman blubbered while encircling her in a warm embrace and stroking her long auburn hair.

Mother Goose stepped over to give Little Jack Horner a big hug. He had been standing off to one side just shaking his head.

"Miracles upon miracles. Praise the Lord," he said.

"My, how you have grown into a fine looking young man,"

Mother Goose said. "I can't wait to show you the pictures in my scrapbook of you with Little Anne. Who would have ever guessed what the future had in store for the two of you? I feel so blessed to be a part of it."

"Everything's starting to come back to me now," Jack said.

Mother Goose introduced Jack to her best friend, who also embraced him with a warm hug and said, "Although I have never met you before, I have a feeling we're all going to be getting to know each other quite well. I had a vision about you, Jack, but I'll tell you about it later. For now, let's just get on home."

They made their way to the luggage turnstile smiling all the way. After retrieving their bags they were able to swiftly move through the holiday rush and walk, right on out the electric glass doors to the winter cold that awaited them.

Anne squealed with delight when she saw Yankee Doodle's sleigh and team of horses.

"Oh, look," she cried poking Jack in the arm, "aren't the horses beautiful? And look at that sleigh; I always wanted to ride in one!"

"Well, you're in luck, sweetheart," said Mother Goose tickled at Anne's enthusiasm, "that's our ride home."

"Really! Are you kidding? I love you so much!" Anne said, jumping up and down.

Ladybird snuggled up against Anne's neck all the way back to Mother Goose's house. When they arrived, she asked Yankee Doodle if she could stay.

"Of course you can. You belong with Anne, not me, Ladybird. I know how much you have missed her." Yankee said.

With a flip of the reins, Yankee set his team back in motion and with a cheerful wave of his feathered cap, bid farewell.

"See you all tomorrow evening. Merry Christmas!"

Once inside, Mother Goose showed Jack and Anne to their room.

"Oh, my, Mother Goose, you have it set up in here for royalty. Wine, cheese, pastry and even satin sheets!"

"Well, my dear Little Anne, I was just talking to someone the other day about this subject. She had never considered herself as royalty but then I told her that I once heard it said that all who believe in Jesus Christ, our God, who is King and our Father, are all princesses and princes. We are heirs to his kingdom, which in essence, makes us all royalty.

"Hey I like that," said Jack. "I think I'll use that in one of my sermons-if that's alright with you."

"Sure, honey," said Mother Goose.

"I like that, too," said Anne "That really gives me a new perspective on being a child of God."

"Yes, it does. I felt the same way the first time I heard that. I have put some fresh towels and washcloths in the guest bathroom for you along with some other bathroom treats you may enjoy. Please make yourselves at home and if there's anything else I can get for you, please just let me know. Right now I'll get out of here and let you two unpack. There's some extra space in the closet here and the top two drawers in the dresser are empty."

"Would you mind if we took a little nap?" asked Anne.

"No, no," said Mother Goose, "we'll have plenty of time to visit later on. You two come out whenever you're ready; I'm sure you could use some time alone."

Mother Goose and the Old Woman were amazed that Little Anne and Jack were back home again. How incredible that the two of them met up again, all the way across the world in Africa, and had gotten married.

Mother Goose turned to her best friend and said, "While they're sleeping I think I'll run into town and pick up a few things. Do you mind?"

"No, go right ahead I'll stay here in case they get up. I'm going to make Little Anne her favorite vanilla pudding pie with bananas in it."

"Oh, that reminds me," said Mother Goose, "when I get back, I'll make Jack his favorite plum pie that I used to make for the kids every Christmas. Jack liked to stick the plums on his two little thumbs. It was so cute… …oh, such good memories. Make yourself at home my friend. I'll be back shortly."

Mother Goose went straight into town to the five and dime store where they had a great toy selection. She still had a box of Christmas stockings in her attic with all of the children's names on them. This year, once again, she would stuff one for Jack and Anne just for fun. Mother Goose picked out two bags of marbles, a slinky, some jacks and a little troll doll for each of them. One of the trolls had green hair and the other had blue. She also found a little plastic purse with fake jewelry in it and a little tiara for Anne. She spotted a little Indian headdress for Jack, along with a plastic bow and arrows with little suction cups.

"Oh, this is going to be fun," she said to herself. On the way home, she was inspired to stop at the jewelry store and pick out something special for each of them. She got Anne a beautiful pair of diamond cross earrings and Jack, a handsome gold tie clasp with a star etched in the middle. A small diamond was set right in the center.

Her best friend was still busy in the kitchen when she got back. She already had her pudding pie done and was now making them all dinner; a delicious mushroom meatloaf that she stuffed with mashed potatoes and goat cheese.

"Oh, yummy," said Mother Goose. "I'll make some roasted vegetables to go with the meatloaf, but first I need to go up in the attic and find Little Anne and Jack's Christmas stockings. Wait 'til you see what I got for them." Mother Goose came right back down the stairs with their stockings in hand.

"Come on," she said and they both went to her bedroom where she had dumped the toys out on her bed along with the little jewelry boxes.

"Oh, how fun!" The Old Woman said looking over the toys and holding up one of the little trolls. Mother Goose showed her the pair of earrings and tie clasp also.

"Very nice," said the Old Woman, "Anne will love those earrings. You have very good taste."

"You think so," said Mother Goose pulling out another little jewelry box she had in her pocket. "And this, my dear friend, is for you, or I should say, us."

The Old Woman looked at her with raised eyebrows and a twinkle in her eyes as she opened the box. Inside were two frosted, etched friendship rings. One was silver and the other, gold.

"Oh, how sweet!" said the Old Woman. "Why didn't we think of this year's ago?"

They both chortled and put on their rings. "By the way," Mother Goose said, "we'll say the stocking stuffers and jewelry are from both of us."

After Mother Goose made her plum pie, they both cut up the vegetables to roast over the fire later on. While they were getting things ready for dinner, the phone rang.

"Heavens to Betsy! Cried Mother Goose, "That phone has rang more times in the last couple of weeks then it ever has."

"What did you expect?" said the Old Woman.

"Hey, Mother Goose," said Jack Be Nimble. "I just got back from the Coast and I have Mary with me. We're going to run out to the little chapel and drop off the candles and Mary's silver bells and cockle shells; then we thought we would stop by for a few minutes if that's alright."

"Oh, of course, Jack, that would be wonderful," said Mother Goose. "I'd love to have you two stay for dinner if you don't already have plans. I have a surprise I'd like to share with the two of you."

"That sounds great, Mother Goose, dinner plus a surprise. You know how I love surprises," he said thinking about the solar greenhouse he was building for Mary. "We'll be there for sure."

Shortly after Mother Goose hung up the phone, Little Anne with Ladybird perched on her shoulder, came out to the kitchen. She looked refreshed like she was ready to start a new day.

"Thank you, Mother Goose. I needed that time alone. Jack and I had a nice nap then we took an invigorating shower using your peppermint mineral salt scrub. My nerve endings are still standing at attention." Mother Goose and the Old Woman chuckled. They could see that Anne's face and arms were still flushed pink from the coarse salts.

"Dinner will be ready in a couple of hours. I'm glad you got a chance to relax and rev up. We're going to be having some company join us for dinner. Do you, by any chance, happen to remember Jack Be Nimble and Mary Quite Contrary?" asked Mother Goose.

"Well, I don't know. Maybe I would if I saw a picture of them," said Anne.

"Hold on a minute," said Mother Goose. "I'll go get my scrapbook….its in my bedroom.

She passed Jack in the hallway. "Anne's out in the kitchen; I'll be right there. We're getting ready to look at those pictures I told you about."

Jack stopped partway down the hall where he noticed the measurements which Mother Goose had kept of all the children, still on the wall.

"Well, I'll be darned," he said. "There I am." Beside his name was another kid by the name of Jack. "Jack Be Nimble, hmmm, that kid was the same height as me." He looked further down the wall about two feet and saw the measurement for Little Anne. "She sure has grown," he thought.

The Old Woman poured Jack and Anne each a nice cup of freshly brewed coffee and then she poured one for herself and Mother Goose.

"Here we go," said Mother Goose coming back into the kitchen with her scrapbook. She set it down on the table in front of Jack and Anne. Anne had moved her chair over so that she was snug up against Jack and he had his hand resting on her thigh. Anne had been scoping out the kitchen looking at all of the children's drawings hung on the walls.

"I can't believe you saved all of these pictures, Mother Goose. They look like expensive whimsical artwork, the way you have them framed."

Mother Goose pointed to a drawing made with crayons over on the wall by her refrigerator. It was a mix of different colored lines and swirls. "I believe that one's by you, Anne."

"Really!" Anne jumped up and went over to look at it. In the corner was an abstract letter A, one N and two almost unreadable E's. "Are you sure this one's by me Mother Goose? My names not spelled right."

"Yes, I'm sure. Remember, Anne, you were only three years old and you were the only Little Anne I ever took care of. Go look in the living room. There's also a clay piece you made in there. I also have a watercolor over the mantle, piece that you did, Jack. It's very advanced for a young boy."

Anne and Jack both got up and went to take a look. Anne stopped by the dining room wall with Jack right beside her, when she spotted her little clay sculpture sitting on a pedestal. It somewhat resembled a rabbit, but overall, it looked more like a blob of clay with ears. She gently picked it up and turned it over. On the bottom she saw her abstract letters again and included, was the extra N. Minus one of the E's. She got teary-eyed, as she truly knew a Mother's love.

Jack put his arm around her and said, "Your little sculpture here, babe, reminds me of Isaiah 64:8

> *'But now, O Lord, Thou art our Father, we are clay; and Thou our Potter, and we are all the work of Thy hand.'*

Anne snuggled closer into her husband's chest. "Even back then, babe, in your tumultuous little life, God's Holy Spirit was with you and molding you."

"Thank you," Anne said.

Both she and Jack were amazed to see the painting he had done hanging over the fireplace. It was a picture of Jesus holding a star in his hands looking up to heaven. Jacks' Jesus was obviously Jewish. He had a rather large hooked nose, brown skin and short, black, curly hair. He gave him a modest beard and mustache upon his weathered face. His, Jesus, wore a long purple robe and stood on bare feet. Overall he looked like your average guy, there was nothing pretty about him to draw attention; just a simple man holding a golden star. Jack painted his sky rather dark and dotted it with gold. The darkness lightened as it reached the feet of Jesus. Over the entire picture, including Jesus, Jack had whitewashed the entire portrait with shades of red and white giving it a sublime effect that was out of this world. Both Jack and Anne got goose bumps looking at the watercolor. It seemed to draw them in, making them a part of it, as if they were actually standing there with Jesus. They found it hard to turn away from this beautiful work of art.

"What do you think of your painting, Jack?" asked Mother Goose.

"I'm stunned," said Jack as he sat back down at the table next to Anne. "It's beautiful. It's hard to believe I did that."

"I believe you met your calling becoming a preacher. Do you still draw?" asked Mother Goose.

"Well, actually, no. Not anymore. Just a doodle here and there."

"As soon as we get home, Jack," said Anne, "I'm going out and get you some watercolors and an easel with some good drawing paper. I want to see what other heavenly creations you come up with. Your portrayal of Jesus looks nothing like the white hippie-looking Jesus you see everywhere."

"Amen to that," said the Old Woman. You're right, Anne, either you see a picture of some long haired good-looking white dude dressed in a brown robe tied at the waist with a rope, or you see someone's idea of his crucifixion with him hanging on a cross in a dirty diaper. There's nothing vulgar or presumptuous about your Jesus, Jack. According to Scripture I believe you have captured the true essence of his being."

"I agree," said Mother Goose, "your picture of Jesus is the only one I have ever seen, or thought, to hang on my wall. I love it."

While Jack and Anne had been in the living room, Mother Goose flipped through her scrapbook and found a couple of pictures of Jack and Anne together.

"See here," said Mother Goose pointing to a picture of the two of them in the sand box. Jack was helping Little Anne build a sand castle.

"Look at us," said Anne in a soft voice.

Mother Goose turned to another page which she had marked, "And look at this one, isn't it precious? I just love it."

Jack was down on all fours with little Anne sitting on his shoulders, mind you, not the middle of his back, but right up front. She was holding onto his hair pulling it straight up in her little clenched fists, and her baby legs were locked around Jack's neck. The expression, on the face of five year old Jack, was of sheer pain.

"Geez, Mother Goose, how long did you let her ride around on me like that? This picture reminds me of some stunt you would see on *Americas Funniest Videos* where somebody's truly hurt, and in pain and the person holding the camera just keeps on rolling."

"Oh, Jack," said Anne.

Jack winked at Mother Goose, "You know I love you, sugar plum."

"Whenever the two of you were here at the same time Anne, Jack would always make a beeline straight to you. He was very fond and protective of you." Anne squeezed Jacks hand.

"Speaking of sugar plums, see this picture, Jack," said Mother Goose.

"Here you are eating your Christmas pie." She showed him the picture of himself sitting all alone in the corner of her living room with a plum stuck on one thumb and purple filling all over his mouth and hands.

"Why was I sitting in the corner all by myself? Was I selfish?"

"No, honey, not at all," said Mother Goose. You were just very shy. But, I bet if Little Anne had been with me that Christmas, she would have been sitting right beside you." Jack looked at Anne and gave her a little peck on the mouth.

As they looked at the photos, Mother Goose came across a picture of Jack Be Nimble, Mary Quite Contrary, Bo Peep, Sukey and Jack and Jill all playing together in her backyard during the summer time. They were running through the sprinklers.

"See these two?" she pointed to Jack Be Nimble and Mary Quite Contrary. They're the company were having over for dinner tonight."

"Really!" said Anne. "You took care of them, too?"

"Yes, you all used to play together at one time or another. It's going to be fun to see if the two of them or the two of you remember each other."

"Everything's really coming back to me now," said Jack. "I think I do remember playing ball with Jack and another little boy named Tommy. I noticed the measurement chart in your hallway. Jack Be Nimble and I were the same height; I wonder if we still are?"

Anne was tapping the picture of Mary Quite Contrary with her fingertip. "You know, I think I do remember this little girl. She used to help me dress my Barbie dolls didn't she?"

"You have a good memory, Anne. Yes, she did. Mary adored you. You were like a baby doll too her," Mother Goose said.

"She looks a lot older than me, Mother Goose."

"Actually, Anne, she's only two years older than you. Between the ages of three and six a child can grow a lot and continue to go through growth spurts until they reach adulthood."

"What do Jack and Mary do now?" Asked Jack. "Are the two of them married also?"

"No, they're not married," said Mother Goose. "I think Jack would like to get married but I don't think Mary is quite ready for that. She's still trying to figure out who she is. I'm just glad they are still close. I think Jack is really good for her. Jack works for the Candlestick Maker, here in town, and also has a couple of jobs on the side. He's a very ambitious young man."

"And Mary, well she moved to the Coast awhile back and she opened her own business. She sells her homegrown flowers to various shops around the area and also at the Saturday market. She does very well for herself. She's a delightful young woman. I know you'll like her Anne. They should be here in about an hour so I'll let them tell you more about themselves when they get here.

For now, why don't the two of you bundle up and take a little walk around the neighborhood and we'll finish getting dinner ready. What do you say?"

"That sounds like a great idea," said Anne. "It's so beautiful outside with all of the snow and everything. Thank you for showing us the pictures."

"The Old Woman put her mushroom loaf in the oven to bake and then set the dining room table while Mother Goose roasted the vegetables over the open fire.

Chapter Twenty-Seven

WHEN JACK AND MARY arrived, Mother Goose told them to go on into the kitchen and help themselves to a cup of coffee. Mary noticed the scrapbook still on the kitchen table and sat down to take a look.

"Oh, look! Jack, there's pictures of all of us kids in here. Here's one of you and I together picking flowers in Mother Goose's garden!"

"Wow, this is a trip," said Jack.

Mother Goose came into the kitchen with a platter of roasted vegetables and set them on the stove.

"Hey, Mother Goose," said Mary, "I don't think you've ever shown these to me before."

"Oh, yes I have. You've seen them before, sweetie. It's just been along, time ago. I keep my scrapbook in my bedroom now because sometimes at night before I go to sleep I like to look through it."

"How come there's places where it looks like a picture used to be but now there's not?" asked Mary.

Mother Goose hadn't expected this question and thought a minute. "Oh I just took some out that I wanted to label on the back," she fibbed. The missing photos she had copied were all still in her craft room on a shelf. Mother Goose quickly changed the subject and got Little Anne's book, *On Fire for the Lord,* to show Mary and Jack be Nimble.

Mary read the back and inside covers and then screeched, "Oh my God! What a life-and look at her now." She looked at the front cover again, "She's so beautiful and peaceful looking. You would never guess that she had been through so much just by looking at her picture."

Jack read the covers also and remarked, "I can hardly wait to meet Jack. I've never met a minister my own age before. This will be like meeting Jesus." Right after this statement, he and Mary both got up to go look out Mother Goose's front window.

Anne and Jack were just coming up the walkway to Mother Goose's house. Jack had his arm around Anne holding her close and Jack Be Nimble couldn't help but notice the look of envy on Mary's face as they approached.

Mary quickly opened the front door and said, "Hi! My name's Mary. You must be little Anne and Jack. I'm so glad to meet you.

"Hi. Nice to meet you," said Anne.

"Come in, come in," Mary instructed. "Wow! Your story is incredible, Anne. I can't wait to hear more about it."

The two Jacks shook hands and Jack Horner sized Jack up. They still were the same height; not that it mattered. "Hey man, nice to meet you," said Jack Be Nimble.

"Nice to meet you, too," said Jack Horner. Mother Goose and the Old Woman began placing the food on the dining room table.

"Come on in and sit down, kids," said Mother Goose. "Dinner's ready and we have all weekend to visit."

While sitting around Mother Goose's beautiful mahogany table, enjoying their meal, Anne shared her story of abandonment with them. She also told how Jack and she met up again over in Africa, fell in love and were married.

When Jack told his side of the love story, it was sprinkled with Jesus and you could practically see the wheels spinning in Jack Be Nimble's head. Mary, herself, was overflowing with admiration.

When Jack Be Nimble got a chance to ask the question he was longing to know the answer to, 'What's it like being a minister, Jack?' the meaty conversation then commenced.

"For me, I would say it's like being able to provide a home for a homeless person and filling it with nourishing food for life. You can see the fullness of people's spirits come alive with hope when they receive their daily bread. Our goal at the hut, that's what we call our church, is not just to give the people something or someone to believe in, but to give them a solid foundation to build their faith upon. We teach that, through Jesus Christ, all things are possible. There are no legalistic holds or boundaries. That includes any other persons, myself included, limited identification or experiences with Jesus and the Holy Spirit. We all have the same equal opportunity to access God's blessings, no matter what nationality we are, what religion we have practiced, what we have done wrong in the past or where we fit into the food chain of society. God's royal majesty sees us all as individuals and reads our hearts as such. Nothing, absolutely nothing, is impossible to those who, with fidelity, have put their heart in total allegiance with God's word. We have seen many miracles happen within our fellowship and those with their newfound love give freely to others."

"Man, that sounds awesome. I'd like to be a part of a ministry like that," said Jack Be Nimble.

"You can be. That's are main goal at the church", Jack continued. "Once a person is established in their faith, they are capable of ministering to others-and that's exactly what they do. We have huts all over Africa where the faithful now serve 24/7. Anyone at any time can go to the hut for council or worship or just to hang out and have fun. There's always some kind of activity taking place, whether it be playing games, learning how to make something or just sitting around shooting the breeze."

"That's outstanding, Jack," said Mother Goose. There is an overwhelming need for churches like that which are open at all hours of the day and night, where a person can find love. Not just on Sundays...."

"That's the great thing about ministering out of a hut, Mother Goose. Anyone can build one and there's no overhead. It's just like ministering in an open field. Like the Bible says, '*A church is not a building but where two or more are gathered in my name.*' All of us ministers, including my senior and my mentor, share the gospel for free. There is no basket passed at our services. Jesus gave of God's word freely and so do we."

"Well, what do you live on then?" asked Jack Be Nimble.

"I have a contractor's license. I help build schools and do repair work around Africa when I'm not preaching and Anne works part-time at the orphanage bringing in a little extra money, she also volunteers there when she's off the clock. Our combined income is enough to sustain the hut we live in and also allows us to financially help others in need. Myself, and other skilled members of the church also teach others a skill or two so that they, also, are employable."

"I am totally enthralled," said Mother Goose. "I have never heard of such a divine ministry."

"Neither had I, Mother Goose, until my family and I went to Africa.

"What about your senior pastor and his wife, Jack, don't they get paid?" asked the Old Woman Who Lived Under a Hill.

"No, after being involved in the civil rights movement here in America, they moved to South Africa and began work with Nelson Mandela to dissolve the apartheid. At that time, they were paid generously and were able to put quite a bit of money away.

After working with Nelson Mandela, they saw a need for a revival so my senior and his wife, along with the help of some village people built the hut where I now work, and their new mission with the Lord took off. My mentor says that Jesus' goal was to teach his disciples the truth and instill in them faith so that they could also be pastoral shepherds and guide his flock back to love."

The Old Woman was soaking in all of this information like a plant dying of thirst. Mary, through the whole conversation thus far, was pondering Jack Horner's statement earlier concerning fidelity and allegiance to God. She knew that she believed in God and she tried to read his Word everyday but, like a lot of Christians and other people who considered themselves spiritual, she held back when it came to personal sacrifice. Giving up what she thought to be fun or making a change she wasn't sure, of wasn't easy. She excused her behavior as just plain human nature but she knew better. Truth be told, she lacked faith. She didn't quite believe Jesus when he said all things were possible. Her self-will and pride, kept her from experiencing the Holy Spirit's total peace and splendor.

"What about the poverty in Africa, Jack? What's being done about that?" asked the Old Woman.

"Well, just like here, it's taking a slow turn, for the better. The capitalists and the middle class have a "me first" attitude. "Me" never seems to have enough. "Me" wants this or that. "Me" doesn't have time. And, "Me" doesn't know how to give; just take. "Me" doesn't want to share. Worst of all, "Me" doesn't know you; you're a stranger."

"You hit the nail on the head," said the Old Woman.

"Yes, it really is an atrocity," continued Jack. "A lot of people call themselves Christians but they still put themselves first and rationalize their behavior. Jesus taught that we are not to hoard up treasures here on earth and that we are to give freely and to help others when need be. I'm sure we all know the story of the Good Samaritan. I like, in particular, where James says in the Bible, *'If ye be a hearer of the word and not a doer, he is like unto a man beholding his natural face in a glass.'* My dream is that soon people will really open their hearts to the Lord's teachings and truly follow them. When this happens, there will be no poverty, or children going to bed hungry."

During Jack's commentary, Anne sat in rapture of her husband's love for the Lord and his children. He had a true desire for the world to live in harmony.

With true admiration, the Old Woman said, "I like the way you think, Jack. You have burning coals of righteousness in your soul. I have often thought about what's going on in our own community. We have approximately 55.000 people living here during the school year, 25,000 who are college students and, give or take,

7,000 children. That leaves 20,000 adult residents who reside here year round. I have it figured out. If the 20,000 gave just one dollar a month to help those in need, by the end of the year, there would be a total of $24,000 dollars. Just think how many jobs could be created with that money and how many people could be helped without government assistance! Then, say that the college students were required also to give a dollar a month during the nine months that they lived here in our little town, that would bring us to a total of $465,000 dollars; that's almost half a million dollars! In just one year. This amount more than likely would exceed half a mil, because of the more generous donations from people who already gave freely. I love how the book of Corinthians speaks of the value of giving. 1Corinthians 13:5 says:

> *'Charity seeketh not her own and verse 13 says, 'And now abideth faith, hope, charity, the greatest of these is charity.'*

After the Old Woman had said all this, Jack Horner was very much taken with her being. He could see and feel her passion and also, her pain.

Mother Goose and the Old Woman had often talked about her vision to end poverty, not just in their little community, but all over the world. They both knew that some people would argue her theory just for the sake of debate. And there would also be those who would turn her idea into something much more complicated than need be. God forbid they would have to give up one dollar a month to help someone in need; especially someone they didn't know or who lived in a far off land.

Between Jack Horner's story of Africa and the Old Woman's

ideas, a light bulb came on in Jack Be Nimble's head. What if he built a hut of his own out in a field or set up a tent and started his own church? Maybe he could get everyone in the community to step out of the box of bureaucratic thinking and donate a dollar a month to his own mission. He could then turn Babylon into a paradise in no time at all.

After dinner, they all went into the living room and sat around the fireplace where they talked some more. They all had a lot to share with one another concerning the events that had taken place in their lives over the past several years. The four young adults were taken with the Old Woman's story about how she and Mother Goose met.

"Yes," continued the Old Woman, "that same night after Mother Goose and I met at the library and exchanged phone numbers, my Old Man was killed while riding home from work on his old Indian Harley. I was told by a policeman, that he hit a sheet of black ice and was tossed into a tree on the side of the road and that he was killed instantly. Mary gasped and Anne let out a sigh and began to dribble tears.

"No need to cry, it's alright now, girls. I can still feel his spirit with me, especially out at our dream home under the hill. He even runs with me through the forest and, at times, I can hear him talking. The whole experience has brought me closer to the Lord then ever. And, look at this. She held up her right hand and wiggled the finger with her new friendship ring on it. I even gained a best friend from the whole event."

The girls giggled and Mother Goose held up her hand as well so the girls could see her ring. Then, she patted the Old Woman's leg.

Anne looked at Mary and said, "I think you and I ought to get a couple of rings like that. I've got a feeling that you and I are going to be friends for a long, long time." Mary's eyes lit up with great, delight.

The two young men also hit it off right away. Jack Be Nimble wanted to know everything about Jack Horner. He wanted to know how he became a minister at such a young age and also how it affected his relationship with Anne. He was learning a lot, already, about love just by listening to him talk and watching the way he interacted with his wife.

Around ten o'clock, they could all hear the wolf call of a Harley off in the distance. It sounded like it was headed their way.

"I wonder who that could be?" asked the Old Woman as they heard the bike pull into the driveway.

Mother Goose jumped up, all in a tizzy, and said to her, "Did you tell that "trombone guy" at the Coast, where I live?"

"No, of course not, but maybe he looked it up on Google earth," said the Old Woman.

Mother Goose's systolic heartbeat went bonkers and she began to feel a bit wonky. In a panic, she said, "Those computers have no right to share private information."

"Just calm down," said the Old Woman, "he's harmless."

Not being able to restrain themselves, they all got up and looked out the front window. They were surprised to see a beautiful shiny black and white Harley Davidson with a sidecar attached to it parked in the driveway.

Mother Goose looked at her best friend questionably, "I have no idea....." said the Old Woman.

No one could see the man's face, because of his helmeted head, as he walked right up to the front door and rang the bell.

"You answer it," Mother Goose told the Old Woman. And she did. On the small stoop stood The Baker with his helmet in his hand now, smiling like a little boy with a new pony.

"Good evening, ladies," he said.

"Oh, for heaven's sakes" said the Old Woman. She turned to Mother Goose who was now conspicuously pulsating with emotion and asked, "Did you know he rode a Harley?"

"Nooo, I never would have guessed," Mother Goose said as if there had been some sort of misunderstanding.

The Baker chuckled and said, "I'm sorry I showed up unannounced. I didn't realize you were having company tonight, love. I just thought I would come by and see if you would like to take a little cruise with me and look at the Christmas lights. Then, maybe later, we could attend the midnight service at the church downtown."

Mother Goose was overwhelmed and tingling with excitement. The Old Woman and the four young adults were having just as much fun watching The Baker and Mother Goose's exchange.

"Well, I don't know. This is quite a surprise," said Mother Goose. "My friends here are visiting all the way from Africa."

They all chimed in, "Go, Mother Goose, go! We will still be here when you get back."

"Well, I don't own any leathers and I don't ever intend to put another pair on," Mother Goose declared.

The Baker threw back his head and roared with laughter. The Old Woman laughed so hard she was gasping for air as tears ran down her cheeks.

"Don't worry, my love, I wouldn't want you to. I much prefer you in dresses....although you did look quite stunning in your friend's leathers. I had a leather fleece-lined snuggie made special. Just for you."

Mother Goose flushed with embarrassment as she wrapped her arms around herself.

The Old Woman crinkled up her face with her arms wrapped around herself also, playfully mocking her, "Well that's settled," she said. "You have your own original leather outfit. Now, you go on." She held up her finger with the friendship ring on it and said, "Remember; kindred spirits. Enjoy the ride."

"Oh, alright, I'll go but I would like to be back here by midnight. Jack here is a minister and he is going to give us a private sermon."

"Whatever you want, my love."

Together, they all walked outside and watched as Mother Goose got into the sidecar. When she held out her arms so the Baker could slip on her black leather, fleece-lined snuggie, the Old Woman giggled under her breath.

"Oh, be quiet," said Mother Goose, "you're just jealous you don't have a leather snuggie.

The Baker tucked the snuggie in around Mother Goose and gave her a little kiss on the forehead. He then climbed on to his Harley. *Vrooom, Vrooom* growled the engine as he knocked back the kickstand with his black leather boot. With a smooth shift they were set in motion moving down the road like rolling thunder.

Back inside, Mary Quite Contrary asked the Old Woman, "Did you hear that? The Baker called Mother Goose "my love."

"Yes, I did dear," she said with a smile and not another word.

The Baker, with Mother Goose at his side, cruised all over town looking at the Christmas lights. When they passed the big Old Historical Gingerbread House, Mother Goose saw Cross Patch standing in the window and waved at her.

Cross Patch waved back and then she turned to the other gals sitting in their living room and said, "You won't believe who I just saw ride by; it was Mother Goose! She was sitting in a sidecar beside some big biker dude driving a Harley."

"No, I doubt it," said Polly. "Not after her experience wearing the Old Woman Who Lived Under a Hill's leathers. That guy named "Trombone" scared the daylights out of her."

Mother Goose was thoroughly enjoying herself snuggled up in the sidecar beside The Baker on his roaring chariot. After an hour or so of sightseeing, they pulled up in front of a charming little cottage tucked away in an alley not far from the riverfront.

"Where are we?" she asked.

"This is my home. I wanted you to see it. Please, come in," The Baker said.

The Baker's home was very warm and inviting; yet very masculine. In the living room was a small fireplace with a hearth in front where one could sit down and enjoy the warmth. The fire, he had set before he left was still glowing adding to the earthy ambiance. Over the dark, cherry mantelpiece was a large, framed silhouette of a man in a chef's hat. Below in gold calligraphy were these words.

Refine Me, Refine Me
And Always Remind Me
You Are The One Who Made Me
And Guides Me.

Mother Goose giggled and said, "I love that. Where did you ever find it?"

"Oh, thank you. I made it myself," said The Baker. "I like to dabble a little in the arts of writing and photography."

In front of the fireplace was a brown leather sectional couch with fluffy sheep skins draped across the back. The couch was carefully placed on a large brown, black and cream-colored rag rug that partially covered the beautiful hardwood floor. Next to it were a couple of stained glass floor lamps with fringed lampshades.

Mother Goose hadn't noticed it when they walked into the house, but when she looked to the right of the fireplace at the waxy-leafed palm tree, she saw out of her peripheral vision a little masterpiece. On the other side of the room, by the small bay window, stood a black baby grand piano.

"Gracious sakes," said Mother Goose, "don't tell me you play the piano also?"

"Yes," said The Baker and he sat down and played for her, *My Satin Doll*. Mother Goose reeled with desire as she watched his agile fingers caress the keys, while his soulful voice massaged her heart.

On the built-in shelves, tucked into the corners on either side of the small bay window, he had on display various framed photographs of jazz and soul artists who he had met over the years. On top of the baby grand was a tasteful ebony and ivory sculpture of two naked people entwined.

"Come on, I'll show you the kitchen," said The Baker to Mother Goose. She was speechless. He took her hand.

"What do you think? I just remodeled it," said The Baker.

She oohed and awed at the custom woodwork while The Baker poured them each a glass of burgundy wine. He had redone all of his cabinets using old barn wood leaving the fronts of the cabinet doors open with just some screening covering them. He also made shelves out of the weathered wood, which he filled with mason jars containing all the dry ingredients you would need for baking, along with a huge assortment of herbs, spices and nuts. The glass containers sat snuggled together beneath The Baker's grape motif wallpaper border. He also, had made himself a table and benches out of the same wood to fit in his kitchen nook.

On the kitchen walls hung a few more pieces of The Baker's framed poetry. Mother Goose read each one aloud while The Baker drank his wine and thrived on her natural beauty and thoughtful delivery of his art.

By the refrigerator one read:

To you who made the stars and Son,
Thank you
For showing me how to make fruit bars and buns!"

Above the kitchen sink another read:

My sweet Jesus, I love you so.
You taught me to bake and
To knead the dough.

And on the wall in the kitchen nook above his rustic dining set another poem spoke to you:

Holy Spirit, you're on my side
Showing me what to put inside.
Olives and cheese, sprinkled with thyme
Braided Bread; I made a rhyme!
Blueberries and cherries, brown sugar so fine,
You are the one I need for all time.

For this poem, The Baker had made the frame himself, using a mixture of flour, salt, cornstarch and water.

After reading The Baker's poetry, Mother Goose turned to him, covered in goose bumps and said, "You are the most delightful, interesting and surprising man I have ever met in my life."

The Baker took the glass of wine Mother Goose held in her hand and sat it on the counter. He pulled her close to him and with one arm wrapped around her waist and the other hand cradling her head, he gave her a big, soft pillowy kiss on the lips. Mother Goose melted into The Baker feeling as if she had been transformed into a vapor, rising on the wings of love while embraced by The Baker's immortal spirit.

He held her close until she returned from her transcendental experience and then he looked longingly and passionately into her gold-flecked hazel eyes and said, "Well my love we had better get going so you don't miss the midnight service."

Chapter Twenty-Eight

THE BAKER AND MOTHER Goose arrived back at her house just a little before midnight. Both were moonstruck. Their faces were aglow and their eye's emblazoned with the light of love. Mother Goose, of course, invited The Baker to stay for Jack Horner's service.

Jack Be Nimble, Mary Quite Contrary and the Old Woman Who Lived Under a Hill were acquainted with The Baker but none of them really knew much about him except that he was an extremely nice man and owned the best bakery around. As soon as Mother Goose and The Baker walked through the front door, they all began to inquire about his Harley Davidson.

"Where'd you get the bike?" "I didn't know you rode." "Who is the sidecar for?"

"Slow down, slow down," said The Baker, "it's a long story but I'll make it short. I've had the bike for years, but it's been parked in my garage. I got it a long time ago, after I got out of the army. I used to ride it a lot until I moved out here and opened my bakery. Just recently, I got inspired to ride it again by a spunky little woman all dressed in leathers pretending to be a biker."

Mother Goose quickly responded, "I wasn't pretending any such thing!" Everyone burst out in laugher.

The Baker winked at the Old Woman and said, "Well that's when I ordered the sidecar and had the leather snuggie made especially for her. This past week I have been busy assembling my dream."

"Is that why you cancelled our dinner date?" asked Mother Goose.

"Yes, love. I didn't want you to take it personally, although my reason had everything to do with you."

Mother Goose's old grandfather clock struck midnight and they all sat down in the living room and listened to Jack Horner's sermon.

"Ukhisimusi Omuhle! That's Zulu for Merry Christmas," said Jack.

"Merry Christmas!" everyone said in return.

"May we all bow our heads for a moment of prayer before I begin?" Everyone humbly complied.

"I'm sure you're all expecting me to give a sermon on the birth of our God, Jesus Christ, but I'm not. Instead, I am going to talk about his death and the indwelling of his Holy Spirit. If it were not for his dying for our self- will, none of us would be redeemed. It is through the indwelling of his Holy Spirit that we all have a chance to live a full joyful life."

"Hallelujah!" said The Baker. "Excuse me."

"No need to apologize," said Jack and then continued.

"Jesus knew what his mission on Earth was from the time of his birth. He came to speak the truth and to share the wisdom and light of his Father with us. He says here in St. John 12:49-50:

> *'For I have not spoken of myself, but of the Father which sent*
> *me, he gave me a commandment, what I should say, and what*
> *I should speak. And I know that his commandment is Life*

Everlasting. What so ever I speak therefore, even as the Father said unto me so I speak.'

Jack went on to point out the Scripture where Jesus talked about He, and the Father being as one. Then, he spoke another truth.

"Jesus also knew," said Jack, "that he would be crucified and that he did not have much more time to share the words of his Father with us here on Earth.

In John 7:33, he says:

> *'Yet a little while I am with you, and then I go unto him that sent me. Ye shall seek me, and shall not find me: and where I am, thither ye cannot come.'*

"When Jesus said these words, some people were angered and others felt lost. They didn't want him to leave them," said Jack. "Chapter seven goes on to say:

> *'In the last day of the great feast Jesus stood and cried, saying If any man thirst, let him come unto me, and drink. He that believeth in me, as the scripture hath said, out of his belly shall flow rivers of living water.'*

"I find that very touching," said Jack. "Here in the next verse it says:

> *'But this he spake of the Spirit, which they that believe on him should receive; for the Holy Ghost was not yet given; because he was not yet glorified.'*

"Jesus knew, not just what his purpose here on Earth was, but also that his earthly being would return to his Father and yet he would return to us through the indwelling of his Holy Spirit. Then, all things bright and beautiful in heaven would then be made manifest to those who had faith, even as Christ himself."

Jack continued to share his thoughts and Jesus words with strong emotion. John 14:15-18

> *'If ye love me, keep my commandments. And I will pray the Father, and he shall give you another comforter, that he may abide with you forever. I will not leave you comfortless: I will come to you.'*

Jack patted his heart and said, "You see, he's still here." The Old Woman whispered to Mother Goose, "Remember my Old Man's letter?"

Mother Goose squeezed her hand and whispered back, "Yes, dear, I do."

Jack went on to share more Scriptures about the teachings of Christ and about some of the miraculous healings that people had witnessed. He also said that it is through Jesus Christ, Holy Spirit, that we all are capable of giving and receiving love. Not only that, we also have the power to heal others through our own actions.

He ended his sermon with a quote from the book of Revelation:

> *'Fear not; I am the first and the last I am he that liveth, and was dead; and, behold, I am alive for evermore.'*

Mother Goose got right up from the couch when the sermon was over and gave Jack a big hug and said, "Jack, sweetheart, that was the best Christmas sermon I have ever heard in my life. Thank you for sharing "your" Holy Spirit with us."

The Old Woman stood and raised her hands in the air and said, "Praise God. May his Holy Spirit reign throughout the world tonight and every,day." You could see the flame of the Spirit alive in her eyes as she gently swayed back and forth.

Jack Be Nimble and Mary Quite Contrary didn't quite know what to say. They had never witnessed the power or the gentleness of the Holy Spirit before in someone so young. Anne sat still, basking in the knowledge that the Lord had chosen Jack, this wonderful God-like man, to be her husband.

The Baker shook Jack's hand and said, "You know, young man, I have never been much of one to attend church but, if we had a minister like you here in town, one so obviously filled with the love and sincerity of the Holy Spirit, I believe I would come and listen to you."

Mother Goose looked at the Old Woman and said, "I believe now would be a good time to tell Jack about your vision."

She then excused herself and went into the kitchen and poured everyone a brandy snifter of Christmas eggnog; a blend of light rum and blended whiskey with nutmeg sprinkled on top. She also cut up some generous slices of her best friend's vanilla pudding pie and some of her own special Christmas plum pie. She returned to the living room with her large silver serving tray and passed out the drinks and deserts.

After the Old Woman told Jack about her vision at the little abandoned chapel, and how God had spoken to her and said that soon the little chapel would be up and running again with Jack, being the church's minister, Little Anne was ecstatic!

"Oh, Jack, what do you think? We could still take missionary trips back to Africa. During the years that we have been there, you have taught many others to minister to those in need and have brought the Lord to, many of the villages. I'm sure that they would be just fine if we moved on."

Jack Be Nimble jumped in right behind Anne, "Yeah man, that would be great. I'd love to hear more of what you have to say."

Mary added in her Mary way, "Come on, Jack, that would be awesome. We could all hang out together and Anne and I could be best friends." She turned and gave Anne a big toothy smile.

Jack Horner held Little Anne's hand as Jack Be Nimble and Mary spoke. He knew how much she loved Mother Goose and also how much the Old Woman Who Lived Under a Hill had meant to her. He felt that Jack and Mary had now also been put into their lives for one reason or another. The Baker reminded Jack of his mentor and senior pastor. This made his decision even more captivating.

"With all that has been revealed over the last few days," said Jack, "I think that the Lord just may be calling us here. Let's take a few days to pray about it," he said to Anne. "I would appreciate it if all of you would pray about this too."

After finishing their pie and eggnog, everyone exclaimed what a wonderful Christmas Eve they had had. Now that it was well past midnight, although no one was really feeling tired, they all knew that they had better get some sleep before the big Christmas event in the forest.

Jack Be Nimble drove Mary to the new Hilton Hotel where he had made reservations for her. He knew that she wouldn't be able to sleep after having met Anne and her husband. He felt the same way. He also knew that with the kings and queens staying at the hotel, Mary would really, be wound up.

"Hey Mare," he said, "do you want to stay up and talk some more? We can just hang out in the lobby and visit. We don't have to meet everyone at the chapel 'til tonight, so we can still get some sleep later today."

"I'm glad you asked. Yeah, I'm really wound up; come on in." Mary complied with his request to stay not only because she was wound up but more than anything, she didn't want him to leave.

Jack and Anne were the next to excuse themselves. They retired to their room ready for some time alone. They had a lot to think and pray about.

The Old Woman Who Lived Under a Hill, Mother Goose and The Baker all talked a while longer and expressed their feelings of admiration for all of the kids and marveled that they had all grown into such lovely young adults.

Both Mother Goose and the Old Woman immensely enjoyed The Baker's company that evening.

The Old Woman said to him, "I would venture to say, from what I have felt, from you tonight that you are a man of many talents and deep spiritual content. I have no doubt that we will have the pleasure of spending more time with you."

"Well, thank you very much," said The Baker. "If my prayers are answered in the direction that I hope them to be, I believe you will be seeing much more of me. I also enjoyed your company this evening and getting to know you, a little better. Are your insights, or should I say visions, always accurate?"

Mother Goose nodded her head at The Baker, "Oh yes," she said, "she just hit the nail on the head about you didn't she?"

"Well, I don't know about that," said The Baker modestly. The Old Woman didn't answer his question. She just raised her eyebrows and gave The Baker a knowing look and then picked up the scraped pie plates and empty mugs and headed for the kitchen.

Mother Goose walked The Baker to the door where she personally thanked him for a wonderful evening then said, "By the way, how did you get my address?"

"It wasn't hard. I just followed the goose feathers laying along the sidewalk."

"Ha ha," she said, "no, really?"

"Your friend, Old Mother Hubbard, The Butcher's wife, told me where you lived."

"Oh, well, that makes me feel better. I thought maybe you looked it up on a computer. I really hate those things."

"No, love, I would never do that. I don't care much for computers myself," The Baker said.

"I'm so glad you came by. I had a truly wonderful evening. Riding alongside you on your growling Harley was an absolute thrill. And thank you for showing me your home. It's just charming."

"Well, my love, I hope to show you the rest of it one of these days. Thank you for sharing this evening with me also and inviting me in. You have very eccentric taste; I like that about you."

Mother Goose's emotions, again, were beginning to make her weak in the knees and she thought to herself, "I could spend the rest of my life with this man."

"I had better go now, my love, so we both can get some sleep before the party tonight." The Baker pulled her to him and gave her another soft, pillowy kiss. This one, in French. Mother Goose's tongue fluently responded to his and then, before she got completely carried away not only from his kiss but also by his alluring smell of Frankincense, she pushed him out the door feeling flushed and light-headed like a champagne's fizz.

When she turned around, she saw her best friend standing in the kitchen doorway with a big grin on her face. "Now that is one charming, multifaceted man, my dear."

"Yes, I know," said Mother Goose. "I feel like I have bubbles in my head about to burst with happiness. Come on now- let's go to bed. I need to calm down." The Old Woman chortled and they headed for her room.

Once in their nightgowns, Mother Goose couldn't wait any longer. She knew now was the time to give her best friend back her memories.

The Old Woman ran her hand over the top of the package and felt the Harley Davidson pin underneath and the leather lacings down the side. With a sudden tingle of goose bumps, she slowly unwrapped her present. With tears balancing on her lower lids, she stared at the pin and carefully unlatched it from the book and opened the locket. Her tears jumped over the ledge and she began to sob when she saw the picture of her Old Man and her, once again, cheek to cheek.

With gasps and shudders she asked, "Where in the world did you find this?"

"While we were in the mystical clearing setting up the tables just before I came back into the chapel and you had had your vision," said Mother Goose.

The Old Woman turned the locket over and whispered, "My Old Man." She opened the book and slowly turned the pages filled with memories of love. She devoured her husband's image which she had so long been without. When she came to the last page, she read the rhyme Mother Goose had written for her entitled; One Misty, Moisty Morning. She read it aloud.

> One misty, moisty morning
> When cloudy was the weather
> I chanced to meet an Old Man clothed all in leather.
> He began to compliment and I began to grin
> How do you do, and how do you do
> And how do you do again?
> For my best friend with love always
> Your half-baked Goosey old friend XXXOOO

The Old Woman laughed now, with still more tears cartwheeling down her cheeks, but this time they were tears of joy.

"This book is beautiful. I love the black leather cover and lacing. Thank you so much. Well, since we're exchanging gifts, I'll give you yours now, too,"

She got up off the bed to get her backpack she had placed over in the corner of the room. She then put it on the bed where she pulled out a small gift-wrapped box and then tossed her pack back on the floor in the corner.

Mother Goose carefully unwrapped her gift also, and with gentleness, she opened the box. Inside was a diary; one made for a young girl with a little lock and key. She held it up and looked at its sky blue leather cover decorated with a few colorful flowers.

"Ohhh, I haven't had one of these since I was a child," she said as she placed the key in the lock and gently turned it. The first page read:

> To my Bestest friend ever, Mother Goose. I have been truly blessed to have a woman friend such as you. One who gives of herself so lovingly and freely not only to me but to all she encounters. I thank the Lord daily for his Holy Spirit bringing us together and I will always treasure our relationship.
>
> Kindred spirits and Best friend,
>
> Forever I love you!
>
> XXOO
>
> From the Old Woman who now lives in the dirt under a hill because of you! Har, Har Har!

Mother Goose laughed and gave her best friend a hug and a little kiss and said, "Hey that was your dream not mine."

The diary was filled with supernatural events that had occurred while the two of them were together. The first entry was about their meeting at the library. Next, their experience digging out the Old Woman's home under the hill, then their making of the labyrinth and the Holy Spirit's descent upon them in the mystical clearing.

The Old Woman included many more miraculous, spirit-filled events that they had experienced together over the years; many of which Mother Goose had forgotten about.

As Mother Goose read some of the entries she began to cry. "What a beautiful, thoughtful thing to do. I will treasure this book the rest of my life," she said.

"Oh, quit blubbering," said the Old Woman, "you're not planning on going anywhere soon, I hope. I plan on writing several more entries in another diary I already purchased. And the way the Holy Spirit has been revealing himself these last couple of weeks, by the time the party's over, I have a feeling I'm going to have to go out and buy another book right away."

They chortled some more and hugged one another and then crawled under the covers.

"You know, my dear friend," the Old Woman said to Mother Goose, "I had completely forgotten that you had that box of pictures of me and my Old Man. I even looked for them not long ago and thought I had lost them just like I had the locket. I have felt so guilty." The tears ran from heart again and spilled out of her eyes.

Mother Goose slipped her arm under her head and held her close. "Go on and cry, I have heard it said, *"Tears are the safety valve to the heart."*

They both said their prayers and also said a special prayer regarding whether or not Jack and Anne should move back to town.

Just when they started to drift off to sleep, Mother Goose sprung out of bed and shrieked, "Oh, no!"

"What's wrong?" asked the Old Woman.

"I can't believe it! I forgot to hang out the stockings."

The Old Woman chuckled, "Someone's had too much chocolate."

"Oh, that's a good one, smarty pants," Mother Goose said as she quickly gathered up her pets' and Jack and Anne's Christmas stockings. She swiftly took them out to the living room and hung them from the mantle with care.

Chapter Twenty-Nine

CHRISTMAS MORNING MOTHER GOOSE woke up a little after ten a.m. to the smell of freshly brewed coffee and eggs. On her nightstand was a note that read:

> *Rise and shine. I made breakfast after I had a quick cup of coffee. There is a quiche in the oven waiting for you. Your, Fine Gander, bless his little heart, offered to fly me home. Anne and Jack are out in the kitchen doing their Bible study and waiting for you to eat. They have something to tell you.*
>
> *Merry Christmas my dear friend I'll see you this evening.*
>
> *XXX OOO*

Mother Goose put on her robe and slippers and joined Jack and Anne in the kitchen for breakfast.

"Good morning, Mother Goose! Merry Christmas!"

"Good morning, my sweet children! Merry Christmas to you, too! Did you sleep well?"

"Oh, yes" said Anne. "Sleeping in those satin sheets was like being nestled in a silk cocoon. After we went to our room last night, we prayed for a couple of hours for the Holy Spirit's guidance and then peacefully fell right to sleep. This morning, when we woke up, we both had a resounding answer to our prayers; we're moving back, Mother Goose!"

"Praise the Lord!" said Mother Goose and hugged them both. She looked at Jack, "Are you sure about this?"

"Yes, Mother Goose. I have never felt so sure about anything in my life except for when I accepted Jesus into my heart and when I married Anne."

"This is the best Christmas ever," said Mother Goose.

After they ate, Mother Goose took them into the living room to open their stockings. Her Fine Gander wasn't back from the Old Woman's home yet and Goosey Goosey Gander, Madame Goose and her Fiddling Cat were outside playing in the snow so she decided to wait until her Fine Gander got home before she gave them their stockings.

Mother Goose pointed to the mantel and said, "Oh look Santa Claus was here, Anne."

"Oh my!" Anne squealed. "Look, Jack, those two stockings have our names on them. I didn't notice them when we went out to the kitchen."

"I used to hang these up for you when you were kids. I thought it would be fun to do it once again," Mother Goose said and Anne giggled with joy like a little girl.

In the top of Anne's stocking, Mother Goose included a bag of her homemade roasted sunflower seeds for her Ladybird. She was perched on Anne's shoulder singing Christmas carols.

Anne placed her on the mantel and poured some of the treats

out for her then proceeded to look through her stocking filled with toys. Jack was now wearing his Indian headdress. Anne found her tiara and put it on.

"This is so much fun," she said while stroking her little troll's blue hair.

"These toys bring back so many childhood memories," they both exclaimed.

Anne had a childlike quality that was very refreshing to see in a young woman, especially, in this day and age. When they got to the bottom of their stockings and found their little jewelry boxes, Anne opened hers first.

"Ooooh, these are beautiful! Look what my momma gave me, Jack," she said. Anne lightly touched the little cross diamond earrings with tears threatening to spill over onto her cheeks. Jack put his arm around her and gave her a little hug.

"I looove these. Thank you, Mother Goose, and I loove you too!" Anne got up and gave Mother Goose a big hug then went into the bathroom to put her new earring on where she could see herself in the mirror.

"Mother Goose, you have no idea how much those earrings mean to her," said Jack. "Over the years she has cried on occasion when one of her friends received a special gift from their mothers. She always felt so left out with nothing to show them." When Anne came back into the room she was brimming with self-worth.

Jack opened his little box with the gold tie clasp and little diamond in the center and said, "Well, I know one thing for sure, I'm going to be the best dressed minister in town even if all I have on is pair of jeans and a tie."

"Oh, Jack!" said Anne smacking him on the knee.

"Thank you, Mother Goose, this is very nice."

Anne excused herself and went back to their room and returned with three beautifully wrapped packages for Mother Goose and set them in her lap.

"Goodness, gracious! Are these all for me?"

"Yes, momma."

Mother Goose set the packages down on the floor in front of her and picked up the one on top wrapped in colorful construction paper.

"That one's from the children at the orphanage where I work and volunteer," said Anne. "I told them all about you and that we were coming out here to visit you. They all wanted to give you something."

Mother Goose opened the package and found inside several very colorful drawings that the children had made for her. One drawing in particular stirred her emotions. The longing was obvious. It was a picture of a goose and on top sat Mother Goose with her arms around a little black girl with braids sticking up all over her little head.

"Oh, how precious," said Mother Goose, "these are all priceless. When you go back to get your things I would love to go with you and meet all of the children if that would be alright."

"Of course it would be," said Anne. "Right, Jack?"

"Yes, of course we'd love to have you go with us. The children would love to meet you and we could show you around the villages and the hut where I minister. I would also like to introduce you to the senior pastor and his wife," said Jack.

"They are an amazing couple. I'm anxious for you to hear their stories about their experience during the Civil Rights movement and their work with Nelson Mandela. They have taught both Anne and me about true courage, strength and love. They also taught us all the old gospel songs that they grew up singing."

"We sing them before and after service at the hut," said Anne. "You would love it, Mother Goose, the music is totally uplifting and spirit-filled. People even get up and dance."

"You're right, Anne, I would love that. In fact, the Old Woman Who Lived Under a hill and I both love gospel music. We were just talking about how wonderful it would be to have that kind of uplifting, gospel church here. And, by the way things are going, I think we just may in the near future. I know a few talented musicians around here that I am sure would love to be a part of this."

Anne handed Mother Goose the next package and said, "This is from the senior pastor and his wife. You're going to love what they made for you. They're the nicest people."

"Oh, my," said Mother Goose, "they made something for me." She opened the box and found inside an exquisite hand-batiked caftan of blue and gold with a touch of burgundy, and a head wrap to match. Tucked in around them were little wooden carved animals; a rhinoceros, a giraffe, a spotted leopard, an elephant and a zebra.

Holding up the caftan, Mother Goose admired the intricate design. "This is just exquisite. I have always wanted a caftan. I've seen pictures before, in National Geographic, of African woman wearing them with their head wraps. They look so elegant and colorful, I can hardly wait to try these on."

"One of the old women in the village taught the minister's wife how to batik," said Anne. "She also taught her how to make all kinds of African clothing, along with wall hangings using the material. She wears caftans all the time, herself, and her husband likes to wear the shirts she makes for him along with muslin drawstring pants. An old man in a nearby village taught him how to carve the little wooden animals."

"I can hardly wait to meet these people," said Mother Goose. "What a generous exhibit of love."

Mother Goose got up and went over to her fireplace and placed the little wooden animals on the mantel among the fir boughs around her angel.

"There," she said, "now my angel watches over the children and animals in Africa."

Anne smiled, "They needed an angel. Thank you." Mother Goose sat back down and picked up the last box.

"That one's from me," said Anne. "I made it myself. I hope you like it."

"Of course I will, sweetheart, you're my little girl."

Anne looked at Mother Goose when she said this with a big smile making her dimples stand out like a little bruises on an apple.

Inside was an exotic necklace made out of silver and hand-painted African beads. In the middle hung a round, silver disc with the words '*I AM*' etched in black, right in the center.

"Oh, Anne, thank you. This is exquisite. I love this!"

"I AM is another name for God, you know," said Anne.

"Yes, I know," said Mother Goose. "This is very unique. Where did you get the disc?"

"From an old black woman who was sitting along a dusty road side selling beaded bracelets along with some of her friends. She had it in a box with some other medallions and stray beads. When I saw it, I knew it would be the perfect piece to add to your necklace."

Mother Goose got up and hugged both Anne and Jack, who were already dressed for the day and said, "I better go get dressed now myself. Then, what do you think about us all going over to the new Hilton and greeting our other out of town guests? We'll also check in on Mary Quite Contrary."

"That sounds great," they both said. "But, wait a minute, alright?" Jack said.

"I have something else I want to give you." He went back in their bedroom and opened his Bible. In it he kept a quote written by Nelson Mandela. His senior pastor had given it to him shortly after they met; he had treasured it ever since.

Jack came back out to the living room and handed the quote written on a thin piece of pounded bark to Mother Goose. She read it aloud.

> *"Religion is one of the most important forces in the world. Whether you are a Christian, a Muslim, a Buddhist, a Jew or a Hindu, religion is a great force and it can help one have a command of one's own morality. One's own behavior and one's own attitude."*
>
> *Nelson Mandela*

"This is a very profound writing," said Mother Goose. "I don't believe I have ever heard religion summed up in such a humane and exact way before. Did Nelson Mandela actually write and sign this?"

"Yes, he did," said Jack. "My senior pastor gave it to me. He has lots of quotes from him. I want you to have this one. I see here on your walls that you appreciate the spiritual teachings of other cultures, along with Christianity, and I think it would be nice for you to include this quote from a man who has truly experienced diversity, and overcome terrible hardships."

"I am honored that you would give this to me, Jack. Thank you. I will display it with gratitude."

Mother Goose propped the quote up against her angel, among her African wildlife, and then went to her room. She put on her new vibrant-colored caftan and head wrap and then fastened on her new necklace admiring her new ensemble in the mirror. "Mmm,mmm,mmm," she thought, "I bet The Baker would really get a rise out of this outfit."

Jack and Anne ooohhed and awwwed when she came back out, "You look like an African queen," said Anne.

"I feel like I am one," said Mother Goose fondling her necklace.

Chapter Thirty

WHEN THEY GOT TO the hotel, it was poppin' with energy. The hotel staff was scurrying around everywhere making sure that everything was just perfect. With royalty lodged at the Hilton, the security was large, in more ways than one. Mother Goose went up to the front desk, feeling very cosmopolitan in her new outfit, and she inquired as to the whereabouts of Mary's room and also of the kings and queens.

"Who, may I ask, would like to know?" asked the hotel manager looking at her suspiciously with his squinty little eyes, while pulling on his Groucho Marx mustache. He also eyed Jack and Anne, who stood aside with zipped lips. {This situation called for drastic measures.}

With ruffled feathers, Mother Goose said, trying not to sound too condescending, "My name is Ukhisimusi Omuhle," remembering Jack's Christmas greeting in Zulu. I am the Queen of Africa and I have important business with the Queens and Kings of England. And, for your information, Mary is my oldest daughter."

As she spoke she intentionally fiddled with the necklace

around her neck as she could see that the manager was inspecting the silver disc.

The manager pointed to Jack and Anne with his boney ET finger. "And, who are they?" he snorted.

"They are my children, also. Now listen, I don't have all day to play Clue with you. Just tell them that Mother Goose has arrived."

He shook his head and thought to himself, "Must be some sort of code name."

"Please, young man, let them know we are here or lead us to their rooms. If it had not been that you were already booked up, we also would all be staying here and there would be no need for concern. As it is, we are staying at a small bed and breakfast in town instead."

Given Mother Goose's, a fortiori, and convincing African attire, the manager rang Mary's room. "The Queen of Africa is here to see you, miss. Shall I send her up?"

"Who? What?" said, Mary.

The manager slightly shook his head and said, "Mother Goose has arrived."

"Oh! Mother Goose. Tell her I'll be right down."

Mother Goose told the manager that she would first like to visit with her daughter and then she would have him contact the kings and queens.

"Sure, whatever you say, your majesty. Just let me know when I can be of further assistance."

Mary came running out of the elevator and over to Mother Goose and Little Anne and Jack who were now all seated in the lobby over by the grand fireplace. It was decorated with a huge wreath and life size nutcrackers standing on either side of the hearth. Talk about deck the halls with boughs of holly! The entire hotel lobby was overflowing with Christmas cheer.

"Merry Christmas!" Mary said and started rambling on about how she and Jack Be Nimble had stayed up all night and so on and so on. When she caught her breath, she told them that Jack was still upstairs asleep.

"Oooohh," said Mother Goose.

"We didn't do anything wrong, Mother Goose, really! We stayed down here in the lobby awhile and then went upstairs so I could lie down. We just talked and then finally put a movie on and fell asleep on top of the covers."

"Calm down, sweetheart, I believe you. I figured you two wouldn't be able to sleep after meeting Jack and Anne. I just wanted to check in with you. For now, why don't you and Anne and Jack all go back up to your room and visit some more while I go check in with the kings and queens?"

"Sure," said Mary, "that sounds good. Have fun visiting, Mother Goose!" Mary grabbed Anne's hand, pulling her toward the elevator and waved at Jack. "Follow us," she said.

Mother Goose went back up to the front desk and said to the manager, "Kind sir, I am now ready to see the Queen of Hearts. Could you please give me her room, number?"

"All of the queens are in the spa and the kings are all in the parlor playing chess."

"Well, for now, could you please just direct me to the spa?" Mother Goose said.

"I will need to call ahead, first," he said.

The attendant at the spa answered the phone and the manager said to her, "Go tell the queens that the Queen of Africa, I mean, that Mother Goose has arrived."

"What's a Mother Goose?" asked the attendant.

The manager snapped, "Just! Tell, them."

The attendant returned to the phone, "Send her right in!"

Mother Goose walked into the luxurious spa filled with plants and heavenly aromas and, at once, was greeted by the attendant who showed her to the hot tub where all of the queens were relaxing and drinking champagne.

> *The Queen of Hearts*
> *She made some tarts,*
> *All on a summer's day.*
> *The Knave of Hearts,*
> *He stole the tarts,*
> *And took them clean away.*
> *The King of Hearts,*
> *Called for the tarts,*
> *And beat the knave full sore;*
> *Brought back, those tarts,*
> *And vowed he'd steal no more.*

"Hello, my dear!" called out the Queen of Hearts. "My, oh my, you look like some sort of ambassadress or the Queen of Africa. Mother Goose burst out laughing and told them about her encounter with the hotel manager. They all hailed, "That's our girl!"

They invited Mother Goose to join them but she said she didn't want to be gone too long since she had Jack and Anne with her, along with Mary and Jack Be Nimble. She briefed them in on Little Anne's story and also about how the four of them had met the day before and told them that they were all upstairs visiting.

"Well," said Old King Cole's wife, "call the girls on down here and they can join us. Sounds like a good time for the boys to talk alone, don't you think?"

"That sounds like a wonderful idea," agreed Mother Goose. "Are you all sure you wouldn't mind? I know the girls would be thrilled."

"No! No! Call them down and get out of those clothes! The water's great in here! It's a hot, brutal, pulsating anodyne. It will soothe those weary old bones of yours."

Mother Goose raised her eyebrows at the queen's description and gave her a look of superiority saying, "I am neither old nor weary. I am like a well-seasoned, faithful, cast-iron skillet"

"Now, now, Mother Goose, there's no need for logomachy, now get in here before we all turn into shriveled up old prunes."

"Be quiet you old bag," said Mother Goose and then went to strip down.

Mother Goose and Old King Cole's wife always bantered this way when they were together. It came naturally, like mold on a well-aged piece of gourmet cheese.

The girls came right down and were led to the spa after Mary had convinced Anne that her husband, Jack, would be just fine without her for a while. Mary had noticed the evening before, and even now, how Anne clung to her husband and vacillated in her personality. Mary thought of her as a woman-child or as being co-dependent. At times, she seemed to be very docile, unsure and childlike when speaking and in her mannerisms, and, at other times, very much in control of her womanhood, articulating what she had to say with a mature command of her words and posture.

Mary wanted so badly to share her observations with Mother Goose but she didn't dare go there. She remembered a conversation she had once had with her and the Old Woman Who Lived Under a Hill about another friend of hers who had behaved in much the same way as Anne.

"Yes, Mary, I noticed your friend's a little different," Mother Goose had said. "I'm sure some people who attend twelve step meetings with a follow-the herd mentality cwould label her as being co-dependent or an adult child of an alcoholic or say she grew up in a dysfunctional family. Her family did function, maybe not just as smoothly as others. Which isn't a fair assessment either. No family runs smooth all the time."

Mother Goose continued to say, "Since counselors and so-called professionals started using these terms, there has been a rash of books out on the subject. For my own insight on these new so-called forms of mental illness, I have read several books on the matter. *Co-dependent No More, Woman Child, Man Child, Adult Children of Alcoholics*, the list goes on. They all are filled with the same hogwash; ditto, ditto, ditto."

"You don't think there's any truth in them?" asked Mary.

"Oh, yes, Mary, I do. The thing is you can take their long lists of symptomatic behaviors and apply them to just about any human being, who has any feelings at all. These labels and books are just another avenue to exploit a human being's need for validation whether their behavior is right or wrong."

This conversation had drug on for over an hour with the Old Woman Who Lived Under a Hill growing more and more irritated and finally ended when she said, "Why don't you just love your friend the way she is Mary and try and help her forget her past by making wonderful new memories? The Bible says that we are all unique and that we are not to dwell in the past and that we are to forgive and move on."

After Mary's recollection of this intense conversation, she prayed that she would not continue to put her new friend, Anne, under the analytical microscope of her societal, altered mind.

Mary and Anne felt privileged and pampered, already just entering the elegantly decorated spa with its gold pillars and plush, velvet seating area; along with marble-topped tables. Upon entering the room with the hot tubs they both gasped. There were three large hot tubs with lighted steps leading in to them. The tubs were recessed in teak wood flooring that was covered with lush potted palm trees and tropical plants. The walls were all black marble with laces of gold inlay running through them except one, which was a colorful mosaic of Egyptian women carrying pots of water on their heads. In the center of the three pools stood a rock sculpture with continuous water flowing over it.

They both stood at the edge of the big, tiled hot tub wide-eyed, looking at the bubbling pool of water with steam rising up all around the queens, and Mother Goose.

"Wow! Cool!" Mary said. "I've never seen a hot tub like this before; for that matter, I've never been in a spa before either. This is great!"

Anne stood with her hands in front of her as if she were praying. "This is absolutely incredible. Nice to meet you, your highnesses," she said.

All of the queens laughed and King Arthur's wife said, "Well don't just stand there girls, get out of those clothes and come in and join us. We have a whole day of pampering before us."

When good King Arthur ruled the land,
He was a goodly King.
He stole three pecks of barley meal,
To make a bag pudding.
A bag pudding the Queen did make,
And stuffed it well with plums,
And in it put great lumps of fat,
As big as my two thumbs.
The King and Queen did eat thereof,
And noblemen beside,
And what they could not eat at night,
The Queen next morning fried.

Mary and Anne looked at each other with smiles stretched across their faces from east to west. After the attendant showed them to the dressing room, where they got undressed, she then handed them each a new, terry cloth robe to wear with the words "Hilton Luxury Spas" embroidered on the back in gold satin thread. She also gave them each a plush, white bath towel to dry off with when they got out of the hot tub. She told them that when they left the spa, the bathrobes were theirs to keep. Mary and Anne were thrilled, a souvenir to take home with them from the royal Hilton Hotel.

The girls came back out to the steamy room, and hung their robes on the gold hooks which lined the black marbled wall. The spa attendant had placed a little gold plaque, with each of their names on them, above a hook so they would know which robe was theirs. Mary and Anne stepped down carefully into the hot tub and seated themselves on either side of Mother Goose.

Anne was feeling somewhat shy and tried to keep her breasts below water, until Mary told them all about the weekend before when Mother Goose and her best friend had come over to the Coast to visit, and they had all gone skinny dipping in the ocean. The queens all erupted with hysterical laughter at Mary's story and playfully splashed water at Mother Goose. Anne quickly relaxed after seeing how friendly and fun-loving the queens were, and after realizing that no one was paying any attention to anyone else's nakedness.

After they soaked in the hot tub for about an hour, they all got a massage. Anne lay on a table next to Mary and told her more about her relationship and marriage to Jack. Mary just couldn't seem to get enough information.

"Anne," Mary asked, "don't you feel somewhat stifled being married; especially to a minister?"

"What do you mean, Mary?"

"Well, you know, like say you want to go out with your girlfriends dancing or you see some good looking hunk you'd like to spend some time with or you just feel like being alone."

"I never feel those things, Mary. I really love Jack. In fact, I don't just love him, he's my best friend. I totally enjoy his company. Sometimes, like today, coming down here to the spa, I hesitate to leave him because I might miss something. He's full of wisdom and a lot of fun to be with."

"Wow, I've never heard anyone say that about their husband before. Does he try to control you? Him being a minister and all."

"No, no, Mary, he's not like that at all but I know what you're talking about. In Ephesians 5:25 it says:

> *'Husbands love your wives, even as Christ also loved the church and gave himself to it.'*

"To Jack, that's what marriage is all about. He loves me unconditionally and never tries to force his will on me."

"Well," said Mary, "what about in the Bible where it says, a woman is to obey her husband.

"I believe what God intended was for men to be Christ-like, like it's explained in Ephesians and many other Scriptures. Then, a woman will want to obey or, shall I say, follow her husband because she trusts him and knows that he loves her. Have you ever done something you wish you hadn't, Mary?"

"Yeah, of course I have."

"Wouldn't it have been nice, at the time, if you had had a husband that was watching out for you and not trying to control you, but just pointing out the consequences of your actions that may lay, ahead.

"Yes, I guess that would be nice. Sometimes I don't make the wisest decisions on my own," Mary admitted.

"In 1Corinthians 7:3, Mary, it says:

> *'Let a husband render unto his wife due benevolence; and likewise also the wife unto her husband.'*

"What does benevolence mean, Anne?"

"I wondered that also when I first read it so I looked it up. The dictionary defines it as a disposition, to do good, an act of kindness, a generous gift. Pretty neat, huh Mary?"

"Yeah, it is. I never knew that. I thought it meant being subservient or something like that," said Mary.

"No, 1 Corinthians 7:4 then goes on to say:

> *'The wife hath not power over her own body, but the husband and like wise also the husband hath not power of his own body but the wife'*

"How's that song go, Mary? *I've got the power, la, la, la, I've got the power.* I think it was by a group called Snap."

Mary cracked up. She was liking Anne more and more. "This is great, Anne, having you explain all this to me. I always thought marriage was about kissing ass. Oh! Excuse me, I need to work on my mouth."

Anne giggled, "No, the way Jack and I see it, marriage is a two-way street, give and take, just like the Bible says. What about you Mary, what's your relationship like with your Jack?"

"Well, let's see. I know I love him as a friend and he's a great guy. He reminds me a lot of your Jack in some ways. He's extremely kind and giving and he's really patient with me. I think he wants to be more than just friends and sometimes I think I do too. But…."

"But what, Mary?"

"But… I really like my freedom. I've been with some really exciting macho guys and Jack is just soooo different."

"Different, meaning?"

"Well, you've seen him Anne. He's not very big and he's nothing to brag about as far as looks go. Also, he's really soft spoken. I can't even get him to raise his voice. I've tried to get a rise out of him but he just calmly sits there and lets me rant and rave. If I were him, I'd slap me, or yell. Do something!"

"Mary, looks have nothing to do with love. Our bodies our just a housing for Holy Spirit and our souls. I have met some of the homeliest people, not so attractive because either, they had an illness or were just born that way, and they had more love inside of them then a whole slew of beauty queens or GQ men. And, I don't understand why you would want to antagonize Jack to the point that he would yell or hit you."

"I don't really do it intentionally; he's just so boring sometimes."

"Have you two ever gone somewhere or done something really exciting?" Asked Anne.

"No, not really. We usually just sit around and talk. Sometimes we go down on the beach and take a walk or go out and get something to eat. That's about it."

"Well, that could make for a pretty boring relationship. You hear about couples in that same trap all the time. Why don't you do something different?"

"Like what," said Mary.

"Say, go bungee jumping together or go someplace where you could swim with the dolphins. Take a raft trip down a wild river. Ride the highest roller coaster you can find or take a dance class together or some other class you two might enjoy. Maybe if you did something different and fun, you would see a more vibrant Jack than you do now. Compliment him. Get involved in his homeless project."

Anne's last statements pretty much summed it up for Mary. She had been the one that was boring, selfish and set in her own ways. Where was her sense of adventure?

After their massage, all of the queens and Little Anne and Mary got their hair washed and styled. Mother Goose decided to wear her hair down like she usually did but she did opt to have it washed and have a white rinse applied to really make it shine. She talked with the queens while they had their hair set up in rollers and dried.

Anne had never had her hair set and styled before so she decided to have hers put up in a French twist. Mary did the same as she was quite taken by Anne's decorous nature and felt that she was a good role model for her. She wanted to emulate her in every way possible, which wasn't easy considering how rough around the edges she was. The hairdresser added a special touch to each of the girls' hair. In Anne's, she twisted in a sting of fake pearls and sprigs of holy. In Mary's, after hearing about her prized silver bells and cockle shells, she twisted in some blue beads and attached little silver bells all the way up the back of the twist with some baby's breath lined up in between.

For a final touch, they all had a facial and makeup applied while another cosmetologist painted their toes and fingernails. Mother Goose enjoyed the facial, along with everyone else, but she decided to apply her own makeup. She wanted to try out her new Mary Kay products which she had gotten from Bonny Lass.

As they were getting their makeup applied, they could all hear Old King Cole's wife instructing the cosmetologist.

"Good heavens, dear, draw the eyeliner out further. I don't want my eyes to look like two golf balls encircled in black. And don't skimp on the foundation. I have a lot of wine spots to cover up.... if you know what I mean."

Mary and Anne were just giddy with their new looks. They couldn't quit looking at themselves in the mirror.

"Wow, Anne, you look gorgeous. You should be a model," said Mary.

"I couldn't do that," said Anne. "Besides I'm way too short. You don't think this too much?"

"Oh, God, no! Sorry, you look great! Jack's gonna love it," Mary gushed.

"You look like a movie star yourself. You remind me of Kim Bassinger. She's so pretty and voluptuous; just like you," said Anne. Mary couldn't have been more pleased with the complement.

The queens and Mother Goose also expressed how elegant and mature they looked. You could really see in their postures how grown up they felt.

"Now, ladies," said Mother Goose, "the queens and I are going to go into the parlor to visit with the kings for a while. If you don't mind, I'd like you to go back upstairs and I'll call you down as soon as I'm ready to go." She knew the girls were dying to get back upstairs now and show off their new looks.

"No, go ahead, Mother Goose," said Mary giving Anne a little jab with her elbow. "Take your time. We'll be upstairs waiting for you."

After Anne and Mary thanked the queens for the spa treatments and expressed how wonderful it was to meet them all, they gathered up their robes and a few other complimentary gifts the attendant had placed in a bag for each of them.

Besides their plush bathrobes, they each were given a bottle of luxury shampoo and conditioner along with a gold plated hairbrush and a wide toothed comb. The cosmetologist included a small makeup kit with an assortment of eye shadows and blushes. There was also a powder foundation to match their individual complexions. They were pleased to find a little manicure set with an assortment of miniature nail polish in the bottom of their gold lamé tote bags also.

They were, so excited as they passed back through the lobby that they almost fell over the luggage rack the bellhop had placed by the elevator, while he confirmed a room number at the front desk. The manager couldn't help but smile as they waved at him and stepped into the elevator.

Upstairs, Jack Be Nimble and Jack Horner had been having a wonderful time of their own talking about God, love and marriage. Jack was particularly interested in what Jack and Anne did for fun. To him it seemed that his and Mary's relationship had come to a dead-end where entertainment was concerned.

"Anne and I never let the river run dry," said Jack Horner to his new friend and attentive listener. "I believe this is one of the keys to a happy relationship. Anne and I mix things up. We take turns cooking and trying out new recipes on one another. Sometimes we co-write poetry together just for fun, and we go out to visit other people and also have others over, to enrich our own lives. On the weekends, we take turns planning fun excursions."

"One weekend, we went over to East Africa and I took Anne to the Serengeti National Park. It was spectacular. The landscape is vast and beautiful with rolling grasslands that serve to feed enormous herds of herbivores and predators. Between May and November there is what's called the Great Migration where more than 2.5 million wildebeest, zebras, antelopes and other grazers storm northward across the land in search of fresh food, even crossing the Mara River. Then, between August and September, they return to breed. We could feel their hooves beating against the Serengeti floor; it was like a flash mob of wild energy."

"Wow man, that sounds awesome. Weren't you and Anne scared?"

"Not me, but Anne was a little, even though the guides kept everyone back at a safe distance. I told her, not to worry, that these incredible animals were on a mission and that they didn't have time to run off track. You should have seen Anne-she clung to me like a baby baboon to its mother!"

Jack Be Nimble laughed then asked, "What else have you guys done for fun?"

"Well, let's see….we went scuba diving off the Coast of Mozambique, in the Indian Ocean. Anne wanted to see a manta ray up close. They reminded me of flying saucers with wings. I got scared when Anne reached out and touched one. She was so thrilled that she spit her mouthpiece out and when I saw the bubbles escaping all around her and her wiggling around like a worm on a hot rock, I thought she was a goner, but thank God, the instructor got to her in time and everything turned out alright. She did get a scolding, though, from the instructor when we surfaced. You really ought to try scuba diving sometime if you already haven't. The ocean floor is like a terrestrial landscape filled with exotic, plant life and tropical colored fish."

"Sounds like a lot of fun. Maybe I can get Mary to try it with me. Heck, she lives on the Coast. I'm sure, there's plenty of classes we could take. Tell me some more. This is really interesting," Jack Be Nimble said.

"One of my favorite forms of exercise is hiking so we went hiking along the Drankensberg, there the highest mountain range in Africa. Up top we were able to see Tugela Falls, which is the second highest water fall in the world. It was breathtaking. The waterfall tumbles down a sheer cliff in five stages. Both Anne and I had to take in the sight in intervals, along with some of the other tourists, because we were experiencing vertigo. But it was worth it. The Zulu call the mountains "the barrier of spears." They are quite menacing to behold."

"I love waterfalls, too. I think there's some not far from here. I'll have to check it out," Jack Be Nimble said.

"Oh, you'll love this trip then. Anne heard about Wli Falls, located in West Africa's Ghana nation, so we went there because she loves bats."

"Bats!?"

"Yeah, bats. Can you believe it? The place is swarming with them. It took us over an hour to reach the falls hiking through the dense jungle. Along the way, we saw some bats, but not many. A leopard tracked our every move. The guide said he often made an appearance when there was enough people in his mind, to impress. After crossing over eleven log bridges, we finally got to the iridescent, cascading waterfall set back in a cool, sheltered combe where thousands of bats make their homes. Anne was in heaven. We spent the rest of the day swimming in the pooled water, below the falls, and visiting with the other sightseers while watching the bats overhead do their aerial maneuvers."

"That night, everyone camped out around the water and after everyone was asleep, Anne and I snuck out of our tent and made love under the waterfall."

"You're kidding me? Anne went along with that idea?" Jack Be Nimble said with disbelief.

"What do mean? It was her idea!"

After this whole conversation, Jack Be Nimble's sense of adventure and imagination was flowing. Yet, he was befuddled and bewildered. His new friend Jack, was a minister for God sakes, and there he was risking his life along with his wife's. And Anne….loving bats, of all things. And, the thought of them having sex outside amongst strangers, really threw Jack, off. Anne seemed so innocent and shy.

"Man, I never in my wildest dreams would have thought a minister and his wife would have so much fun. I want to have a relationship like that with Mary. Ours is so boring compared to yours. I'm planning on asking her to marry me. What do you think Jack?"

"To be honest, I would say for you to hold off on any proposals for now." He said this because he noticed that Jack Be Nimble seemed to be struggling with his emotions and also because Mary seemed to have a wild side about her that he wasn't sure Jack could fulfill.

I would suggest that both you and Mary become well-grounded in your faith before you make a commitment like marriage. Marriage won't solve any of your problems. And, if you're bored now, marriage could even make it worse, by being stuck under the same roof 24-7."

Jack Be Nimble agreed, but he didn't let Jack Horner's view dampen his plans. He truly loved Mary and he was willing to do whatever it took to win her heart.

When the girls came back in to the room all dolled up, except for their Christmas dresses, Jack Horner exclaimed, "Jack, my friend, I think we just died and went to heaven. Either that or we have standing here, before us, the two most beautiful angels here on earth!"

Jack Be Nimble raised his hand and gave Jack a high five and said, "You got that right!" His face and actions were animated beyond any expression Mary had seen before. She and Anne were tickled pink at the guys' reactions.

Jack Horner stood up and put his arm around his wife and said to Mary and Jack Be Nimble, "Hey, you know what? I just had a brainstorm. Do you two think you could take some time off from work?"

"Yeah, I know I can. I pretty much make my own hours," said Mary.

"How about you Jack?"

"I don't think it would be a problem since the rush to make holiday candles is over. Why do you ask?"

"Well, how would the two of you like to go back to Africa with us for a week or two while we pack up our things and tie up some loose ends? Mother Goose will be going with us also."

Jack jumped for joy and grabbed Mary, "What do you think Mare?" Jack told me all about it over there. It would be a blast!"

"Hell, yes," she said, "I wouldn't miss this opportunity for anything. Do you think we can go see some bush people and meet a witch doctor?" she asked Jack and Anne.

Jack chuckled and said, "I think I could arrange that.

Anne moved away from her husband Jack to give Mary a big hug. "You're, going to love it over there my friend."

Old King Cole was a merry old soul,
And a merry old soul was he;
He called for his pipe,
And he called for his bowl,
And he called for his fiddlers three.
Every fiddler, he had a fiddle
And a very fine fiddle had he;
Twee tweedle dee, tweedle dee, went the fiddles.
Oh, there's none so rare,
As can compare
With King Cole and his fiddlers three!

Mother Goose and the queens joined the kings in the parlor where they were still playing chess.

But, before they went inside, Old King Cole's wife instructed them all to surround the table where the kings were seated. "You got to see how I control the old codger," she said.

All the queens and Mother Goose did as they were told. Once around the table, Old King Cole's wife shouted, "Checkmate. Game's over!"

Old King Cole threw up his hands and said, "I just can't win."

The other kings and queens, along with Mother Goose, all exploded with laughter.

"She always pulls this on me at home to get her way, but she's usually accompanied by a few of my knights," said Old King Cole with a chuckle.

The King of Hearts looked at his wife with a wink and said, "Now, don't you be getting any ideas."

All of the kings stood up to embrace Mother Goose with warm

greetings after this show of command and then they gathered some more chairs and made room for the women to join them. Not long after they all had been seated, Humpty Dumpty joined them in the parlor. He had been up in his room having a late breakfast.

He was not aware that Mother Goose was at the hotel until he overheard the bellhop, say to the maid as he was leaving his room with a tray of dirty dishes, "Hurry up. You got to see the queen that just arrived from Africa. She goes by the code name, Mother Goose. She's beautiful, but it's kinda strange because she's white."

"So what?" scowled the maid, as she scrubbed the toilet. "I suppose you think just because I'm black, I come from Africa? Well, I don't. I was born right here in the United States and so were my parents and their parents. My mom traced our lineage, all the way back and not one person came from Africa."

"Well, I didn't mean to make you mad. You don't have to be such a sorehead," said the bellhop and left the room.

Humpty Dumpty went straight down to the parlor after he heard that Mother Goose was there. As he entered the room, he saw that Mother Goose was seated at the round table with her back to him and gestured with his finger to his lips for all the kings and queens who noticed him come in, to be quiet. In his new state of metamorphoses, he sneaked up behind her and tapped her on the shoulder.

"Oh, my goodness," said Mother Goose turning to see Humpty Dumpty. She stood up and gave him a big hug, "You look spectacular, Humpty! Thank you, Jesus. I'm so happy you could make it. Bo Peep read me your email and I haven't stopped thinking about you."

"I was going to call and tell you about my transformation but then I thought that I would like to surprise you. I have never felt better in my life," said Humpty. "If it hadn't been for your constant letters and prayers, Mother Goose, I don't believe I would be standing here today. You gave me the faith that I needed to be healed. You know, I sat on that wall a long time and, sooner or later, I was bound to fall off. I know now that it was all for my own good and on which side of the wall I belong. God and I have a very close personal relationship now and I am also now counseling others who have fallen and are broken. For once, I feel my life is truly meaningful and I have a purpose."

"I hear what you're saying, Humpty. Sometimes we have to get off the fence before we can fly. This Dr. Foster has done a magnificent job with you. I heard that he had amazing healing abilities from the Sprats, not only surgically, but also spiritually. You certainly are a witness to that. I am so grateful, that you are able to be here with all of us for Christmas."

"Thank you, Mother Goose," said Humpty, "you're my angel. Now, what's this I hear about you being a queen in Africa?"

Mother Goose glanced at the clock on the wall. "Oh my," she said, "Humpty dear, I hate to cut this short but I must be on my way. I need to go home and change my clothes and get out to the mystical clearing before everyone starts to arrive. We can talk some more tonight at the party. By the way, where are all the knights and knaves?"

Old King Cole spoke up, "They all went out to the Doodles' farm to visit Yankee and his Fine Lady from Banbury Cross. They haven't seen them since they moved over here to the States and they especially wanted to see Yankee's new team of horses. Don't worry, they'll all be at the Christmas party tonight."

Mother Goose started to leave and then turned back to ask,

"And what about Brian O Linn? Did you pick him up in Ireland on your flight over?"

"Yes, he's here also, said Old King Cole. He went over to visit his old girlfriend, Bonny Lass. He was able to locate her address on some computer site called Facebook."

Mother Goose cringed.

"Brian said she lives someplace here in town in a big Old Historical Gingerbread House called the "Women's Retreat". What is it, some kind of new age place?"

Mother Goose chuckled and said, "No, not exactly, but in some ways I guess you could say that. I'll let Brian tell you about it when he gets back. See you all tonight."

Mother Goose had the manager call Mary's room for her.

"Mary, sweetheart, I'm ready to go now. Tell Anne and Jack to come on down now, will you please? We all need to get back to my house and get changed soon. Come to think of it, why don't you and Jack just grab your things and meet us at my house? It's getting late and you and Jack need to get out to the little chapel to meet the guests before anyone shows up."

"Alright, Mother Goose, that sounds like a good idea. We'll all be right down."

When they came down, Jack Be Nimble said that he had to go home to change because he hadn't brought a change of clothes.

"Remember, Mother Goose," he said, "I was just going to drop Mary off last night. I didn't intend to stay and fall asleep."

"I'm sorry, Jack," said Mother Goose. "Well then, run along. You can meet us back at my house. I'll take Mary with us so she'll be ready to go."

Mother Goose asked the hotel manager to call her a cab but he insisted that the hotel limo take her and her children back to the bed and breakfast where they were staying. He also told her that he would be glad to provide her with free accommodations the next time they were in town.

Mother Goose felt a little guilty about her masquerade, and graciously thanked the manager, before they all went out and climbed into the black stretch limousine. When they pulled up in front of Mother Goose's house, the chauffeur remarked that there was no bed and breakfast sign.

To everyone's surprise, especially to her husband, Jack's, Little Anne said, "Oh it's a very exclusive bed and breakfast. It's only advertised in the finest brochures and you have to make reservations months ahead of time."

"Oh, I see," said the chauffeur. He got out and opened their doors. After he helped Mother Goose out of the long fancy ride, he kissed her hand and said, "I always have loved your sense of humor and ability to have fun. Mom's going to love this one!"

A little shaken, Mother Goose said, "What? What are you talking about?"

With laughter, the young man said, "My mom's the Old Woman Who Lived in a Shoe. I'm her oldest son."

"Oh, for goodness sakes. You're kidding me."

"No, I moved away to college years ago; that's why you don't remember me. I'm now working on my PhD in geriatrics. I want to be able to help my mom out when the time comes and also help put my siblings through college. I was the only one who got the opportunity to go to college before our father left us."

"Well, for crying out loud. I can't get away with anything," said Mother Goose. "Are you living back here now?"

"No, I just took this part-time job as a chauffeur, for the Hilton while I'm here visiting over the holidays. The money I make, will help mom out a little until I graduate."

"I'm sure your mom, is awfully proud of you sweetheart. Are you going to be able to make it to the Christmas party tonight?"

"Yes, I get off work in a couple more hours and then I'm going to go home and help my mom wrap presents and get the other kids ready to go. Her boyfriend, the Crooked Little Man, is going to come over and pick us all up and drive us out to the little chapel."

"Oh, that's wonderful, dear. Tell your mother I'll be looking forward to seeing her tonight, alright? And thank you for the ride, see you tonight sweetheart."

He tipped his chauffer's cap at her and said, "Don't worry, Mother Goose, your secret's safe with me. Amused, he got back into the limo and drove away.

Mother Goose went straight to the kitchen and brewed a fresh pot of strong, black coffee while Jack and Anne went to their room to change and Mary Quite Contrary went to Mother Goose's room to change into her, party clothes.

While they were getting dressed, Mother Goose called her pets in from outside to get ready. But first, she gave them their Christmas stockings. They gleefully dumped them out on the floor and were pleased to see all the treats.

"O.K. kids," said Mother Goose after few minutes, "time to get ready to go. You can sort through your loot later. Now go get dressed."

Her Fine Gander looked grand in his new bow tie and Goosey Goosey looked quite debonair in his green beret. Madame Goose, with her new neck ruffle, looked like the belle of the ball. She spritzed on some of her sparkling feather shine to add to her eye-catching appeal. The Fiddling Cat jumped right into his new tuxedo then made a mad dash to the bathroom and back. He liked what he saw in the mirror.

"What do you think?" he asked Mother Goose.

"Sweetie, I think you look better than the Cat in the Hat!"

"Thank you," he said. "Puuurrrfect." He slipped a little bag of Christmas treats he found in his stocking into his pants pocket to give to his girlfriend, Pussy Cat.

Jack and Anne, along with Mary, all came out at once to the living room ready to go. Anne had on a red velvet long-sleeved dress with a sweetheart neckline and was wearing black patent leather high-heeled shoes. Mary was wearing a strapless, glitzy blue and green rhinestone dress that fit snuggly over her curves and went all the way to the floor. On her feet, she had on her faithful Birkenstocks.

"Wow!" said Mary looking at the geese and the Fiddling Cat. "Don't you critters, all look snazzy!" The geese all ruffled up their feathers and stretched out their already long necks in appreciation and the Fiddling Cat stood up on his hind legs and took a bow.

"My, my, you two young women look like a couple of divas," said Mother Goose. "And you, Jack, look extremely handsome in that suit."

"It's the tie clasp," said Jack looking down at his gift.

"Well," said Mother Goose, "I guess I better get a move on myself. There's some fresh coffee in the kitchen, help yourselves, and I'll go change. She tap danced back to her bedroom as Anne watched her, overflowing with love.

Mother Goose took off the caftan and head wrap and shook out her hair. She, then put on her robe and went into her bathroom too apply her new makeup.

"Oh, my," she said to herself as she looked at her reflection in the mirror. She hardly ever wore makeup. When she did, it was just a little mascara and a touch of lip gloss. The light brown eye shadow she had brushed over her lids really set off her already sultry, deep-set hazel eyes. The soft black eye liner, along with the rose-colored lipstick, made her look very neoteric. She pursed her lips together and slightly cocked her head to one side.

"Hmm, I don't look too shabby for a fine, seasoned, old cast iron skillet." She giggled to herself and then ran a brush through her long white hair. With a last minute thought, she went back out to the living room and asked Madame Goose if she could use some of her sparkling feather shine.

"Sure," said Madame Goose, "but be careful. It comes out in a blast."

Back in the bathroom, she sprayed some on the top of her head. It made her hair sparkle and glow as if she were wearing a halo.

"Oh my, no!" she said. "What have I done? Well it's too late now to wash it out so I'll just have to go looking like a glitter queen."

In her bedroom she put her new dress on and looked at herself in her full-length mirror. What she saw, wasn't a glitter queen at all but a woman in love.

"Thank you, God," she said. "Thank you, Jesus. Thank you, Holy Spirit."

Mother Goose took her new cape from the closet and also a couple of wool blankets for Jack and Anne to use. She then went out to the kitchen where Jack and Anne were patiently waiting.

"Oooh!" Gasped, Anne. "You look gorgeous! They should put you on the cover of *Vogue*. Don't you think so, Jack?"

"Well, I was thinking more like *Victoria's Secret,* the "Angel Edition.""

"Jack," said Anne, "she's old enough to be your mother."

"Yeah, well, she's sexy enough to compete with the best of them in that dress."

Mother Goose blushed, "Do you think it's too much?"

"No. By no means," said Jack. "You look fabulous. I know one thing for sure; your friend, The Baker, is going to have a hard time controlling himself. The way you look tonight is a far cry from your usual peasant dress and leggings. You have extraordinary legs, by the way. You would put those cat walkers to shame. The Baker's going to have some explaining to do to God after tonight."

Somewhat, self-conscious now, Mother Goose said "O.K. Now, where's Mary?"

"She already left," said Anne. "Jack Be Nimble came by and picked her up while you were getting ready. He said they would meet us out at the little chapel."

"Well then, if you two are ready for the flight of your lives, I'll saddle up the geese and we'll fly right out of here."

"You mean we get to ride out on your Fine Gander with you?" said Anne. "I thought we were going to take a taxi like we did to the hotel."

"Oh, heavens no. This is Christmas! Maybe we'll pass Santa Claus and his reindeer on the way."

Anne jumped up and down, while clapping her hands. Her smile was so bright it could have led the wise men to the manger where Jesus lay.

"Anne, you'll fly with me on my Fine Gander and Jack will ride on Goosey Goosey Gander with my Fiddling Cat."

Mother Goose's Fiddling Cat smiled at Jack and said, "Don't worry, I know how to handle these big birds."

Mother Goose put on her new cape and gave Jack and Anne each one of the wool blankets to keep warm. She then saddled up her geese and made sure that all of her books and quill pens (which the geese had made) were tightly secured in their saddlebags and they all climbed aboard.

"Are you ready for take-off?" Mother Goose asked her feathered friends.

"I'm ready and rarin' to go," said her Fine Gander.

"Honk honk," said Goosey Goosey Gander.

"Do you think my feather shine will blow off?" asked Madame Goose.

"No, sweetheart, that stuff sticks like glue," said Mother Goose.

Chapter Thirty-One

ON THE WAY OUT to the forested hills, Anne's little Ladybird tried to keep up with the geese but she couldn't quite do it, so she dove in under the blanket with Anne.

They first landed at the little chapel so Mother Goose could check in with Jack and Mary to make sure that they had found their way out to the mystical clearing. She hoped that her directions had been clear. On the door of the chapel was a note from Jack that read:

> Don't worry, Mother Goose, we found our way to the
> clearing just fine. We're out there decorating the tree right
> now. A big buck deer and his family met us here and led
> the way. He told us that their friend, The Old Woman
> Who Lived Under A Hill asked him to meet us here so we
> wouldn't get lost. No wonder you call the clearing mysti-
> cal. I think it's haunted. It's awesome, It feels like we're
> being watched. Gotta run-I don't want to leave Mary out
> there alone. I just ran back to leave you this note.
> Love You! See you at the party.

Mother Goose was amused and said quietly to herself, "If he only knew."

"Knew what?" asked Anne.

"Oh, it's nothing, honey, the Holy Spirit's got everything under control."

Mother Goose pocketed the note and got back on her Fine Gander with Anne, and then they all flew on over to the Old Woman's home, under the hill.

After Mother Goose sent her geese and Ladybird on out to the clearing to help Jack and Mary finish decorating the tree, Anne then turned to Mother Goose and said, "I love you so much. I have had more fun in these last couple of days than I've ever had in my whole life."

Jack added, "That flight on your goose was the funnest thing I have ever done! Skydiving doesn't even compare."

"Well I have news for the two of you; we're going to have a lot more fun when you get moved back here. I may be old, but I haven't lost my zest for life," said Mother Goose with a look of promise.

Out in the mystical clearing, Mary and Jack felt like they were in some sort of fairy tale. The clearing was alive with the Holy Spirit's energy. What Jack and Mary didn't know was that they really were being scrupulously watched. As Mary hung her silver bells and cockleshells on the wise old tree, she thought about the things that Anne had told her about God and her relationship with Jack. She realized that co-dependent or not, it didn't matter. Anne really loved her husband and Jack really loved her. She fantasized about going to Africa with Jack Be Nimble. Maybe he wasn't so boring after all....

Jack was also thinking about the things that Jack Horner had shared with him. He was trying very hard to keep his emotions under control. He wanted to just grab Mary and give her a big kiss on the lips and propose to her right then and there. But then he thought better of that idea. He didn't want to ruin their trip to Africa in case she turned him down.

It was dark outside now and the little candles on the tree shined brightly reflecting off the water, snow, and the icicles hanging from the trees. The illuminating light created little dancing rainbows all over the place.

Besides the family of deer that had led Jack and Mary into the mystical clearing, there were now more deer and also raccoons, rabbits, possums, squirrels, owls and other birds that usually would be asleep at this time. The dark sky and the lullaby of the bubbling creek had no effect on their regular sleeping habits this night. It was as if all the creatures knew of some imminent event that was about to transpire.

Jack and Mary quickly hung one last ornament on the wise old tree and then Jack handed Mother Goose's Fine Gander the remaining decorations for him and his feathered friends to hang on the upper branches. Jack took Mary's hand in his and they took one more look around the clearing before they left. Mesmerized and tingling with excitement, they both knew that what they were seeing and feeling was brought on by another force imperceptible to any earthbound mortal being.

Under the hill, Jack and Anne fell in love with the Old Woman's home. It reminded them of the hut they lived in over in Africa.

CHAPTER THIRTY-ONE

"This must have taken you and Mother Goose forever to complete," said Jack.

"No, actually," said the Old Woman, "it only took a couple of weeks. The Holy Spirit gave us strength and instruction the whole time. I always marvel at what we can do when we ask him for help and don't try to do things all on our own."

"I can see that you and Mother Goose are very spirit-filled women. It's no wonder my Little Anne here made it through all those difficult years having the two of you as role models."

"That's nice of you to say, Jack, but the way I see it," said the Old Woman, as she laced up her knee high moccasins, "she made it through all those years because she had Jesus on her mind and in her heart. We weren't there for her during her most difficult times. The Holy Spirit, then brought you into her life to be her loving and protective husband."

"You've got a point there," said Jack. "I was forgetting the fact that she was not around the two of you, all those years."

"You remind me of Sacajawea," said Anne as the Old Woman got up off the floor, from tying on her moccasins. "I've always admired what a courageous, strong woman she was."

"Thank you," said the Old Woman. My Old Man gave me this outfit, on our first Christmas together."

She had on a white doeskin dress with fringe that hung down from the neckline and hem. The turquoise, black and red beading, was sewn on in a precise, design. All day long she had felt her Old Man's presence stronger than ever. While she was debating on what to wear to the party earlier that evening, she had heard him say, "Wear your white doe skin to the clearing to tonight."

"You look beautiful said Mother Goose, the spirits in the mystical clearing are going to come alive to night when they see you." The Old Woman did not respond to this remark. Nor did Jack or Anne who weren't sure what to make of it.

Now, before we leave," said the Old Woman to Anne, "I have a gift I made for you and Jack. It's over there under the blanket." She pointed to her workbench.

Anne lifted the worn Indian blanket and underneath she found a willow cradle lined with woven grass and moss. Over one end was an arched hood with a few brightly colored feathers and strings of beads dangling from it. Anne's Ladybird had donated the colorful feathers earlier that morning before the Old Woman had left Mother Goose's home.

Mother Goose, Anne and Jack all looked at one another inquisitively.

"This is extraordinary," Anne said. "Did you make this yourself?"

"Yes," said the Old Woman.

"Absolutely priceless," said Mother Goose.

Jack was looking back and forth at the Old Woman and the cradle. "But we don't have a baby," he said.

"I believe you do now. It's in the oven," the Old Woman said with a smile.

Mother Goose laughed and raised her hands to the Lord above, "Thank you, God, for giving our little Anne the most precious gift on earth."

"You think I'm pregnant?" asked Anne directing her question to the Old Woman.

"Yes, I believe you are. When I came out to the kitchen this morning and was talking to you and Jack, I had a vision. I could see the baby suckling at your breast."

Anne looked at Mother Goose and said, "What do you think?"

"I think you had better listen to your new godmother here because she has an amazing connection with the Holy Spirit."

Anne gave Mother Goose a big smile and then said to the Old Woman, "Will you be my godmother and my baby's also?"

"I would be delighted," she said.

Jack pulled Anne close and whispered, "I love you, sweetheart. Can you believe it? On top of everything else, we're going to have a baby!"

"Praise the Lord," said Mother Goose and clapped her hands. "O.k., now we had better get going." She patted Anne's stomach and said, "That means you too, muffin." Anne giggled with a fountain of joy misting her eyes.

"All right, then," said the Old Woman.

"Here, Jack," you take these," she said as she handed him two large round baskets filled with her stuffed mushrooms. She then put her Three Blind Mice in a smaller basket filled with lamb's wool to keep them warm.

"I'll carry my precious cargo and you, my friend," she said to Mother Goose, "can carry my wall hangings. I already took all the baskets I made for gifts out to the clearing before you arrived."

"What about me? Can I carry anything," asked little Anne.

"No, you just hold on to my hand and watch your step," said the Old Woman.

The Fiddling Cat took Pussy Cat's paw and out the door they went. The Old Woman's Little Laughing Dog barked all the way as he led them out to the mystical clearing. He loved living with the Old Woman now and having his own responsibilities.

When they reached the mystical clearing, they were all totally captivated by its outstanding beauty. Also, like Jack and Mary, they could feel the presence of the Holy Spirit. The Old Woman also sensed the presence of other celestial bodies all around them. She often had encounters with them when she was out after dark, taking her run through the forest or bathing in the creek.

She smiled at Mother Goose and said, "They're here. They came to join the party."

Mother Goose said, "I know." And she smiled back at her with a twinkle in her eyes. "I have a feeling this entry in our new diary is going to be one that no one's ever going to forget."

Anne and Jack went right over to the majestic old fir tree that stood in the middle of the clearing. They stood close together and looked up at all of the little candles, silver bells and cockleshells. Every way they turned, they could reach out and touch a little dancing rainbow created by the light.

"I thought we would have to make a big fire for warmth but, with all of the little candles on the tree and the Holy Spirit's energy here, I see no need for one," said Mother Goose.

"I agree," said the Old Woman. "In fact, I think it might get a bit too warm once everyone arrives."

Mother Goose, put the Old Woman's wall hangings under the tree then, took off her cape. Now, standing in the mystical clearing in her white gossamer dress, she looked even more angelic and ethereal than ever.

After she looked around the clearing a moment, she then emptied out her geese's saddlebags and put the books and the geese's homemade quill pens under the tree, also.

Together, she and the Old Woman then covered the tables with some embroidered Christmas linens they had found in a drawer at the little chapel earlier that week.

While they did these final preparations, Anne and Jack walked around the clearing with an ever-increasing awareness of other beings in the forest.

All of a sudden, they all heard a voice from above like an echo off a mountainside say, "Merry Christmas!" in a strong bold voice. Jack and Anne about jumped out of their skin; they thought it was God. They had never heard his voice so audibly before.

The Man in the Moon
Came down to soon
To inquire the way to Norwich;
The man in the South,
He burnt his mouth with eating cold plum porridge.

Mother Goose waved to the Man in the Moon, "Hello, my dear friend. Merry Christmas to you! I'm so glad you could make it. I was afraid you might be spending the holiday in Norwich again."

"Oh, no, Mother Goose, this is one Christmas party I wouldn't have missed for the world; not even an eclipse could have stopped me from showing up."

Mother Goose replied, "Well, I'm so pleased you made it. Thank you for coming. I know everyone will be glad to see you again. Do you happen to know if Twinkle Twinkle Little Star will be here?"

Twinkle, twinkle, little star.
How I wonder what you are!
Up above the world so high
Like a diamond in the sky!

"Oh, yes!" said the Man in the Moon. "She should be here shortly. She had to guide a soul to heaven, but she'll be down soon."

Mother Goose, the Old Woman and Jack and Anne could all hear the clamoring of excitement as the guests began arriving out by the little chapel. When Mother Goose heard The Baker's Harley approach, she relinquished her pounding heart to the harmonious beat of his own.

"Calm down," said the Old Woman patting her on the shoulder. "Just calm down."

Jack and Mary thought that they would probably have to take turns guiding the guests into the clearing, but to their surprise, everyone showed up on time within minutes of each other.

Jack had everyone get in long line of twos and he instructed Mary to distribute some more candles down the line to help light the way.

"Alright, everyone," said Jack, "lets head on into the mystical clearing. Now, please watch your step and stick close together."

Upon entering the mystical clearing, everyone's mouths dropped open and their eyes lit up with the wonderment of children.

Chapter Thirty-Two

AFTER EVERYONE CAUGHT THEIR breath, Mother Goose graciously said, "We thank you all for coming and we pray that all of you may enjoy this mystical place tonight as much as we have over the years. We hope that you will all have a divine experience." In her native Cajun tongue she added, "Laissez-les bon-temps rouler! Without further, adieu, let the good times roll!"

The tables soon turned into a smorgasbord of delicious entrées provided not only by the Butcher and The Baker and the gals who lived in the Big Old Historical Gingerbread House, but by many other people also brought their own special dishes to share.

As everyone mingled, The Baker, Tommy Stout and his partner, Tommy Lin, set up a self-serve bar with an assortment of fine liquors and wine. They also placed different flavors of fruit juices on the table for the kids; some who were now playing in the labyrinth and others who were sitting around talking on Little Miss Muffet's, tuffets. There were also the enlightened little ones that stood at the clearings edge talking to unseen beings.

The Old Woman Who Lived Under a Hill made a beeline over

to the creek when she spotted Jack Sprat and his wife talking to a man she had never seen before. Humpty Dumpty, Jack and Jill and Jill's husband Johnny were talking to this man as well.

The Old Woman thought to herself, as she headed their way, "That must be Dr. Foster." And, indeed it was. They were discussing the possibility of Jill's brother, Jack, recovering from his paralysis. Of course, the Sprats and Humpty Dumpty had plenty to say about their own transformations.

The Old Woman was enthralled with Dr. Foster's knowledge of medicinal plants and his spirituality. He, likewise, was quite impressed with her and invited her to join him on a vision quest. He gave her his phone number and urged her to call him before the week was over.

Back at the bar, The Baker made himself and Mother Goose each a drink. He carefully poured a ¼ oz. of white cream de cocoa into each cordial glass then added a ¼ oz of slow gin, ¼ oz of brandy and a ¼ oz of light cream on top. Then, with a drink in each hand, went over to Mother Goose who was now standing by the majestic old fir tree. She was talking to the queens and the Fair Lady from Banbury Cross along with Bo Peep and the Old Woman Who Lived in a Shoe.

"Good evening, ladies. I hope you don't mind if I interrupt."

"Oh, no, please do," said the Queen of Hearts. The Baker handed Mother Goose one of the cordial glasses.

"You look heavenly tonight, my love, like a flawless diamond lit from above."

Old King Cole's wife placed her hand over her heart while she flushed with envy and gasped at his words.

"Thank you," said Mother Goose trying to keep her cool. Her feet were dying to break out in a tap dance.

She held up her drink and said, "What do we have here?"

"It's called an angel kiss," said The Baker. Mother Goose started to take a sip, when The Baker stopped her and said, "I was hoping that you would take that as a hint." She moved closer to him and gave him a soft gentle kiss on the cheek.

"Thank you, love. I feel much better now," said The Baker. "Now would any of you other lovely ladies like a drink?"

When The Baker went back to the bar to get their cocktails, the woman all expounded on his charisma and charm. They wanted to know more about this unbeknownst relationship. Mother Goose told them all how she had been sweet on him for some time but it wasn't until recently that she found out he felt the same way.

"Ah ha!" exclaimed Bo Peep "That's where that Big Chocolate Kiss on your cheek came from isn't it?"

The Old Woman Who Lived in the Shoe said, "I remember that. You had that Big Chocolate Kiss on your cheek when you came down to the river and invited my Crooked Little Man and me to the party. I didn't think much of it at the time. I thought maybe one of the children at the park had given it to you."

The Queen Of Hearts couldn't help but say, "Well, I know one thing for sure. That's no child. He's all man and, if I were you my dear Mother Goose, I would hang on to him. He is what I call a real man and a very handsome one at that. Besides, you're never too old for a little lovin."

The Baker returned with a tray of cocktails and, after they each took their drink of choice he said, "If you don't mind ladies, I would like to steal Mother Goose away from you for a little while. I have something I would like to show her."

"No, we don't mind," said Bo Peep noticing the wool blanket he had slung over his shoulder. "Go ahead." She looked at Mother Goose's flushed cheeks and twitched her eyebrows up and down a couple of times at her, then grabbed the serving tray from The Baker. "Here, I'll take that for you. We'll probably need another round by the time you get back."

As they left the clearing, hand in hand, The Baker plucked a little candle off the wise old tree to light their way.

Many of the guests saw them depart from the clearing, including her best friend, the Old Woman Who Lived Under a Hill. She just smiled with a knowing gaze in her eyes and said to herself, "Now that's a match made in heaven."

As they walked up the creek, hand in hand, Mother Goose couldn't stop thinking how handsome The Baker looked in his tailored black suit and deep purple shirt. She loved his royal blue silk tie with the little red pomegranates all over it. The tie reminded her of the poems he had written. His sense of whimsy and love for Jesus was something she had always longed for in a man.

They stopped just a little ways up the creek where there was a fallen tree and The Baker laid the blanket over it.

"Please sit down, my love."

Mother Goose sat down with a strange sensation of being lifted upward at the same time and a knowledge that they were being watched.

"Do you have any idea how much I love you, Mother Goose?" The Baker asked standing before her.

Not quite sure of what to say, Mother Goose responded, "I know that you seem to like me a lot."

"I guess I need to make myself clear," said The Baker and he sat down beside her positioned so that he could look her in the eyes. He took her dainty little hands in his and then, reciting from the Bible, chapter four of the book of Solomon, The Baker poured out his heart:

> *'Behold, thou art fair, my love; behold, thou art fair; thou hast dove's eyes within thy locks; thy hair is as a flock of goats, that appear from mount Gilead.'*

> *'Thy teeth are like a flock of sheep that our even shorn, which came up from the washing; whereof everyone bear twins, and none is barren among them.'*

> *'Thy lips are like a thread of scarlet, and thy speech is comely; Thy temples are like a piece of pomegranate within thy locks.'*

> *'Thy neck is like the tower of David builded for an armoury, whereon there hang a thousand bucklers, all shields of mighty men.'*

> *'Thy two breasts are like two young roes that are twins, which feed among the lilies.'*

> *'Until the daybreak and the shadows flee away, I will get me to the mountain of myrrh, and to the hill of frankincense.'*

Mother Goose listened attentively to The Baker, while at the same time trying hard to suppress her laughter. Not just at Solomon's choice of words, but also because she was overflowing with happiness.

The Baker, continued to recite all sixteen verses from the Song of Solomon and by the time he had finished his proclamation, Mother Goose was completely athirst for him.

"That was beautiful," she said. "Absolutely beautiful. Thank you."

"Need I say more?" asked The Baker.

Mother Goose gently shook her head. "I have had a crush on you from the first time I saw you, too. You had just bought your shop on the riverfront and you were outside washing down the front of the building in your jeans and white t-shirt and you had thongs on your feet. I watched you from the bench across the way admiring your deep brown skin with touches of obsidian showing off a glassy luster as the water drops from the hose moistened your long muscular arms and slender long fingers. The sweat, brought on by the afternoon sun, sent droplets of salt water over your strong brow and chiseled cheekbones of fine cut black glass. Your flared black nostrils reminded me of a black stallion I once saw out in a field whinnying for a mate. I could hardly contain my love for you when you held the hose over your head to cool down. I wanted to run over and sink my fingers in your hair like sheep's wool. And that smile of yours, like a guiding light set high in your tower of manliness, always made me weak in the knees. Every time I saw you or before I came into your shop, I had to steel my emotions."

The Baker gave Mother Goose a warm smile and said, "Well doesn't that just take the cake? Two seemingly confident adults afraid of following their own hearts. I hope what I am about to do will solve this problem."

The Baker pulled from his suit pocket a small velvet jewelry box and got down on one knee in front of Mother Goose and opened it up.

"Will you marry me, my love?" The Baker asked. His heart and soul bared.

Mother Goose looked deep into his onyx eyes. The gold in her hazel eyes flickered with acceptance. "Yes, I'll marry you, my sweet man. Only in my dreams did I ever imagine I would be so blessed to have a man such as yourself; so creative and filled with the Holy Spirit."

The Baker kissed her hand and said, "Now, just imagine what we can create together."

He slipped the blue star sapphire ring, with rubies surrounding the star, on her finger.

At that exact moment, the entire forest lit up with the astounding presence of the Holy Spirit's brilliance. The cherubim that had been watching them came out from their hiding and winged their way around Mother Goose and The Baker. The sounds of a flute playing whistled from their beings as the cherubim winged their way back to the mystical clearing.

Mother Goose and The Baker could hear the guests in the clearing exuberantly "Oooh" and "Aaahh" at the Holy Spirit's unveiling of light. When the cherubim let themselves be seen, there were shrieks of joy from the little children and adults, alike.

The Old Woman Who Lived in a Shoe's youngest daughter yelled to her, "See, momma I told you they were real!"

Exultant, The Baker got up from his knee and gently raised Mother Goose into his arms and they passionately kissed. "My love, what do you say, since we have all of our friends already gathered here and obviously the Holy Spirit's approval that we get married tonight as soon as we get back? We can have our new minister, Jack, marry us."

"I was just thinking the same thing," said Mother Goose. "Yes, I think that's a wonderful Idea. I can't wait to start the next chapter of my life with you."

As they entered back into the clearing, everyone noticed them in the brilliance of God's light. They were illuminated in love.

Little Anne ran right over to them, unable to control her excitement.

She shouted, "Mother Goose, Mother Goose, look around, can you believe it? God's here; you can feel him. And we saw these strange creatures, like in the Bible fly around. Just look at the light!"

"I know, sweetheart, I know"

Jack came up beside Anne with his eyes brilliantly lit and magnified, "This is incredible. I've never seen anything like this before," he said.

The Baker looked at him with his eyes ablaze also and said, "We have all been truly blessed here tonight young man, and if you would, God willing, Mother Goose and I would like to ask you for one more blessing. We have decided to get married and we would very much like for you to perform the ceremony."

CHAPTER THIRTY-TWO

"I would be honored to do that. When do you plan on having the wedding?"

The Baker looked at Mother Goose and asked, "Now how does that saying go, my love?"

"I believe it goes, there's no time like the present."

Anne threw her arms around Mother Goose. "I can't believe this. Now my baby's going to have a grandmother and a grandfather." She looked at The Baker with hope in her eyes.

"I would love to be called granddad and you can call me dad, if you'd like." Said The Baker. Tickled pink, Anne gave The Baker a big with joyful hug.

Mother Goose waved the Old Woman Who Lived Under a Hill over and said to her, "You have been my best friend for a long time now and always will be. Now, how would you like to be my maid of honor also?"

The Old Woman smiled and said, "I was just waiting for you to come back from the woods and ask me."

The Baker got everyone's attention, which wasn't hard to do, and then announced, "Mother Goose was planning on having dinner now but she has changed her mind and has decided to get married instead." Everyone erupted with whoops and hollers and gathered around them.

Humpty Dumpty extended his hand to The Baker and said, "I just knew that someday God, with his infinite love, would send Mother Goose a soul mate. Although I don't really know you yet, I have no doubt that Mother Goose has made a wise choice and that you will love and cherish her for the rest of your life."

"You have good insight, my man. I would be very pleased if

you would stand in for me as my best man. I have great admiration for what you have been through and what you are doing with your life now. What do you say?" The Baker asked.

"I would be much honored to stand up for you," said Humpty.

With that said, Jack Horner positioned himself in front of the majestic old fir tree with The Baker and Mother Goose standing before him. Alongside Mother Goose stood her best friend, the Old Woman Who Lived Under a Hill. Humpty Dumpty stood beside the Baker, like a knight in shining armor.

With the ceremony about to commence, all of the little rainbows gathered themselves together to form an arch over the wedding participants.

Then! Without warning, the majestic old fir tree burst! Into flames. Everyone, including Mother Goose and her best friend, stood completely still in shock.

Out of the tree's massive trunk they could hear Gods voice as that of a trumpet, spew out these words of wisdom.

> *'He that has an ear to hear, let him hear what the spirit saith unto the churches; To him that overcometh will I give to eat of the tree of life, which is in the midst of the paradise of God'*

As fast as the wise old tree revealed its Holy Spirit, just so it returned to its earthly state of being. Suddenly! Seven more people appeared out of nowhere joining the wedding party. Their faces shone like the sun as they stood in unison. Everyone knew at once that they were angels who had come to witness this holy matrimony.

The cherubim, Gods heavenly creatures that protect the way of the tree of life, moved from their hiding places amongst the forest trees again. Each were fitted with six wings and full of eyes and they sang Holy, Holy, Holy.

One, which looked like a lion, positioned itself above the mystical clearing on the East. One, which appeared to be a calf, moved upward to the West. The one who looked like a man, winged his way to the South and the cherubim that looked like a flying eagle settled with its watching eyes to the North, above the crowd.

Although the night was absent of any wind, the trees in the forest surrounding the mystical clearing swayed back and forth while Jack united Mother Goose and The Baker in wedlock.

"Dearly beloved, we are gathered here tonight for a Christmas reunion and with Gods inspired love, to join Mother Goose and The Baker in holy matrimony. If anyone amongst you has any objections please say so now or forever hold your peace."

At that invitation, the cherubim wildly searched the crowd with their many eyes daring anyone to deny this consecration of marriage between their beloved Mother Goose and her chosen lover.

After a few moments of silence, Jack continued to lead the two of them through their vows. When the exchange was completed, he added his own blessing, "May the estuaries of your individual souls flow together, indivisible, to the ocean of Jesus Christ's love, our God forever and ever."

"You may now kiss the bride."

After The Baker released Mother Goose from his embrace, all of the guests cheered and moved to the edge of the clearing making room for the newlyweds. The Man in the Moon hollered down from above, "Play *Moon River*; that's Mother Goose's favorite song!"

Old King Cole did as he was told and struck up the band. After all, who would dare argue with the Man in the Moon? Along, with Old King Cole's band, played Mother Goose's Fiddling Cat, Little Boy Blue on his French horn, and Tommy Tucker on keyboard. They played a jazzy rendition of Henry Mancini's old time favorite, *Moon River*. With Mother Goose in his arms, The Baker led his wife around the clearing like a feather on a pond. After this traditional opening their friends joined in twirling like tops around the majestic old fir tree.

The cow even jumped over the moon in synchronized time and Twinkle Twinkle Little Star pulsated to the beat. Everyone danced until they could dance no more.

But, before they all sat down for the Christmas feast, the Old Woman Who Lived Under a Hill cajoled Mother Goose to sing. Mother Goose finally gave in and sang Billy Holiday's, *God Bless the child who's got his own; who's got his own. Like there was no tomorrow.*

Everyone raved at her outstanding voice and performance along with The Baker who also trembled with desire. He had no idea she could sing. With all of the guests still standing and clapping, Mother Goose now coaxed The Baker into singing one more song with her. Together they sang the most beautiful, seductive version of *Somewhere over the Rainbow* that you have ever heard. Mother Goose's soulful voice harmonized in perfect golden key with the velvety, smooth voice of The Baker. If you had had your eyes shut you would have thought you were listening to the master himself, Mr. Marvin Gaye. Again, everyone applauded while the cherubim winged their way around the mystical clearing one last time, before they disappeared.

With everyone seated and enjoying the feast, Mother Goose glanced around the tables at all of their friends. She noticed that Bryan O'Lin was sitting at a table next to Bonny Lass and on his other side, sat a young woman she had never seen before. Bryan had his arm around her and looked very happy. Apparently, Bonny Lass had introduced her friend to Bryan when he had gone over to talk to her. There were no hard feelings between the two of them and there had never been any mistaken identity on Bryan's part.

The Old Woman Who Lived in a Shoe and the Crooked Little Man were scrunched together at a table with all of her children and were having a grand old time.

The Butcher and his wife, Old Mother Hubbard, and their son Simon, were sitting at a table with Dr. Foster. Along with Jill and her husband, Johnny; Jack, Jill's brother had his wheel chair positioned next to him. The Sprats and Mother Goose's best friend were all marveling at the presence of the Holy Spirit and reveling in his healing powers. Simon, for some odd reason, {go figure} was speaking quite understandably, yet the good Dr. Foster had yet to fix his jaw line.

> *Simple Simon met a pieman*
> *Going to the fair.*
> *Says Simple Simon to the pieman,*
> *Let me taste your ware.*
> *Says the pieman to Simple Simon,*
> *Show me first your penny.*
> *Says Simon to the pieman,*
> *Indeed, I have not any.*

Of course, Jack and Anne sat at the table with Mother Goose along with Jack Be Nimble and Mary Quite Contrary. Jack and Mary were now twined together like a pair of shoelaces tied in a double knot. Alongside The Baker, whose arm was draped over Mother Goose's shoulders like chocolate syrup on vanilla ice cream, sat Humpty Dumpty; proud as punch to be The Baker's new friend.

After dinner, while everyone was enjoying The Baker's scrumptious deserts, Mother Goose and her best friend passed out their gifts to their friends. They were all dazzled with the Old Woman Who Lived Under a Hill's artistic creations. And they were especially touched with Mother Goose's books of rhymes and memories. They laughed at her fitting and whimsical portrayals of themselves.

"Before we all depart tonight, I would like to say something," said the Queen of Hearts now standing. "I believe I speak for everyone here tonight. This has been the most spiritual, mystical, enchanted evening of my life and I would like to thank you, my dear friend Mother Goose, for inviting us all. Mostly, I would like to thank your best friend here."

The Queen of Hearts walked over to the Old Woman Who Lived Under a Hill and placed her hands on her shoulders.

"Thank you, my dear, for sharing your backyard and secret sanctuary with us. I see why Mother Goose considers you her best friend. You have been truly blessed and are a blessing to us all."

Everyone stood and echoed her praise, including Mother Goose, who was feeling blessed beyond imagination to have all of her friends.

"Come here, my dear friend," said Mother Goose. "I would

like you to lead us all now in prayer before we say goodbye.... if you would."

Getting up from her seated position, the Old Woman walked over to the edge of the clearing and stretched out her arms and said, "Please, everyone, join hands with me in this sacred circle." Mother Goose quickly went to her side.

"God our Father, in Jesus' name, we thank you for all your ways and for showing us your, Holy Spirit tonight. May your light continue to shine in everyone's life when they leave this sacred place tonight and may your love continue to grow in each of our heart's, Amen."

"I have one last thing to say," said the Old Woman. "At a Native American gathering in the desert, one year at summer solstice, I heard a Hopi elder say."

> *"The time of the lone wolf is over. All that we do now must be done in a sacred way and in celebration. We are the ones we have been waiting for."*

Mother Goose smiled and whispered in the Old Woman's ear, "That was a lovely prayer my dear, but I didn't think you liked peppered jerky."

The Old Woman gave Mother Goose a playful smirk and said, well, with all the goings on tonight I figured you didn't get your share today so I thought I'd just take a bite for you."

"Mmmmm, I see," said Mother Goose with an amused smile.

Before departing, everyone vowed to keep in touch and to make it a Christmas tradition to spend each Christmas together in the mystical clearing.

No photometry could measure the light of the Holy Spirit's brilliance.

Nor was the photokinesis of the trees swaying in the windless night explainable by man.

The whirling cherubim in the sky; only God knew them by name.

The manifestation of the Holy Spirit to those who dwell in the kingdom of God is beyond a doubt the most rapturous experience on Earth.

I wish you God Speed and Blessings on your journey home.

Goodnight

References

http://www.andiquote.co.za/authors/Thomas_Jefferson.html

https://www.youtube.com/watch?v=s2LDNIYxzUQ
    Somewhere over the rainbow

http://www.brainyquote.com/quotes/quotes/a/alberteins164169.html

http://www.goodreads.com/quotes/19814-true-compassion-is-more-than-flinging-a-coin-to-a

http://www.azlyrics.com/lyrics/dianaross/aintnomountainhighenough.html

https://www.youtube.com/watch?v=NSq9tvwM5_c
    Walk Over Gods Heaven

http://www.goodreads.com/quotes/44714-the-snow-goose-need-not-bathe-to-make-itself-white

http://www.goodreads.com/quotes/424094-be-certain-that-in-the-religion-of-love-there-are   *Rumi*

http://www.carolhansengrey.com/Quotes/Native_Quotes.html
    Time of the lone wolf is over

http://www.goodreads.com/quotes/258364-if-thou-speakest-not-i-will-fill-my-heart-with   *Rabindranath Tagore*

Rhymes taken from:
Mother Goose
Illustrated by Tasha Tudor
Copyright 1944 Henry Z. Walck.Inc

The Real Mother Goose
1916-1966
Rand Mcnally & Co.Chicago

Self-Pronouncing Edition
The Holy Bible
Containing The Old and New Testaments
Authorized King James Version
The World Publishing Company
Cleveland And New York

About the Author

Marta Maxwell is a retired hairdresser, bartender, waitress, truck driver.   And at one time was an alcohol and drug counselor at a boy's home. For a time, after she got off work in the evenings she did standup comedy and was a Cher impersonator in nightclubs. Today she fills her time writing and making needle felted sculptures and helps those in need whenever possible. She, has written two unpublished stories for children and many, a poem. A Mother Goose Chocolate Christmas is her first published work. To view her wool sculptures go to www.blackpeopleaologc.com and Pegasus frame studio and gallery.